Rock God

Jeremy Eads

UNVEILING NIGHTMARES PRESS

CONTENTS

ROCK GOD

The recruits of Alpha Rock 1st Platoon 1-48th Infantry Division were infected with a distorted hysteria. Every male in the Platoon decided to shave their balls. A communal shearing of nether regions. I'd missed the memo. Everywhere I looked naked men, groins slathered in shaving cream, scraped razors over their most sensitive parts. The recruits laughed, joking with each other, oblivious to the strangeness of communal pubic scalping. Just another day of military training. Hooah.

Standing in the entrance to the men's bathroom I felt almost afraid to cross the threshold. Sunlight filtered through the glass blocks near the border of cinderblock and ceiling. "Did I miss something?" I asked, confused and horrified at the group insanity I was witnessing. One of my bay mates, they slept us eight men to a room, walked up to me, naked and freshly shaved with a can of shaving cream in one hand and his razor in the other, "Shave your balls man?"

"We're not that good of friends."

"Nah man! You wanna shave your balls?" he asked offering the supplies in his hands, pushing them toward me. Little curly hairs stuck between the razor blades. Gross. Everywhere foam, pubes, laughing recruits.

I had a calming influence on the guys in my bay. I was a bit older, more traveled. Seasoned. They trusted I knew what I was talking about. Some of the time I did. I had been training with these guys for seven weeks, two more and Basic Training was a memory. We were almost through. A 10-kilometer march out to the site of our final training exercise, a week in the field, followed by a final 15-kilometer march back to the barracks and we would no longer be recruits. We would be soldiers.

Something had happened, I wasn't sure what.

"Why would I want to shave my balls before a march?" I backed up a step shoving his arm away. I knew what happened when a razor dragged across skin unused to rough treatment. I thought about Rae. In a day or two the hair growing back would transform into its own little ring of hell, the added benefits of razor burn notwithstanding. Every male just volunteered to up their suffering this next week by a thousand percent. Except me. Hadn't any of them ever lived with a woman? Girlfriend? Sister? Something? At eighteen and nineteen probably not. For most I imagine the military was the first real adventure of their lives, their first solo attempt at anything.

"Dude, shaving your balls will keep the ticks off you. Ticks are bad out in the field." He looked so sincere, genuinely worried hordes of voracious Missouri ticks waited in the woods to devour my hairy testicles and the only way to stop them was shaving the hair off. Maybe he thought a tick couldn't get a grip on a smooth sac.

What the actual fuck? Ticks?

"Battle, you know I love you guys, but shaving my balls to keep ticks off might be the dumbest thing I've ever heard. Ever." I said moving around him to try and find a space on the benches clear of shaving cream or short and curlies. All I wanted was a shower.

"Nah, man. Drill Sergeant told Kermit right after we were dismissed from formation. He told us."

Kermit bunked over me. His oblong face combined with his Army issued Birth Control Glasses earned him the nickname. He looked like a pale version of Jim Henson's famous frog but lacked charm. I didn't like him. Though not strictly a bad guy, he was arrogant. And worse still, Kermit pretended wisdom he didn't possess and would get aggressive if challenged.

I had asked the Drill Sergeants to pair me with him during hand-to-hand combat. Slapping him around was the highlight of my basic training experience.

After we straightened things out on the mat, Kermit did whatever he could to avoid me, hard to do in such close quarters. Which was fine because I didn't want to deal with his stupidity any more than I had to. I eyed the disgusting razor again.

"Kermit is a moron. Why did you listen to him?"

"He said it came from Drill Sergeant." During basic, a message from Drill Sergeant is akin to a message from God. Divine, holy and never questioned. Kermit's claim of a tip from Drill Sergeant took advantage of the soldierization process causing the entire platoon to lose their collective minds. Well, the male half had. Marching out tomorrow would be a good time when the prickles started growing back. I wondered what the female recruits were going to think. I wondered why my battle buddies believed in a correlation between ticks and pubic hair. What happened? I was going to be a rock star. Now I was Eads instead of Annie. I hung my towel on the hook above the bench and went to get my shower. How did I end up in a room full of foamy dingle dangles?

I am a Southern boy, emphasis on Southern. I don't do winter. I'd managed to get myself stuck in a nowhere mountain town nobody ever heard of in Southwest Virginia. You could drive 15-20 minutes north or south and tell people you lived in Summit Valley, and nobody would know where it was. Hidden in the mountains, the people who called it home rarely traveled, and didn't seek attention. Summit Valley resisted growth and avoided change. No major businesses, tourist attractions, restaurants, colleges, universities, nothing. My family owned a best bed and breakfast/restaurant in the area. We were on a lake, not the creepy B&B in Summit Valley's dying downtown. I worked for my folks trying not to spend any more time at the business than absolutely necessary. No late night, nothing to do really after eight p.m. Most people in Summit Valley lived weekend to weekend. DFF. Drink. Fight. Fuck. No reason to come here, every reason to leave.

But there I was. Static. Stationary. Stagnant.

. I was enrolled in a local comedy college, half-assing my way toward an English degree, no real idea what I wanted to be when I grew up. Stuck in the general apathy which hung in the air over the town like an invisible malaise. I trudged through my days same as everyone else. Paycheck to paycheck managing to remain one step ahead of disaster. No real desire to do anything but make it through another day.

The bed and breakfast sat on three and a half acres with eight hundred feet of private beach on Caldera Lake. I don't know why they named it Caldera Lake as it's manmade and as far as I know there aren't any active volcanoes in Virginia. I'd probably have liked it more if I didn't work there. Washing cum covered sheets takes the charm out of any job. My time was spent doing various chores, whatever needed doing, killing wasps. I killed a lot of wasps.

The house was located on a hill overlooking the lake. Wasps love the lake. Every few days I checked the perimeter of the house, under the stairs to the beach front, in the bushes, the mulch around the flower beds, and the boathouse for new nests. Bald faced hornets, mud daubers, even bumble bees wanted a home by the lake. Except yellow jackets. They liked the mulch or burrowing into the hillside. They're hard to find and they're mean as hell. Yellow jackets are serious assholes.

Honeybees, and Virginia's gigantic fuzzy neon green bumble bees were the only things that fly and sting I didn't kill. I liked them. They make their homes where I can't find them. Plus, I appreciated a don't fuck with me, and

I won't fuck with you, attitude. They never bothered me or our customers.

It could be argued I'm lazy. I don't think that's the case. I work hard when I'm interested. The problem is not much interests me. And I've never learned how to fake it. What's the point? My father lived by a philosophy of, "Life is Work, and Work is Life." Worked himself to death disapproving of his lackadaisical aimless son. My own philosophy seems to be more along the lines of "Why Bother?" In the last year of his life, Dad told me that he wished he hadn't spent so much time chasing the all mighty dollar and spent more time being a better father and grandfather. He died in the yard of heart failure.

He had excellent credit.

I paid my bills when I had the money but if I didn't, oh well. You can only do so much with what you have. What are they going to do? Ruin my credit? Ha! Mine has never been good, it never will. I pay outrageous interest until I can't. Then I don't. Zero fucks given. Life continues. Another amusing side effect of aimlessness, indifference to my own lack of fiscal responsibility. Whatever.

Then that window hit the floor. *Whump!*

Three years ago, the window fell to my faded green worn out shag carpet with a muted thump and the winter wind followed behind. I don't do winter and a sudden cold wind will motivate you to take action. Any action. The winter wind forced me out of my chair. Pausing the game, I put down the controller. I had to ACT. Fuck. The situation had to be dealt with *right now*! I hated having something to do while stoned. Fuckity fuck.

I tried to prop it back in the empty frame. A half assed attempt, I know. If it had stayed, I would deal with it later. Maybe tomorrow. Whatever. If the glass had broken, there wouldn't have been a point in trying to fix it. I would have to jam something, a t shirt or blanket, in the hole and hope it would be enough to keep the winter out.

Virginia winter, at least Southwest Virginia winter, is no joke and every day I'm glad I no longer have to deal with it. The temperature dips into the single digits with wind chill ten degrees or more below zero. Yes, it might not be cold to those living in Yankee states where a million inches of snow defines a typical winter. I don't live up north. I'm a Southern Boy. By the grace of God, I am of a tropical people. Yes, I'm Irish - Tropical Irish. We crossed the ocean. On a boat. Look, the point is, winter is meant for penguins, polar bears, and walrus, not sweet southern meat like me.

I checked the kitchen for some tape. Masking tape, Duct (in the South, pronounced DUCK) tape, Scotch tape, packing tape, painter's tape, glue, or anything to hold that stupid pane in place. Nope. Nothing. I couldn't even find something to stuff in the hole where the pane used to be.

Old Man Winter dancing around my living room made it difficult to think of what to do besides shiver. My apartment was shaped like a rectangle, tiny, couch beside the door, hole to wintry hell blowing directly at the couch. Snow was blowing in, piling up on the raggedy carpet. The shades banged against the window frame. A saving grace was the hole was by the door and my electronics, my TV, my old PlayStation, sat on the wall opposite. My German Shepard watched from his corner of the couch while I searched for tape, eventually abandoning me with a dissatisfied grunt at my poor effort, for the relative warmth of the bedroom. Even the dog was too cold. Traitor. The Boston, my Boston Terrier, remained beneath the covers on my bed, situation normal there. She stayed under the covers on my bed. No support from her, ever.

My neighbor across the hall pulled up, stomp snow from his boots, come inside the building, and head into his, likely, warm apartment. According to the clock on my phone it was almost one in the morning. I didn't know the neighbor, he and his family had just moved in. The truck I always saw him in claimed he worked for the phone company. His wife was much younger than he was.

I also knew she wore thong underwear. I found a pair on the stairs to the basement where we all did laundry. Her face was bright red when I returned her tiny, lacy, metallic gold piece of lingerie. I tried to keep a neutral air about myself, she was another man's wife. She was cute in a country girl kind of way. Her underwear probably meant she was a bit wild, so I thought it prudent to act indifferent around her. Still, Ashley's gold panties flashed through my mind every now and again when I rubbed one out or heard her with her husband. Her name was Ashley.

I wasn't thinking about rubbing anything just this second. I was hopeful a guy who worked for the phone company had tools. Or duct tape. Then I could return to my game and a pleasant little beer buzz. Hopefully, I wasn't about to disturb a psychopath or maybe that was only the weed talking. People are crazy. Last thing I wanted was shot in the face for knocking on the door so late.

I had to. The winter wind would not be ignored. Even the damn dog bailed out. I left my door open, so he could see into my apartment, see I wasn't lying. Also, so Adam, my German Shepard, could get out and rescue me should the neighbor decide I needed to be punched in the face for disturbing his family at such a late hour.

One in the morning isn't late to me, never has been. My blood doesn't really get pumping until around ten pm or so. I don't like the morning. Nothing good has ever happened on a day started in the morning. All the most interesting things occur in the dark. The first breast I ever saw, I saw at night. I also got a hand on it. Not to brag. My first drink, at night. The first high was on a hilltop in the woods of Kerrville Texas, at night. I work night jobs during night hours. Traffic isn't bad, if you watch your speed, the cops aren't either. I recognize the whole world doesn't operate the way I do.

He *did* come in at one in the morning. Had he been at work all day on some phone guy emergency? Was this a regular thing for him? The room got no warmer with me waffling directly in front of the hole. Fuck that *wind*!! Ugh!!

That hole wasn't going to fix itself. I didn't have a solution in my empty little apartment. Freeze solid or seek help. With the door open behind me I decided to nut up and knock. I convinced myself the worst that could happen

shot in the FACE

was he might tell me to go fuck myself.

I heard the guitar as I crossed the couple of steps between apartments. I loved that guitar. Another thing I knew about my neighbor was he played a magical guitar unlike anything I've ever heard. He could attack the strings with a ferocity bordering on manic frenzy reminiscent of Jimi Hendrix. I'd also heard him playing a melody riding harmonic feedback to the ragged edge of disaster with the tonal control of David Gilmour. Yes, I compared my neighbor in this do nothing, cousin fucking, drunken, redneck town to two of the most amazing musicians ever. Not a comparison I make lightly. I'm a fuck up in almost every area of my life but I know my music.

And I love those who make it. Music brings color to the world. It's oxygen when you're smothering. Musicians make living, the drudgery, boring everyday fuckery of life tolerable. Music is the medicine that keeps me going. It still does.

Music makes the blood, pain, tears, sweat, sacrifice, and daily awful seem somehow worth it. Like maybe it all means something. And if not then fuck it, at least we got to rock. I stood transfixed, listening, staring at the peep hole, hand poised to knock.

What lights your darkness? What keeps you hanging on? Did you ever think about your reasons for not putting a gun in your mouth and ending it? Yeah, for me, that's music. The soundtrack of life. Rock and roll, bass and drums, some screaming lead guitar interwoven through complex layers of melody. Also, all the good in my life occurred to a soundtrack. Every single thing worth remembering happened to music.

My first kiss? I'll Remember You by Skid Row. First high? Judith, by A Perfect Circle. The first time alone behind the wheel? Black Sunshine by White Zombie. Sex always happens to a soundtrack. I don't think I've ever been with a woman without music playing. Gotta get the right rhythm. Pink Floyd to Sara McLaughlin, Tool, The Smiths, The Cure, Depeche Mode, Massive Attack, Death Cab for Cutie, Anthrax, Aerosmith, Ice Cube, Metallica, Run DMC, Sugarhill Gang, KMFDM, Counting Crows, Lords of Acid, Primitive Radio Gods, Sonic Youth, Oasis, Jimi Hendrix, Fats Domino, Digable Planets, De La Soul, Gorillaz, I could go on and on.

I didn't want to interrupt. My arm grew tired and I let it fall back to my side. Outside, nothing moved but the snow covering the parking lot, illuminated by his living room lights and my own. The guitar continued its beautiful song.

So many times before I sat in the hall listening to him play. Sometimes he played for a few minutes, sometimes for hours. I'd hide on the stairs, where I couldn't be seen from the peephole, journeying with him on his nightly sonic forays. I'd float away on those chords, as sure as the man playing was himself drifting. He'd never play covers, just his own music. And the songs were unlike anything. Chords which made me yearn for things I couldn't put voice to. I'd lose myself on those stairs until my ass went numb. I'd sit there as long as he'd play.

And I'd want. I'd want distant beaches I'll never see and exotic women I'll never be with. I'd want something intangible. Primal. Essential. Unknowable. But his music made me want it anyway. A late-night feeling, the pull to somewhere else. Hiding from the light of day, an ache, a need, deep in the chest causing your heart to ache. If you don't understand what I'm talking about, I feel sorry for you. If you've never wanted something you couldn't explain, never felt there was something lost you needed desperately to find, then I wonder about the state of your soul. Sometimes at night, in the still quiet hours, I hear that guitar. And I still want.

I knocked. Quiet. Gentle. I didn't want to wake the whole house. I just wanted the guy to know someone was at the door. I'd only ever seen him from a distance. I wasn't prepared for the face who answered. He was tall, taller than me and I'm 5'11", not quite six feet tall. I never did break that six-foot mark. Denied, always denied.

My neighbor, easily 6'3", skinny, wearing those 80's style squared off aviator glasses. Goofy. Fuck ugly. Sandy blonde hair was feathered in the front, long enough in the back to curl on his neck. A mullet. An honest to God mullet, at least fifteen years past its prime. A severe brow over a slightly hooked nose completed the picture of what was honestly one of the ugliest men I've ever seen before or since.

He looked concerned but not angry that I was knocking so late.

"I'm sorry to be knocking on your door at one in the morning but I need some help. I'm your neighbor by the way." I tried to maintain eye contact. I had a habit of staring at my feet when nervous. I was trying, and failing, to appear as normal as possible.

"Yeah, I've seen you coming in and out. I'm Gideon."

"Benedict."

Gideon. How perfect was that?

"Right, so, you aren't going to believe this, but my windowpane just fell out of the window frame."

"Did it break?" He asked, looking over the top of my head into my apartment.

"No, no. If it had, I wouldn't be bothering you." I said.

"So why are you bothering me?"

My cheeks flushed hot and I shifted my weight from foot to foot. Another quirk of nervousness. "Do you have any tape or glue or something I can use to stick that pane back in? It's so cold in my apartment." Maybe a little sympathy will help motivate him! My dad would say I was playing him psychological. That's me, a master of playing 'em psychological.

"Well, let's take a look."

Yes! Maybe I won't freeze tonight!

He stepped across the hall. I showed him the trouble. Winter happily rampaged around my living room. The carpet beneath the hole, faded and raggedy as it was, was wet from snowmelt. He looked at the hole and went back to his own apartment without saying a word. He went inside and shut the door behind him.

Well, damn, so much for playing 'em.

A few moments later he came back out. I was standing in the hall awkwardly trying to decide if he was coming back or if I was well and truly fucked. In his hand was a fat silvery roll of duct tape.

YES!

My face flushed again, and I nodded as he said, "Let's close that hole."

After we taped the pane back in place (duct tape for the win), bless the soul who invented duct tape, he asked if I'd like to come over while my apartment warmed back up. I'm not about being cold when I don't have to be, and this guy seemed nice enough even if he was ugly as death backing out of a shithouse, (and that *hair*!! *A mullet*! An actual *mullet!! Feathered*!) so I said yes.

We went inside, and I spotted the guitar propped up against a tan overstuffed couch. There was a small Marshall amplifier in front of the corner of the couch which he moved out of the way like I'd seen something dirty.

"You want a beer? Do you drink?" Gideon asked.

"No, thanks," I answered still riding my buzz. "I smoked something earlier."

Gideon grinned, "Well, that's what I was getting around to."

As it turned out I had no need to be worried. In the entire apartment complex, we were the only night owls. We hung out at night after the world went to sleep. Everyone else worked days. Normies. Technically Gideon did too.

He was an on-call phone repair technician. He worked in prisons but only when there was an issue. Not a bad gig, as things in prison are designed to last. He rarely worked. And he was paid forty hours a week regardless. Plus, overtime.

But when the phone rang, he headed to prison. Thank you, no. He could have it. Before I met him, and we became friends, prison had no real context for me. An abstract. A concept. It was a word people used, not an actual place. I didn't understand prison is a place of suffering. A prison is a house of death. I had no context by which to judge or experience to draw from. I'm not completely brain dead, I knew on an intellectual level what prison is, or I thought I did. I had HBO. I'd seen OZ.

Where was his wife?

I went with him on a call once. And only once.

After driving for hours, we arrived. I imagine if the devil had a McMansion it would look something like Queen Hill Penitentiary. Square buildings with tiny, barred window slits were surrounded by high fences topped with razor wire. Fences that were in turn surrounded by deep moats filled with jagged rocks guaranteed to break legs or ankles and were circled by even more fences and razor wire. The outer fence, bordered by a road encircling the compound, was monitored by guards in a pickup truck. The circuitous route lasted ten minutes exactly. I timed it.

Every ten minutes. All day. All night. Riding in that truck doing its endless left turn must be its own unique ring of hell. I hope whoever drove got paid well, but why would anyone want to?

Rolls of razor wire lined the bottoms of the fences inside and out. Along the outside lay an occasional dead animal which had the bad luck of getting tangled up in the horrible stuff. Razor wire wraps tighter with struggle. It cuts deeper, longer the more you fight. From my seat in the parking lot, small lumps of fur were clumped in random places along the fence line. Unfortunate possums, squirrels, skunks, rabbits, even the occasional deer died hard. Gideon told me while riding back, deer received the mercy of a bullet.

There was also the stink. Sure, rotting animals lined the outer fencing, but everything there was bad. The air, the ground, the squat toady buildings, the people within, everything here had soured. Prison scared me on a fundamental level. Even today, I don't speed.

Gideon asked if I wanted to go inside. Um...no. No, hell no, no way, no fuck no, not today, not any day, I'll wait in the truck. I've seen every season of Oz. Prison lifestyle in any capacity absolutely did not appeal, even a brief trip in and out. I brought a Batman graphic novel with me. The Killing Joke, fucking awesome story. He shrugged and went to do his job. Two hours or so later the Citra I drank on the way down returned to haunt m. I had to pee. There was nowhere to go except into reception.

Going inside was the last thing I wanted. Queen Hill Penitentiary scared the hell out of me. If I went in, would they let me out again? This place didn't like letting people go. Once you went through those doors you stayed there. I got out of the truck. I seriously considered pissing in the parking lot. Shifting my weight back and forth, the pressure in my bladder was becoming unbearable. Twin metal doors covered in signs like, *Anyone entering subject to search! No exceptions! Property under 24 hr surveillance!*, stared right back at me, daring me to perform a little public indecency. I thought if I cut loose in the lot, they'd drag me through those doors. Guards would appear from everywhere and drag me, dick in hand, into the Queen's squat gaping maw.

Welcome to your new home, dumbass! Enjoy your piss? Picked the wrong parking lot, didn't you? You're never leaving! Hope you fed the dogs!

I had to pee. Urgent pressure from my bladder demanded immediate attention. I must have relief from the unrelenting urge that was not going away but growing in intensity by the second. I waited as long as I could. Things were about to go all kinds of wrong below my belt. I went inside. A generic cinderblock government lobby, painted industrial blue, with cheap black and white parkay linoleum greeted me. It stank of Pine Sol, puke, years of despair.

I approached the reception desk where a fat, bored guard sat.

"Help ya." A statement, like I'll help ya the fuck out of here without your teeth longhair. I've seen plenty of YOU already.

"Uh...yeah...I'm with the phone guy." I said.

"Great. Glad to hear it." For someone who looked as bored as this guy did, impatience was coming off him in waves. Dude was for sure not a people person.

"Yeah....so...I need to use the restroom."

"You trying to bring drugs in here? Bad things happen to people who smuggle contraband in here." He was starting to look less bored and more predatory. I took an involuntary half step away from the counter. He leaned forward. I was completely terrified, and this fat bastard was lapping my fear up like his sisters cooter.

"NO! I mean no sir. I-I just need to use the bathroom." I had to go...BAD. I didn't want to entertain this jerk anymore.

"Really. You look like a fucking drug addict to me. We see a lot in here just like you. Why don't you get a haircut?"

A haircut? Really? Fuck this desk jockey. Anger flared up within me. My Dad told me to get a haircut, or a real job, daily.

"No, I just need to go to the bathroom. How about I go right here, and you can inspect it for contraband." Hard to believe I'd known him less than a minute.

"Wait here. When a guard is available, he'll take you potty." With that the guard left his position at reception, disappearing behind a steel door into the guts of the prison, leaving me alone. After ten awful minutes trying not to piss my pants, pacing, and doing the pee pee dance, shifting my weight, another guard finally arrived. As he walked me to the bathroom I saw a sign hanging in an administrative area:

WELCOME TO QUEEN HILL PENETENTARY. IF IT'S NOT DOCUMENTED, IT DIDN'T HAPPEN!

If it's not documented, it didn't happen. How did the longhair get stabbed? I don't know, it's not documented. Guess it didn't happen. My escort saw the look on my face. He told me to remember the sign in case I wanted to get cute. Bad things happen, undocumented things, and no one can say differently.

Cute? Nope. I don't do cute. I desperately needed relief.

He stood watching me. I tried to handle my business disregarding his unrelenting stare. I tried to tell him I was bladder shy. Now, as bad as I needed to go, I couldn't. Things didn't flow when I had an audience.

"I don't care. Hurry up, I've got things to do."

Undocumented things?

Gideon's wife worked nights as a candy striper in the hospital. I thought she was a candy striper anyway. Eventually, I found out she was a full-blown actual factual registered nurse, probably the breadwinner. Gideon was coming home from bringing her lunch when my window fell out. Gideon told me how lucky I was he was a night person. I wasn't the only one who kept an eye on my neighbors.

While Gideon explained my good fortune, I checked out his guitar, and sipped on my Dr. Pepper. A beautiful royal blue Ibanez, sleek and mean. I saw a Floyd Rose lockdown on the neck. The strings were so close to frets they almost touched. I hoped he'd pick it up.

"You play?" Wait. He was talking to me...a response was necessary.

"I sit on the steps and listen." I blurted it out. A gushing fanboy. I don't know why. My brains apparently leaked out of my ears. Gideon appeared to be reconsidering his decision to help me.

He gestured toward the guitar.

"Does it bother you? Sorry man, I thought I'd turned the amp low enough."

"No. It doesn't bother me. I like to listen to it. It's become one of the best things about living here." I said.

Gideon nodded his head, reaching for the Ibanez. "Well that's alright then. You like rock and roll?"

"I do. Although I like the classic stuff more than the canned corn you hear on the radio."

"Canned corn?"

"Yeah, you know, it's all the same. Like looking into a can of corn."

"Nice. I like that. You mind if I play a little."

Yesyesyesyesyesyes!

"Do it, man. I was hoping you would."

"I can't explain it but since I moved in here I have the itch to play all the time. I used to be in a band in the 70's but I wasn't anywhere near as good compared with what I'm doing now." Gideon said.

I know it sounds like bullshit, boasting, male bravado, he was telling the truth. It wasn't bragging. It was fact. A simple truth. Gideon's talent was undergoing a metamorphosis. Sitting on those stairs all those evenings I'd heard the truth of it. Intricate melodies floated around in his head all the time. Twisting his fingers in ways he couldn't have dreamed of as a young traveling musician. Chords flowed in an unending ever-changing cascade. I sat with him, me in the recliner, him on the couch, not talking, listening, for hours and never heard the same thing twice.

How many musicians out there can do that?

Gideon's melodies and harmonies danced with each other for hours. Always sensuous, turning, writhing, never the same. And it boogied all night long.

"You want a beer?" Gideon asked, ever the genteel Southern host.

"Nah, I'm working on this Dr Pepper, but I'll be honest, I'd smoke the hell out of a joint if I had one." I said, still riding my buzz from home.

"Well, that's what I was getting around to. A little extra motivation never hurts. I don't have a joint, I think they're kind of wasteful. Most of the weed burns off into the air. I got this." And he pulled out a small green glass bong. It wasn't decorated with pot leaves, tie dye, or any ridiculous stoner culture markings. It fit the man. Tall, ugly, understated, filled with mind blowing potential.

When I went home, completely stoned, dragging myself back across the hall he said to me, "Come visit sometime. No one else does."

Poor guy, married, and he was lonely as I was.

That was the first of many evenings we would spend together. Ashley left for work at nine p.m. and he would be knocking on my door at nine fifteen. I'd follow him over to his house, take my place on the couch, open my Dr. Pepper, and we'd share the first of many bong hits. Following the opening ceremonies, we indulged in all manner of insanity. Goofy conversations I won't repeat here, funny only to a couple of French-Fried Freaks, food, VCR repair or round after round of Mortal Kombat, and of course music, always the music, composed our routine evening after evening. It was good to have a friend. After our first winter hanging out, he asked how I felt about forming a band.

I didn't know anything about forming a band. I'd never been in one, other than the obligatory middle school foray. I come from a musical family. My mother played the piano, my dad, the harmonica. Harmonica counts right? *Anything* had to be better a bed and breakfast.

Asking our youth to decide what they want to do for the rest of their lives when they don't even know who they are is incredibly unfair. Little wonder the average person changes careers half a dozen times.

Most people don't find their lifelong pursuit until they're nearing what would otherwise be a conventional retirement age. So many find their love at the end. Or maybe I'm just making shit up. Twenty hard years taught me what I'm made of. Blood, fire, and death taught me. Surely it must mean something.

Pink Floyd, one of my favorite groups, has a line that becomes more and more relevant. They say, "Life is long, and you are young and there is time to kill today. Then one day you find ten years have got behind you, no one told you when to run, you missed the starting gun." Amen brothers. A-fucking-men. I wonder how many of us are crouched on the starting line waiting for someone to tell us to run.

I wonder if motivated successful people put on blinders and focus on one thing to the exclusion of everything else. Is that what it takes? Why? Why is that success? You grab the brass ring, sure, but miss everything else around you. The thought of such solitary focus is awful to contemplate. How do you know what you're missing? Isn't it better to experience a lot of different things? Shouldn't a person pursue several interests? Is being a dilatant such a bad thing?

Maybe this next thing is *the* thing.

Or maybe not.

So, I joined the band.

I didn't have an instrument. I didn't even have the trumpet from middle school anymore. I didn't know how to play anything either. But hey, I was *in the band*! Hell yeah! I had no idea what I would be doing, or what I was supposed to play, or how I might contribute, but I was most definitely *in the band*!

The band consisted of me and Gideon. I harbored no doubts it would soon blossom into a rock and roll juggernaut. How could it be anything else? The music was hypnotic, undeniable, and all I'd heard of it was the guitar! It could only get better as instruments added more depth. Look out Rolling Stones, Gideon and I are coming for ya!

Gideon knew a bass player. A guy that he played with back in the 70's. When I first saw him, I wasn't sure what to think. His name was Chadwick. Like Gideon he wasn't likely to end up on the cover of GQ magazine. The guy was an introvert, painfully shy, and seemed to want to play on his computer more than he wanted to play bass. He also seemed old to me. Really old. Farting dust old. He was, 'I hope he doesn't break a hip rocking out' old. Even in my younger years I wasn't ageist, but *damn!*

Thinning white hair hung dry and stringy around the base of his neck. Chadwick trimmed it himself keeping the bangs cut back from his forehead in a shaggy Moe. And his sad mop of hair had been all but used up. The limp thinning strands did little to hide the liver spots on his scalp.

Chadwick was skinny. I learned over time his diet consisted of two frozen premade hamburger patties cooked on a George Foreman grill when he got home from work. Chadwick ate two patties a day without buns, ketchup, mustard, lettuce, or condiments of any kind. The rest of the day he drank coffee. His cup was never empty.

I wasn't sure if I should pity him or slap him on the back of the head and tell him to go buy some damn groceries. Chadwick was also obsessed with women, and sex. Under no circumstances would he speak to a female. Communicating with the opposite sex on any kind of normal plane didn't happen. If a woman ever spoke to him, he kept his eyes firmly on the floor. Chadwick often told us about seeing this girl or that girl out in the world somewhere. Never a story about actually *talking* to one. We could also count on a new pornographic desktop photo, or collage of photos, whenever we came over. It became a game. Guess Chadwick's kink today!

Would it be lesbians? Chadwick liked lesbians. Oral? Vaginal? Anal? Solo masturbation? Group masturbation? Micro bikinis? Baby oil? Bondage? Group sex? It was always a surprise. What would Chadwick have on the monitor? We never knew. The pornography gave us something to talk about while smoking the initial joint before practice. We never questioned our demented pre-game ritual. It was routine. And routine breeds indifference. We considered it a little bonus to get us going. Extra motivation never hurt.

Chadwick didn't discriminate either. I never knew him to see something too deviant, too vile. If he had a limit I never saw him reach it. There was never a time when he looked at pornography and said, "This is too much, too disgusting for me."

Midgets, amputees, fecalphilia, bukkake, golden showers, bestiality, and worse held a special place in his heart. Turned out I'm way more vanilla bean than I thought. They ran me out of the room more than once exploring random websites in search of more. Always in search of more. Bigger, juicier, more repulsive! Chadwick didn't care. If there were breasts and vagina to be ogled, Chadwick was all about it. No butt hole out of bounds. Context didn't seem to matter. Restraint was nonexistent.

Nothing like naked women in naughty poses to get you in the mood to rock.

Despite his proclivities Chadwick rocked the bass. It was frightening how hard that old pervert rocked. And he understood Gideon well enough to maintain a bass line while my neighbor floated around in the stratosphere. Then they would fall right back into sync. Only professional musicians and old lovers are capable of that kind of synchronicity.

I wasn't too worried about my role *in the band*. True I didn't play an instrument. It didn't matter. I'd work something out. After all, I was *in the band*, and when you're *in the band* you don't sweat the petty things (like no instrument) you pet the sweaty things!

Chadwick knew a woman who wanted to join a band and asked us to go jam with her. I was shocked, an actual live woman. I didn't believe Chadwick talked to those. While they were going to play, I was to work the sound board. I wasn't sure, but hey, why not? Chadwick taught me even though the board looks scary, all knobs and sliders, it's really about the ear. A good sound man is all about the ear.

Once you understood the board, how to work the knobbies and sliders, the low, mid, and high range frequencies to tweak the most out of each individual instrument, a rough initial process but once dialed in there isn't usually a need to change it. You then blend the levels of the individual instruments to create a complete sound. This is where the magic is, why a quality soundman is as critical to a rock band as a good guitarist.

A soundman knows when to turn something up, give the lead a little more punch or, more importantly, when to reign something in. Everyone has been to a show where there was a generic setting for bands, no actual soundman, and the music became a shrieking nightmare. All vocals, or all lead, no blend, a horrible blaring mess. A soundman in the crowd making sure the acoustic levels are where they should for the space maximizes emotional punch while fending off loud clanging and banging, keeping the people on your side.

We rode over to meet Chadwick's friend. Optimistically, he might have stumbled onto a new member. Chadwick said she was of like mind. She wanted to write and perform original music. Things were beginning to shape up. More and more it felt like we were taking the right steps. We were upbeat up to the point where she answered the door.

She was in her mid 40's to early 50's and dressed like she never got out of the 60's. I don't remember her name, only it was something hippy-ish I doubt her mother gave her. Flower, Rain, Rainbow, Serenity, Leaf, Sunshine, Joy, Frog face, something that made me want to spew my McNuggets all over her tie dye. I instantly disliked her. She was at the same time both aggressive and condescending, a charming combination.

Thinking about her, I still kind of want to punch her in the face. I don't advocate violence where women are concerned, but this chick needed it. Badly.

She was dressed in a giant billowy tie-dyed thing cinched at the waist. The garment, shirt? Dress? Sailcloth? Hid her tiny arms within giant sleeves a pirate wouldn't wear. I thought she'd take flight in a good breeze. Maybe she was wearing a squirrel suit. If the police raided her home she could leap out the window and sail away to safety.

Skinny, hairy legs poked out just below the knee. Her feet wrapped in hemp sandals. Hemp sandals are worn by people who've stuffed sanity in a bucket and kicked it off a cliff. George Carlin said, "You go far left or far right, you've gone too far." One hundred percent correct.

Get too far out you lose sight of the world becoming lost in the vacuum of your own echo chamber, and anyone who disagrees is an enemy. Never mind logic and fair points. Point a finger, gaslight, accuse of isms and ists, and always be a victim. Far left folks tend toward perpetual victimhood, overly opinionated, condescending, passive aggressive, snotty, entitled ass holes.

"Ooh. Do you know what that symbol is hanging around your neck?" she asked me.

I wore an ankh on a strip of leather. An old girlfriend made it for me, wrapping it in some type of thin gold metal. It wasn't gold. It wasn't worth anything, except the sentimental value. To me it was special. A few weeks after August gave it to me, she was killed in a car wreck. It wasn't anyone's fault, an awful accident.

"Yeah, eternal life." I answered stepping back from her questing fingers.

"Actually, that's not correct."

"Ok." I didn't care if it was correct or not. A person I cared for, who no longer walked the earth, gifted it to me.

"No. It's the key to the Nile. Or the key to life after death. After death," she emphasized raising a finger, pointing the tie-dyed nail at me, "there's a difference. Life. Death. Then afterlife. You probably shouldn't wear it if you don't understand the culture. Appropriation is a sign of white supremacy. Are you a nazi?"

What the actual fuck? I'd known her less than two minutes. I always seemed to bring out the best in people.

Oh boy. "No." I didn't want to speak to her anymore. The arc of this conversation was obvious and on the other side I'd look like an ass hole. Picking silly fights with a woman for no actual reason. I stepped past her, into the dark pachouli scented air beyond, to plug up the soundboard. If I opened my mouth, anything I said would be wrong.

Liberal and free thinking, until you disagree, then unleash the rage. I used to identify with the intolerant left before they became so feral. Not that the far right is any better. Somewhere along the line we lost the ability to speak to each other. Listen to one another's ideas without becoming combative. We lost our ability to argue. A simple disagreement becomes a battle cry to rally for complete obliteration of the opposition. Only the opposition isn't an enemy. It's people. Plain folks concerned about the state of the world who've allowed passions to run amok, surrendered logic and reason for rhetoric and one-line gotchas. Too far one way or the other you can't converse like a normal human. If preachy bullshit can even be called conversation. The world doesn't exist in black and white. Us. Them. Ally. Enemy. Whatever the fuck that means.

Life is finding a balance. I don't believe anyone, or anything has a higher claim to my life, liberty, or property than I do. Don't seek control over your neighbors. Don't look to governments for safety and authority. Pull together, watch out for each other, and be kind. Being kind doesn't take any more effort than being rude. Hold people up, don't do harm, don't steal, it's basic stuff we've lost. Laugh at a joke. Not everything is worth a war. And rudeness isn't strength, it's a character flaw.

Of course, she wore hemp sandals.

I looked at Gideon. He looked at me. No words necessary. He and I were both thinking the same thing. This bitch wasn't going to make it. We stayed for the jam session, anyway, might as well. We were there. Gideon hooked up his guitar and I took a seat behind the sound board.

Chadwick plugged in his bass spending an unusual amount of time staring at the ground. Maybe he missed his porn. Maybe he was unnerved being in a room with an actual human female. She spent most of the afternoon fussing. I wasn't getting her vocals right. Or I wasn't getting the right tones from her mandolin. Or Gideon's guitar was too loud. Didn't I understand *balance?* Wasn't I *listening?*

She wanted to sing covers of Grateful Dead or Talking Head songs. Of course, she did. We didn't want to play covers because no one does a song better than the original artists. You won't get anywhere doing someone else's stuff. We wanted to do our own music.

Ms. Flower Power 2012 thought the way was to cover another group's music. Every song ever sung was first an original tune. Original music. Our own voice. Our own songs. There was a basic philosophical difference here we couldn't get past. We didn't want to get past it. Neither Gideon nor I wanted to get into the music game with the intention of goofing around for a few beers on the weekend. We didn't want to just jam out at a local bar for tips. Never mind almost everything she did scraped my nerves raw like a cheese grater down my spine.

We wanted to build something special. There was an idea of a Cycle. Our own personal holy Trinity. The great Cycle consisted of Get High, Play Music, Get Paid. No matter where you were in the Cycle something good waited for you. Oh! It's time to get high! Now it's time to play music! Yea! Now it's time to get paid!

I moved my pointer finger in a circle whenever the Cycle needed an explanation. Our dream was one day entering the Cycle. No longer forced to report in at shit jobs with shit bosses working shit hours for shit pay. All of us wanted more from our lives than to pay bills until death working to make someone else rich. One of my greatest fears at the time was twenty years from now I'd take a lunch break and realize I'd done nothing with my life.

More than twenty years have passed at the time of this telling. As I write I realize in a way my fear has come to pass. I have no legacy. This story is a cathartic venture. One thing I can leave will let people know I was here. We were here. And for a little while we rocked as hard as anyone. There was a reason, a purpose, I didn't see at the time.

I hope so anyway.

I didn't want to fade into the black unknown. I hated to think dad might have been right; Life is Work and Work is Life. Would entering the Cycle have meant more satisfaction? Changed anything? I can't say.

The hippie was not going to work.

"Take me to the *rrrrrriiiiiiiiivvvvvvvvvvver*"

"Drop me in the *waaaaaaaaattttaaaahhhhh*"

We didn't have a river, but we were dropping her for sure. She wasn't going to work. Something else we discovered wasn't going to work was me on the soundboard. Not that I didn't *listen* because I did. I didn't have the people skills necessary to deal with musician's ego. I had a balanced sound, and the hippie thought her vocals should be louder. Her mandolin should be louder, in fact, everything should be louder than everything else. She could go be louder, but not with us. I wish her luck finding suitable decibel pressure.

Gideon and I were riding home in his truck discussing what a fat waste of time going to the hippy's house when he casually said, "You know man, what we ought to do is get you a keyboard. That way you could be a part of the band." Toss a grenade out like nothing.

"I AM part of the band. Besides, I don't know how to play anything." I said turning to him where I'd been watching the scenery pass.

"Yeah, you are, but I mean a creative contributing member. It'll be easy. All we really need is some oooh's and ahhh's in the background. One note filler. Simple shit. No problem. I'll show you."

Creatively contributing? Yeah, I liked the sound of that. We smoked some more and made more jokes about being dropped in the *waaaaatah*. I bought a Yamaha PSR-530 61 key keyboard along with a hard-shell case from Musicians Friend the next day. Gideon said hard shell cases were the best for travel. They arrived in the mail a few weeks later.

That is how I went from being in the band to being *in* the band. A few simple words had convinced me to completely change my life. I was terrified I'd fuck it up. Maybe I'd be too dumb to learn an instrument and get booted like hippy chick. If I sucked, then what? Playing music for a living sounded dreamy. I would never work harder at anything than I would at being a "creative contributor." I had no idea what I had gotten myself into. I used to be way too trusting.

The next few weeks I spent in a haze of smoke and practice. True to his word, at first, things really were one noters, ooohs and ahhhs. Pretty simple stuff. I split my time between school, work, Gideons, and my apartment. School in the morning, work the afternoon, finally I went home to practice. Gideon and I would hang out in the evening until the late night/early morning hours. Next day I would get up and do it all over again.

How was I able to keep a roof over my head and pay my bills with a schedule like that? Easy. My grandmother owned the small apartment buildings I lived in and I worked for family. You might think my family had money. Maybe they did, but it was never shared with me. I worked for the little bit I had.

One business my family owned was a bed and breakfast overlooking Caldera Lake where I did odd jobs. Accounting, pay taxes, cut grass, cook, wait tables for large groups, wash sheets (ugh…disgusting. Anyone who has ever changed sheets at a hotel has my sympathy. They know exactly what I'm talking about.), answer phones, book reservations, sell wedding packages, cut grass, dust, kill mud daubers by the boathouse, yellowjackets on the hill, roll silver wear into the cloth napkins, research new recipes, landscaping, shovel mulch, and cut more grass. I cut a metric fuck ton of grass.

The other business was a catering company run out of the kitchen of the bed and breakfast. When my father retired as a major from the Air Force after twenty-two years he thought he'd like to relax on some waterfront property. (Down by the *waaaaaaaaatahhhh*.) He even bought a pontoon boat. After two months he decided there was entirely too much relaxing. Life is Work and Work is Life. And there wasn't much work getting done. Dad was never happy unless he had a project to do, or, better yet, a project for me to do. The only thing he liked better than a project was supervising someone else.

When I turned fourteen, he signed a release so I could go to work. About stinking time. Because you can't have fourteen-year-olds lying around the house like.... like... a kid. Gotta get them to WORK! Fourteen years already wasted doing little of nothing, so I went to work at Burger King. I hated it. I hated him. I loved him. I was terrified of him. After a couple of months, I quit. I didn't tell him. I let him continue to drop me off after school after which I would get something to eat from Robin Hood Subs and go play basketball. Fuck Burger King.

When he retired, he decided he needed to leave a legacy, a project to hand off to his child, his grandchildren. Such wisdom as Life is Work and Work is Life and Playin em Psychological wasn't enough. In the months before he died, he played the lottery. Twenty to fifty dollars every week. I wonder if he knew time was coming to an end and he was desperate to leave something behind. Sometimes he would call to ask me if I was in. As in had I bought a lottery ticket. I would tell him I was. It made him happy. Sometimes that was even true.

He started multiple businesses. My mother complained she never worked as hard as she did after dad retired. Truth. He had visions, I think, of becoming the head of a hospitality empire based in Southwest Virginia. Then he would pass the business off to his lazy son, no longer lazy, and he would take the empire worldwide. Summit Valley Hiltons.

Sadly, our empire never made it much further than the planning phase. The lottery never hit either.

I didn't want to work in hospitality or food service. I didn't really want to work with the public, charmer that I am. I wanted to be left alone. I wanted to play video games. I wanted to be a rock star. I wanted happily useless.

I put in enough face time at the businesses so people couldn't complain too much when I cut out. I would take my dogs with me, a small bonus. Then we'd head back to my apartment where I looked forward to a solo evening of video games and cigarettes. That changed after meeting Gideon.

I was scared to tell my parents. If you're not getting paid it isn't real work according to my father. It's a hobby. Men went to work. Men support their family. Learning an instrument, keeping up with the prodigious amount of music Gideon produced, along with work and family obligations, was exhausting. When I was able to get to bed, I crashed so hard. I fell instantly to sleep, unmoving, a couple of steps above death, until it was time to get up.

The building may burn down around me, and I'd never notice. I would open my eyes, look at the sky, reach for my keys and head out. Smoldering wreckage unnoticed.

During this time, we found a drummer, Bruce, a guitarist, Shawn, and another guitarist Sean. Shawn worked as a paramedic so three days a week he was on duty he was out of action. His friend Sean, who was a better musician, worked in construction. He was free evenings and weekends. Bruce worked as a forklift driver in a warehouse which also kept him free evenings and weekends. Bruce's house had no air conditioning. During the summer months constantly complained how his house was too hot to sleep in.

Bruce was good to have around. We were all relieved to find him. Finding a competent drummer is a more difficult task than you might think. We interviewed several I doubt could even beat their meat. Interviewing a drummer is a pain because it requires he bring his kit to the band house, set up, try to play a couple of our songs which he's more than likely heard only once or twice, if at all, impress us, prove his chemistry mixes with ours, break his kit down and get out.

A doubly painful process when the drummer in question can't keep time or vary his style. And if you can't keep time, you're not a drummer. If you can't work with the bass, you aren't a drummer. If you only know one beat and apply it to every song, you aren't a drummer. Bruce had a little trouble keeping time, he got fast when he got excited. A small consideration we thought we could work through considering he got so much else right.

The keyboard player, yours truly, never played an instrument before joining the band. Still, after each practice Shawn, Sean, Gideon, Chadwick, Bruce and I couldn't help but feel a sense of destiny. There was an aura of a larger hand at play. Guiding us. My own playing improved by leaps and bounds.

Instead of the one-noters I originally thought would be my role, I carried the melody in several songs. My mistakes were loud but my confidence grew. I could dance in and out of Gideon's lead keeping things interesting when he dropped out or was preparing to come back in. Sean and Shawn were cuing off me. The music grew. So did we. The first album was done. We had enough music for another two full albums.

We began to talk about going somewhere to play live. A test run to see what the public thought. A good idea, I thought, practicing at my parents' house, on my mother's piano while my Boston scrabbled around the basement. They asked me to bring her over to battle a mouse terrorizing the basement. She caught the offending vermin, a mole, not a mouse. Right in the middle of the bridge in one of our best songs, she dropped the offending critter at my feet. I gave her a congratulatory pat and dried chicken strip, disposed of the body, and returned to the piano. While I waited for them to return from a catering gig, I played a little more to pass the time. A celebration! The reign of varmint tyranny was over!

I got into what I was doing and didn't hear them come home. I looked up at one point and they were standing in the doorway staring at me. Dad's mouth was hanging open. Mom was in tears. That's when I began to really think going live was a good idea. If I could get that kind of reaction from people who thought I was just going through a phase, certainly we could rock a few strangers.

We had been working on the title track from the first album when the artist designing the album cover showed up with his latest offering. With him, one of his friends from school who wanted to see what the fuss was about. Word spread around Summit Valley. A new band had formed and supposedly were good. Unlike most rumors there was truth to this one. We were better than good. We were fucking incredible.

Gideon and I were picking out a keyboard melody to accompany the guitar. We weren't paying attention to the coming and going in the band house. And by band house, I mean we'd taken over Chadwick's home in downtown Summit Valley. Traffic moved through all the time. We acknowledged Turtle, our artist, and continued. He sat down with his friend on the couch. After a while we noticed a smell coming from the couch. Rather than leave the music and miss something, Turtles friend shit himself. He ran out when we stopped playing. We never saw him again. We never even got his name.

Gideon and I looked at each other and laughed. You know you have a powerful product when someone would rather crap their pants than leave the music for five minutes.

We needed a new soundman if we were to start playing live as I was now *in the band*. We also needed someone to work on the stage show. We slowly gathered some effect lighting, lasers, a fog machine, and built some homemade PAR cans using industrial cans from the family catering company. The former home of vegetables became eight blue, eight red, eight green, and eight yellow cans. We also had a few DMX controlled lighting devices programmed to run with the show. Spotlights were also programmed in for Gideon, Shawn, Sean, Chadwick, Bruce, or me depending on who was soloing.

Controlling the lights in the band house was easy because there was always someone, usually Chadwick, close by to run the board while playing bass. The sound was already configured for the room and rarely needed adjusting. Out in the world, that would be a different story. We would need someone who had an ear for our sound, someone who *listened*, and could adjust on the fly. Without doubt the most important job outside of the making of the music. We needed a sound man.

The problem of manning the boards, both light and sound, was solved by another guy from Gideon's past. Vincent Michael Pagliato. We called him Arizona Vito. Gideon had been romancing him with stories about our progress, sending him CD's, doing his best to convince Vito we were for real. This was the one. We had to convince

Vito quitting his job and moving back to Virginia was a good idea.

Vito had been guiding us on what DMX devices to buy and what recording software to use from Arizona. His advice had been essential in building our makeshift studio. Vito heckled us to upgrade our four-track recorder. Because of Vito we had the capability of recording 128 tracks per song adding untold depth to the music.

We could correct wrong notes, run effects, refine our sound because of Vito's guiding hand and software knowledge. Most of the band thought Gideon, Chadwick, and I were the ones coming up with the forward moving ideas. In truth, Vito was usually the source. He and Gideon spent a great deal of time on the phone. We needed him. I like to think he needed us too. Even if he didn't know it yet.

Vito worked construction in Arizona. He had saved a little vacation time and we convinced him to come to Virginia to spend it with us. Check us out, get a feel for how we interacted as a group. We wanted him to know how serious we all were about this thing. Showing is better than telling.

I showed up at Chadwick's house for Saturday practice. Saturday's were my favorite because we arrived at noon spending most, if not all, of the day playing music and smoking marijuana. Two of the three spots in our Trinity were covered on Saturday. We played music. We got high. We played more music. We smoked more dope.

Standing in the kitchen was a guy I'd never seen before. Barely over five feet tall and dressed in dirty, sun-bleached jeans that seemed to have Arizona desert ingrained into the fabric. He wore a faded red t shirt underneath a denim vest with the same issue as his jeans. I wondered how his neighbor on the flight out enjoyed sitting next to a human dust bowl. Vito's shaggy shoulder length hair, dirty as his clothes, hung in limp greasy tendrils from underneath a filthy John Deere trucker hat. He was a real-life version of that old Charlie Brown character Pig Pen.

Vito had a large dusty beard as well. He wore thick aviator style glasses which magnified a pair of watery red rimmed eyes faded pale blue by the unforgiving Arizona sun. Vito was wiry, quick, both with his thoughts and actions. His tiny frame barely contained his enormous personality. Vito vibrated all the time like a wire with too much power running through it. He had a filthy mouth, I was never sure what might come flying out of it. I wondered if he might either explode or pass out.

He whipped around, looked at me, and said," That's a great big motherfuckin' case. You're the keyboard player. I'm Vito, fuckin pleased as hell to meet you."

He shook my hand with a dry leathery hand rough with callouses. I expected him to have nasty body odor, but he didn't. He looked so dirty. A faint smell of old spices and sandalwood hung around him. He smelled like the desert, maybe the desert at night completely at odds with the way he looked.

Motherfuckin' hard not to like the guy.

"Fuckin A man, glad you could come out." I said.

"Get that big bastard in the house and set the fucker up." He said, gesturing at my keyboard case with his chin, "Fuckin peyote is kicking in and I'm ready to hear some fuckin rock and roll."

I set the fucker up. Vito sat at the control board having booted Chadwick out. Chadwick looked like a child who expected the clumsy adult to break his toy. He was hovering close. Vito ignored him completely. He made a few adjustments to my sound before the rest of the band showed. Vito looked like he'd always been a part of the group. A master of his domain and the rest of us trusted he knew what he was doing. Everyone but Chadwick gave him space and freedom to do his thing. Chadwick hovered close, answering Vito's questions, and stealing quick nervous glances at the equipment.

Gideon came in surprised that Vito had taken the captain's chair. He grinned, asking how long Vito had been playing with Chadwick's stuff. I told him long enough for Chadwick to work himself into a fine froth. Vito wasn't about to let Chadwick tell him what to do. I realized Gideon was nervous.

It hit me this wasn't a normal Saturday practice. We were engaged in a very real audition; our first serious try out. At stake, a soundman extraordinaire whose leadership and guidance could be the thing we needed to take our game to places we had only dreamed of. Vito could very well be holding the key which unlocked the door to the Cycle. We had to blow his mind. Vito needed to believe.

Once everyone arrived, we passed around a couple of joints. We smoked our cigarettes to give the weed time to kick in. The right perspective matters. Mindset is important when doing anything creative, be it playing music, writing, cooking, painting, sculpting, acting, programming, dancing, or whatever right brain activity you engage in. Inhibitions need to be low for a leap of creative faith.

Putting yourself out there is a scary thing. Not everyone can do it. Not everyone wants to. We tell children anyone can do anything if they put their mind to it. The reality is fear can keep you from doing, sure as a lack of talent or motivation. Believe what you are doing is worthwhile. Trust what is moving through you is good. Belief and trust are difficult to do, maybe the hardest of things.

I'm never surprised to hear of an artist overdosing. Fear is a motherfucker. Sometimes a little chemical courage is necessary to move forward. Some people don't need it. For others it's a necessity not unlike water, or oxygen.

Once good and stoned, we turned off the house lights. Vito brought the stage lights up. The opening number lasted thirty minutes. Three songs joined together through a wind effect. Our own El Duende, the wind for poets and songwriters blowing soul into the faces of listeners. The first thirty minutes we rocked hard driving guitar into slow bluesy pieces that always made me think of places I'd never go.

We laid it out. The music took us all. El Duende raged with hurricane force propelled by souls of giants. The music spoke. And that afternoon the music didn't just speak, it roared. Rampaging around the house with such force I didn't know where I was until the last notes died away. Afterward, Gideon and I were shaking. Our instruments hit with all the yearning, all the passion, of the never was and the never will be. I never had a doubt. Vito sat at the board, dirty hat in his hands, rheumy eyes welled with tears, "Well God damn ya'll. That just fuckin happened."

Vito wouldn't have given a shit if Chadwick didn't trust him. Vito backed up his talk. He knew sound, he understood the console controlling the lights. He didn't want or need any input from us. If one of us tried to tell him to make a change, we had to be prepared to argue our case like a trial attorney in front of a hostile judge. And unless we had a rock-solid argument, and I mean completely airtight, odds were good we'd be walking away not only failing to get the change, but ears burning for bringing it up in the first place.

He heard things which needed correcting before the musicians did. Vito's competence combined with an innate stubbornness helped him deal with the dreaded musician's ego. He was a small guy, soft spoken, intense, but once he started rolling, he seemed to grow. People caught on the wrong side of Vito might later swear he was twelve feet tall. Arizona Vito was a raging force of nature.

Vito went back to Arizona to make plans to sell his house and be our full-time sound man. Meantime we decided on a public test run to gauge how the masses reacted to our sound. To play a public show, we needed a temporary sound and light man.

Even from Arizona, Vito swooped in again to save us again.

He knew a guy he trusted to sit in for him. The guy would do it so long as he didn't have to take any time off work. Fine by us. We didn't plan on playing any shows during the week. A Friday or Saturday night crowd in a party mood is what we wanted. Folks who had to go to work the next morning weren't going to cut loose. Working stiffs weren't going out to bars to check out bands during the week anyway. They were home cooking dinner, bathing children, going to bed, and generally being responsible.

Chadwick had two children, one of which lived with him full time. His ex-wife divorced him and moved to North Carolina. Chadwick joked she gave him so little sex, when he did get some, he wouldn't take a bath for a week. Maybe more baths would have led to more sex. I don't know. I wasn't there.

Gideon had a wife and a son, not in North Carolina, in his house with him. Shawn had a live-in girlfriend. I suspected she cheated on him. I had no evidence, and she never did anything overtly sexual towards me. Still, my suspicion lingered. She seemed like that kind of girl. Sometimes I caught her staring out of the corner of my eye. She came to practice every now and then and when she did, she always displayed a lot of skin. Shawn didn't like it but what could he do?

I had a girlfriend, Dawn, who spent more time at my house than she did at her own. We didn't exactly run wild in the streets. The band was a business. We were in business to make money. We were serious about success.

Alcohol on band time was a no no. Drunk people were sloppy. Drunken people got mean, started fights, had accidents, got dick fingered, forgetful, and couldn't function in the professional manner we demanded. People who drank to excess were usually trying to hide, mask, or medicate. Emotional pain can be avoided temporarily but never completely dismissed. It's always there. Waiting. And when it makes the scene bad things inevitably follow. There was no room for bad things.

Alcohol was a sure way for us to send you with your suitcase. Showing up drunk or on anything worse than marijuana was a no go. Nobody lives in a world of absolutes. Life is an infinite cascade of shades of grey. Sometimes it isn't fair. Sometimes you don't like the current shade. Many times, in the years that followed, I've heard how hypocritical we were to allow weed but nothing else. People have said to me, usually as they were about to get fired, it shouldn't be okay to have one vice band sponsored and others black balled. Life is filled with little disappointments.

Marijuana is a completely different animal. We could function while high, still play, create, work the control boards, and run cable. It helped our focus narrow to laser precision.

Running cable was the biggest part of set up and tear down. When we played a show, I needed my section be done right so I set up my four keyboards, ran the wire, and plugged them into the monitors and sound board. And in the beginning there really wasn't anyone else. If I didn't take care of my area, it didn't get done. Later, I wanted to be the only one who took care of my area.

It's not that I didn't have confidence in our crew, I did, but I was so paranoid, a side effect of the weed, my section be done right I didn't trust anyone else to do it. Knowing my equipment was properly set up, ready for the show, brought peace. Vito's guy, Frank, either understood or was indifferent to the idiosyncrasies of the group and me. Frank never took offense at all the control freaks.

We booked a job at a local bar called Complaints. The location was perfect for the test run; across the street from a college, it drew a decent crowd on Friday and Saturday nights. Even with the proximity to the university it wasn't overly popular with the student crowd. More working-class local people frequented the bar. But being close to the university guaranteed a certain percentage of youthful drinkers and pool players.

A small, elevated stage opposite the main entrance with an even smaller dance floor. Once set up we would barely be able to see over the heads of the crowd. While the back of the bar was visible from the stage area, I doubted people back there would be able to see us. It probably wasn't much of a loss. The bar ran most of the distance along the far wall, dominating the interior. Two pool tables, felt worn thin, pushed close to the door. Complaints maximum capacity was around three hundred and fifty people. Not that we were expecting anywhere near those kinds of numbers.

I borrowed a box truck from the catering business, so we could haul the gear. We would recreate the living room of the band house. We even brought throw rugs. Ambiance matters. Familiar settings helped keep Gideon calm and it also kept the Shawns relaxed. Setting up the stage to mirror where we practiced every week prevented too many jitters.

I found a certain charm in dragging the living room around with us. It was comfortable. The whole world didn't need to know the debauched silliness these carpets and speaker cabinets witnessed. If anyone in the audience had been so foolish to put their face close to the carpet, and I wouldn't recommend it, their nose might detect the ghosts of countless cigarettes and tightly rolled joints.

If they could get their ear close enough and listened in the right way they would have heard hundreds of sexual jokes, misogynistic behavior, frustration over jobs, women, and life. They might have heard our laughter, maybe even heard our desperate hope. Ghosts of our grasping dreams lay all around us. Desire to escape from our mundane, get a taste of extraordinary, had been pounded into those room fixtures note by note. Song by song. We knew it was there, soaked into the fibers of those raggedy throw rugs and ingrained into the finish on the monitor and speaker cabinets. Desperately happy memories were there at a glance if a person knew how to look.

No one else might have supposed why we kept ourselves surrounded in our humble history but that was ok. That was enough. When called on the music answered.

Ferocious, relentless, it would not be denied. We had placed our faith in this thing, this congregation of men, our trust lay in the music. We found our way, our path.

I had gone from a ground zero wanna be sound man lacking any real musical experience to a core component instrument. The music carried me from beginner to sprinting in a little over a year. Gideon and I could read each other and would play off each other, improvising new ways to play old songs all night long.

Striving not to impress a crowd, but the guys who heard the same songs every night. If you could impress them, the ones who had seen and heard it all before, taking it to a group of strangers was easy. How could we be anything but destiny?

That was my theory going into the first show.

We were scheduled from ten pm to one am on a Friday night. We were allowed to start setting up the gear at three pm. Gideon and I were the only ones available for setup. We worked well together. He was my best friend in the world. We instinctively knew what needed to happen next without the need for words. We communicated in laughter and camaraderie. I hid the wire he plugged into the system. One held up a piece of aluminum truss while the other screwed it into place. Lights were hung with military efficiency. Once Chadwick and the Shawns got off work and were able to join us, most of the heavy lifting was already done.

Monitors and cabinetry were set up. The rugs were down. We had rigged the truss and had most of the PAR cans and effect lighting hooked up. Spotlighting was in place. We were down to the detail work of checking connections, running and hiding wire. Gideon and I had it down to an art. He loved playing with the gear almost as much as I did.

There was mechanical satisfaction in attaching this part to that part, securing the pieces with their various screws and bolts, and making sure all these tiny moving parts were working together toward our intended sensory whole. I could tune out and not think about anything. This is the real work of a band. Set up. Tear down. Run wire. Hide wire. And it's done every time there's a paying job. In a sense you work much harder trying to be an artist than you would if you took a straight job.

Finished with my area by five I decided to head home to shower and change. Bruce showed up an hour after we started unloading. He was on scene happily setting up his kit. Wires were hidden, devices were connected, and lights were all functional. Time to shake off the cabinet hand, get my mind right for tonight's performance. Gideon decided to do the same and I rode with him back home. I don't like driving stoned. Gideon did everything stoned. Riding back to the gig with Gideon worked out perfectly.

We got back to Complaints by seven pm; tires crunching in the gravel lot. There was the beginning of a crowd, however, it was still too early for the true weekend partiers to appear. The Shawns were playing pool trying to laugh off their obvious nervousness. They both kept looking at the door, jumping a little every time someone walked in. In their dirty t shirts and jeans the Shawns looked like wanted criminals expecting the police to storm in. Thanks for dressing up, guys!

Gideon dressed in black jeans and a black polo. He had on the battered cowboy hat he always wore when we played. And, of course, the aviator sunglasses. I had on a black bowling shirt with a reflective blue foil worked into the weave. The shirt appeared black but if the light hit it right the foil reflected electric blue. I was also wearing black jeans but of a much looser variety than Gideons. He liked jeans so tight you could count the wrinkles in his cock. I liked my jeans loose. Easy E, founding member of N.W.A. famously said it was for easy access. Amen brother. I also decided to let my hair hang loose rather than tie it back in my usual ponytail, very rock and roll.

Chadwick, in his usual black t shirt and jeans, was with Frank going over some last-minute details. Bruce was wearing a t shirt advertising Budweiser and jeans but had splurged for the show and was also wearing a blue do rag with orange flames. Bruce looked completely at home, totally relaxed. He was teasing the Shawns about more and more people piling in through the door.

Frank was a hard one to read. In a button up shirt and jeans I thought he'd come straight from work. He probably had. He also didn't look a bit concerned with what Chadwick was telling him. Frank brought a couple of guys to help tear down with the promise of free beer. The extra help was appreciated by all. The end of the night is tough. Gideon and I took up a place at the bar near the stage to keep an eye on the gear.

I could already tell the owner of the bar was going to be a dick about someone using his sound board. He didn't want anyone adjusting his board, didn't like strangers messing with his gear, blah blah blah. Gideon shut him up when he told him our operation couldn't be trusted to the house system. We brought our own equipment. The only thing running through the house sound system was the jukebox and only when we weren't on stage. Anyone dumb enough to try to play a song while we were on wasn't going to hear it anyway, not with the stacks we had.

We had more monitor equipment, speakers for the band, than most small bands had for their entire PA system. We didn't bring all our gear to this show either as we would have warped the walls with rock and roll. As I watched the weaselly owner whine over the importance of his sound board *essential* for club operations I thought it might have been worth it. Let him explain it to his insurance company.

Yes sir, I need you to replace my bar because a local band rocked so hard the earth opened and swallowed it.

Dawn came rolling in directly from work in her old Cavalier. She didn't really like the guys but was smiling and excited to see our first show. Her cheeks flushed and brown eyes shined. I bought a Dr.Pepper to give my hands something to do. I nursed it along for a couple of hours before abandoning it. The Shawns abandoned the pool table as the crowd got thicker deciding they too would post a guard on their guitars. I was happily chatting up a pair of coeds, much to Dawn's disdain, when I saw Gideon making the move to the stage. I abandoned the ladies mid-sentence taking my seat behind the keyboards.

The Shawns, right behind me, hurriedly strapped their guitars on. Chadwick was already there holding his bass looking like a man waiting on a bus instead of a man preparing to unleash total devastation. The owner introduced us, telling the crowd this was our first appearance in public anywhere, they were in for a treat. They had no idea what they were in for.

We blew that motherfucker out.

Thirty minutes into the show and I disappeared into the music. Totally gone. The following number was a dreamy ballad about an acid trip. The bar was dark, and haze machines were working overtime. Beam splitters along the ceiling gave the impression of being underwater. Together with the floaty nature of the music it was a powerful combination

I watched the music reach out like a fisherman casting a net, wrap the crowd up, and pull them toward us. People forgot what they were doing. They stood with pool sticks forgotten in hand. Beers were forgotten on the bar while cigarettes sat in ashtrays smoldering down into long delicate tubes of ash. Men stopped chasing women around. They came as one toward the stage mouths open, eyes wistful. Music took control of every single person in the building. The bartender stopped serving drinks. The owner even took a minute off from being a dick.

Security came inside and stopped checking ID's.

The undeniable power of music is God like in its way. They didn't hold up lighters. They didn't scream or yell. They stood there, vessels filled with our collective yearning, our love, our heartbreak, and they drifted.

Willing or not, they went wherever the music decided to take them. But they all felt what we did. They wanted something they couldn't quite define, haunted. Like riding a motorcycle and waiting for the moment when the wheels leave the ground, and you can finally fly. It never happens but you never stop waiting.

I lost myself. I don't remember much else about that night until the music was done. People were clapping and yelling for encores. The only cover we did was Voodoo Chile by Jimi Hendrix. My personal favorite Hendrix tune, I usually hated covers of it. Gideon did it justice. There wasn't a role for me or the Shawns in that piece but that was ok. Gideon on stage, in his element, never disappointed.

It wasn't a full house, but close enough. Every one of those people became fans. Fans buy albums. Fans come to future shows just to experience again the fix only we were able to give them. Fans support us. They wanted to take the ride with us. Music has that power. We created it. It didn't belong to us, it belonged to everyone. Or maybe we didn't create it only opened ourselves to something which then flowed through us. The music spoke to everyone. Secret desires, unfulfilled dreams, lost love, faded glory, better days and better ways all known to the music. And music binds us together in our shared humanity.

I didn't want to cover another band's music. The only cover I have ever heard was the great Johnny Cash covering Trent Reznor's heartbreaking ode to heroin addiction "Hurt". Johnny took that song and made it not about heroin but a lifetime of pain, loss, and regret.

Most people aren't Johnny Cash.

We saved Voodoo Chile for the last of the last of the last of the encores. Only hardcore fans making enough noise got some. Fifteen minutes of ferocity in your face. By the time he was finished the crowd was going apeshit. The coeds invited me to come back to their apartment. I was sweaty and tired. I needed a recharge. My lady begged off earlier in the evening with a headache and went home after the first set. I didn't think she'd be exactly thrilled if I left with two strange women. Tempting as it was, there'd be no ménage a trois for me. I've been barking up that damn tree for years.

We played Voodoo Chile because it felt right the people there, the first to see us, have a treat. Our two volunteers grew to four. They were excited to help *the band*, hang out with guys *in the band*. And if they were willing to heft and tote for the pleasure of our company, who was I to argue?

We sold every CD we brought with us and promised to mail more to people who paid for CD's we didn't have. We had people asking for T-shirts. We had none. It was

now something worth considering. After the show the
dickhead bar owner immediately booked three more at
a substantial increase in payrate. Each successive show at
Complaints sold out. I don't know how much alcohol
the dick sold when we played there, but he always seemed
happy to see us, or if not exactly happy then at least a little
less dickish.

Several things changed for us after that first show. Even
though we were no longer an unknown, our mystique
grew. We were more and more in demand. Local album
shops couldn't keep our CD in stock. People watched us.
More to the point there were people waiting for us. Folks
couldn't wait to find out if we had plans to play live.

We played in public exactly once.

Word of mouth spread like nothing I had ever seen. I
frequented a video store a short hop north on Interstate
81 in the same college town as Complaints. Same street
but the other side of town. I walked in and was happily
browsing movies when I felt eyes on me. The skin at the
base of my neck was crawling and my hair stood on end.
Looking around, expecting to find someone sizing me up

for a robbery, I found instead a group of college students stood outside with their faces pressed to the glass.

They were laughing and pointing excitedly. At *me*! A beautiful blonde broke from the pack and approached. She was the kind of beautiful guys like me would never normally have a shot with. Here she was smiling, cheeks flushed at *me*! She asked if I was in the band, kind of accusatory, more statement than question. She knew who I was. Did she expect me to lie to her? You're *in* the band? A question, but not really.

You're fucking A right I'm IN THE BAND. Holy God am I IN THE BAND. Dear sweet Jesus thank you Lord I am IN THE BAND. She asked me to autograph CD's for them. Huh? Ya'll want MY autograph? Surreal. I felt the ground shifting beneath me. Her smile was all invitation, illicit promise. It scared me silly. I signed her CD's and never went back.

My back up, back up, back up weed guy lived across from the college. As heavy pot smokers it's always good to have back up dealers in case someone goes dry, gets arrested, whatever. I bought from Ash as infrequently as possible. I was used to a much higher quality smoke, but he usually had some when no one else did. Any port in a drought and Summit Valley was seriously dry. Dawn and I stopped by for his cheap homegrown to find a party happening I didn't really want to attend. I knocked on the door. Dawn held her elbows, shifting her weight from foot to foot. The stereo masked the sound. I walked around back. The party had spilled out onto his tiny porch.

I hollered to a random dude.

"Hey man! Ash here?"

"Sure. Who the fuck are you?"

I told him who the fuck I was.

"Dude! In the band? *Dude*! Hang on, man! I'll go...I'll go get the door right now! Wait! No, come around! Unless you want him to come to you?"

I couldn't help but laugh. Relax, I said, and I'd meet him at the door. In the short time it took to walk back around, climb one flight of stairs, and knock on the door (again) word spread through the entire party a member of the BAND had arrived. I've never thought celebrities were worth the attention they get. My own minor celebrity didn't seem anything other than mildly amusing.

The people at Ash's party acted like somebody important was on scene. It was extremely uncomfortable. They stared, spoke all at once, and touched. Arm claps, pokes, back pats, and shoulder grabs. WAY too many people in my space bubble. I didn't play music because I wanted attention. Well, not solely for attention. I played music because I had it in me. If art lies within you, you must do it. I didn't realize it was in me until Gideon showed me

Ten different people were trying to speak to me at once. A group of women walked over, pushing my lady out of their way to get close the way a pack of lionesses will cut out a weak gazelle. They effectively stopped her off from getting back to my side. What was my phone number? Did I want their phone numbers? Would I come back to their place? Could they come back to mine? Where was the band house? Was Gideon with me? Dawn was furious at me for allowing it to happen.

I didn't mind. The blood was currently away from my brain. I was a young man. The attention was nice even if I had to pay for it later. You always pay so might as well enjoy getting in trouble. It's much easier to ask forgiveness than permission.

The second show at Complaints went smoothly. Word of mouth brought larger crowds. There was a wait to get in. I don't think that place ever had a line up to get in either

before or since we played there. The third show saw lines around the building and to the end of the block. Not only were people willing to wait to get in, but that third show took place on a snowy November night. They were standing in the snow! For most of those people waiting out in the weather, they didn't even get in..

The third show tested our professionalism as a group of musicians. During the set up a new roadie stepped on the cord that hooked into Gideon's twelve string guitar. The cable snapped. Rather than own up to what he'd done, the roadie used the cable. We could have replaced it if someone other than this one idiot known what happened. In the two songs we used the twelve string, it was the primary instrument. There were some oohs and ahs on the keyboard and some minor bass and drum accompaniment, but the songs were mainly about guitar.

In the beginning of the second piece the twelve-string died.

Panic. Massive panic. My head snapped up and time seemed to slow. The air turned to syrup, thick, difficult to breathe. The Shawns were off stage so they couldn't pick up the slack. Chadwick was maintaining the bass line and Bruce was cruising along but staring at me. Chadwick stared at me. Mine was the only melody instrument. Oh God. I had to be the one to keep the song moving. The other option was crash and burn live on stage in front of the largest crowd we'd seen up to that point. Embarrassing the group wasn't an option.

I quickly switched over to the piano and continued a rough approximation of the twelve string's part doing my best to dance through the chords. Gideon didn't wait. He grabbed the microphone and continued singing like the unexpected drop of a primary instrument was all part of our master plan. There were other miscues with the lighting as well. Minor issues to be sure, and no one in the crowd had any idea anything had gone astray.

After the show I stormed out the back door to have a cigarette and try to calm down. I was furious everything fucked up. In my estimation, serious errors occurred, and these were failures which could not be tolerated. Up to that point I never let my temper loose. My temper has always been an issue for me. I've always thrown a quick fist and worried about consequences later.

Chadwick followed me outside. Nowhere near as upset about the broken cable or the lack of accountability as I was. He wanted to make sure I wasn't about to kill anyone. The roadie followed Chadwick and seeing how angry I was decided that was the appropriate time to apologize for breaking the cable.

I was getting ready to fire him, unleash some old school fire and brimstone, when another two guys approached bundled against the cold. They heard me yelling and come around the corner to maybe watch a fight. The guy walked up to me and asked, voice muffled behind a scarf, who was *in the band*? I prepared to give him a "fuck you" and start a brawl. I expected him to say something about how bad we sucked. He looked at me and pointed, "You! You're *in the band*!"

I tightened my fist, getting ready to fight.

He then pointed at Chadwick, "You too. You're *in the band*!"

I adjusted my balance as adrenaline flooded my system. My anger blinded me to any possibility other than violence. He pulled his scarf down so I could see his face. Starry eyes, cheeks flushed from beer, cold, or both and a gigantic smile.

"*You guys are fucking awesome! I'll fuckin follow you guys wherever you go!*" He yelled it, voice echoing around the back lot.

All my anger fell away. I felt foolish. Embarrassed at the way I lost my cool. How could I maintain my anger with these two dudes standing out in a back lot with me, freezing their asses off, smiling? His friend stood there happy with identical goofy looks, like they were waiting for a pat on the head. I couldn't take it.

I gave them each a CD and took them around to meet the band. Each guy got their CD signed by the entire group. Gideon told them they could come by the band house and sit in on a practice session. I was honestly surprised by that one. Gideon was normally kind of a recluse. Those two guys left the bar feeling fine. And isn't that the whole point? I still fired the roadie, but I did it nicely.

We didn't do any more shows the remainder of the year. I wanted to start off the New Year with a plan to set up a series of venues up and down the East Coast. I contacted people I felt might aid our cause. Some I had cold called; some I had been introduced to through The Dick. They were all people who had heard us, or at least heard OF us, and wanted to help get the band more exposure.

Christmas was approaching and feeling festive we put a tree up in the band house. Chadwick lived there but Gideon and I were always around we might as well have been living there. Even when we really didn't have anything to do, we were there. I can't say who started it, but somebody's girlfriend put a little bag of skittles on the tree. Other decorations began appearing. Tobacco rolled up to look like a joint, small bags of candy resembling bags of pills. Someone painted EAT MORE ACID on the star in day glo paint that glowed in the dark like spectral writing.

Our Christmas tree became a festive holiday monument to the consumption of narcotics. You don't get more rock and roll than that. Granted, our tree was made up to look like it was covered in illegal substances rather than actually covered in them. We weren't so well off that we could afford to waste drugs.

We sat and drink Citra or Sun Drop from giant cups by the low light of our advertisement for LSD. My personal cup held a tray of ice and two twelve-ounce cans of Citra. It kept cold for most of the evening, and I usually had ice leftover when I cleaned it out before bed. We smoked cigarettes, passed joints, and played music. We made rude comments about the current pornographic pictures on the computer. We laughed and dreamt and felt the comradery of good chemistry both internal and external.

Vito came down to spend Christmas with us. He was still in the process of selling his house, but it looked like he might have a buyer. The Shawns had various girlfriends who would come and go. Dawn had just about decided that she had had enough of the rock and roll lifestyle. We fought. A lot. I can't say I was upset by it. I wasn't. She wasn't the same anymore. I never knew she was pregnant until the doctor told me my baby was gone.

She'd called saying she needed help. She said she had hurt herself and needed a ride to the doctor. I rushed home and when I opened the door there was blood all over the kitchen floor. One of the dining room chairs was pulled out and most of the blood pooled around it. The house stank of sweat and the coppery metallic scent of blood. Blood seemed to be everywhere. I'd never seen so much. Confusion warred with concern which battled plain fear. Had she been attacked? What was going on? Every conclusion my mind jumped to was worse than the one before.

She limped out of the bathroom, blood soaking the front of her pants, eyes puffy from crying. "I hurt." She said. I scooped her up and floored it to the emergency room with the scent of all that blood chasing me. Over and over, I asked, "What happened? Talk to me, Dawn." She didn't respond, just held herself crying. She had almost stopped bleeding by the time we got to the hospital. Nurses took her away from me in a wheelchair through a door I wasn't allowed to pass through. I sat under buzzing fluorescents waiting. Announcements blared inscrutable requests through overhead paging systems in a metallic feminine voice. Harried staff rushed by not speaking to me either. They brought someone else back. Dawn looked the same. Her insides were broken. Shattered.

She finally said she slipped and fell into the chair. She said it was an accident, could happen to anyone I suppose. Plain bad luck. I think about that chair every now and again. I think about it pulled out, away from the table, sitting in a pool of my baby's lifeblood. I wonder if it was in the wrong place at the wrong time. Did I forget and leave it out? Was it the one time I didn't push the chair back under the table when I was done? Was it my fault?

In the small quiet hours of the night I wonder if Dawn decided she didn't want to have a baby with a wanna be rock star. I wonder if she thought she'd be better off without rather than having to deal with the inevitable ugly custody issues. Would life be easier without a baby? Was it better to not have it rather than chase a father who always chased the music? I could never shake the thought it wasn't intentional. I don't know. I wasn't there.

After that she picked fights for no reason. She flashed between clingy and angry faster than I could keep up. We were at my apartment, and I got hungry. I told her I was going to Burger King; I asked her if she wanted anything? Lying on the couch staring absently at the television, she told me she wanted a whopper with cheese, plain only mustard, large onion rings, and a large Dr. Pepper. Check. Can do.

I went and got the food. I came home to a demon waiting on the couch.

"Why couldn't I go?" she asked. Face getting redder as her blood pressure shot up and her anger grew.

"Wait, what?" I asked, confused. Thirty minutes ago, we had been snuggling on the couch watching DragonBall Z. Now a grenade exploded destroying the morning's good vibe.

"You heard me. Why couldn't I go with you? Are you embarrassed to be seen with me?"

"Uh...no."

"Well, why couldn't I go?" She was so hostile. Fury reddened her face, and her breath came in short angry puffs. Her hair was in disarray where she'd been lying on the couch presumably right up to the point where I came back with her fucking lunch. She looked crazy standing there with her fists balled up and her chest heaving. I didn't know what to say. Every answer I offered was wrong.

I thought about a similar incident at a Long John Silver's a few days prior. I love Long Johns chicken. I like to drown the plate in malt vinegar. I don't go there often because I'm a little husky, a bit of a tubby mcfatfat, and everything there is fried. But damn if it doesn't taste good. We decided to eat in the restaurant. Approaching the counter, the girl asked for my order. Two number six's with an extra piece of chicken each. She gave me the total. I paid. She gave me my change and my cups.

That was the extent of my relationship with the cashier.

I got the food and joined my lady at the table she'd selected almost directly in front of the cashier.

"Who the fuck was that bitch?" my lady hissed.

"Wait, what?"

"The slut behind the counter. You two seemed friendly. You fucking her?"

I was honestly confused. "The chick at the counter?"

"Yeah, that bitch."

"I don't know her."

"The fuck you don't."

Conversation devolved from there. The girl behind the counter appeared humiliated, cheeks flushed, mouth hanging open in an "O". She hadn't done anything other than her job. My crazy ass girlfriend had gone completely sideways and dragged all of us for the ride. We ended up screaming at each other in the middle of the Long Johns. The manager came out from the back and asked us to leave. Maybe a better way to put it would be to say he told us to leave. An even better way to put it would be that we should leave before the Sheriff arrived. We left.

I never got my chicken..

Now here she was pulling the same shit again. I don't like getting angry. I have anger issues and try to avoid confrontation. I pursue peace and mellow in my life. Calm. I don't want to do something stupid; prison scares me. I'd never lay hands on Dawn in anger, but I kind of wanted to.

Instead of getting physical I elected something equally dumb. She was standing in the middle of the living room with her chest heaving and her little fists balled up. I decided to argue. Never argue with crazy. You won't win.

"Well, I thought you were a big girl and if you wanted to go with me, I figured you'd unglue your ass from the couch and get in the car."

Exactly the wrong thing to say.

She went off on a twenty-minute rant insulting everything from my parentage, performance in bed, size of my what not, hygiene habits, family, and everything in between. I tried to tune her out but try tuning out a swarm of hornets after stomping their nest.

"Look, you can stay, or you can go, but either way get off my back."

She stopped yelling at me. Maybe she realized I was serious, and I was at my limit. Maybe she had reached hers. Her silence was somehow worse than the noise. She put on her shoes and walked out the door. I ate her Burger King for dinner later that night. Alone.

She decided to get off my back. I never heard from her again.

That's not to say that there weren't plenty of women around. We were a hot new act. I wasn't lonely but there weren't any permanent attachments. Word was getting around that we might be on our way and there were plenty of hangers on who wanted to try and take that ride with us. Truthfully, I didn't really miss her. I was young, full of myself, too fucking stupid to realize what I'd lost. Too proud. Plus, the last few months since the miscarriage were so bad, mainly what I felt when I thought about Dawn was a kind of guilty relief.

I was relieved she was gone. I didn't wish her any harm and I hoped then as I hope now, she found someone who made her happy, someone who gave her what I didn't or couldn't. When she looked at me, she saw either the bad choices she'd made or the terrible accident she had. Either way the resentment she felt for me was something she had to deal with away from me. That's fine. I took her for granted, treated her like a roommate, friends with benefits, cook, maid, chauffeur, and part time compainion instead of acknowledging all the things she did. I never apologized to her for all the awful things she tolerated from me. Dawn cooked dinner, drove me around when I was too stoned to drive myself, spent I don't know how many nights alone while I was with Gideon. I really am sorry, Dawn, you wanted a man and I only played at being one. At the time, I was relieved. Relieved I wasn't subjected to anymore daily verbal lashings.

We decided to throw a small Christmas party to celebrate our accomplishments. While we had initially planned to keep it small, just a few friends, things had a way of quickly growing out of control. Word got out we were having a party at the band house. There were people everywhere.

Most of whom I didn't know. Gideon didn't know. Chadwick didn't know. Bruce didn't know. Arizona Vito didn't know but the Shawns looked suspiciously guilty.

I didn't mind. Women were everywhere. I was downstairs with Gideon, Vito, and Chadwick, close ups of ladies licking lady parts on the computer and happily getting stoned. We were discussing the possible tour locations and financing for the possible tour. Arizona had some good pointers for saving money on the road and I was starting to think he might need to be acting as our manager. Vito loved the board too much for that, but he would make a killer manager. We were running the CD through the monitor system and had the lights set up and running. No one parties like a rock and roll band.

Nearing a perfect state of numbness, the peaking of the high where consciousness becomes detached from the self and rides pure sensation, when a guy came running downstairs saying our temporary sound guy Frank was trying to kill himself. Everyone ran up the stairs, following the sounds screaming. We got into the bedroom just as Frank moved to jump out the window. Franks girlfriend, if that's who she was, screamed again. As annoying as her screaming was, she looked good standing by the door in a pair of panties and red heels. I'm a pig.

"If no one's gonna suck my dick i'ma wanna die!" Frank screamed and jumped.

Gideon and I dove at the same time and managed to catch him by the feet. The band house sat on a hill with part of the hill cut out to provide a driveway. The window Frank tried to jump out of overlooked the driveway and it was a good thirty-five feet straight down onto asphalt. His head would have popped like a melon splattering brains all over my new Firebird. I couldn't have Frank killing himself by my car and from the looks of it someone *was* getting ready to suck his dick. I don't know. I wasn't there.

We pulled him back inside with help from Vito and Chadwick. Frank started crying because we scraped his legs pulling him back in the window. The girl, still making no move to cover up, strutted over, smacked Frank in the face, turned, and left the room.

"Now who's gonna suck my dick?" Frank moaned.

"I don't know, you big idiot." I told him. "Did you really just try to kill yourself?"

"Will you suck my dick?"

"Fuck you, Frank."

He looked at Gideon and Chadwick, tears streaming down his face, "How about one of you guys? Please, *please* suck my dick!"

Gideon asked him what he had taken.

"If I tell you, will you suck my dick? "

"No Frank. What did you take?"

"Just a little bit of acid. Just a little something, now please, please, please suck my dick. I need it."

We picked Frank up off the bed leading him through the gathering crowd by the door. Now that the show was mostly over the crowd around the doorway began moving on to find fresh insanity in other parts of the house.

"Somebody please suck my dick!"

A few people laughed, I couldn't tell who. Frank took it as encouragement.

"Will you suck my dick?" More laughter and jeering.

Gideon and I led him downstairs. Frank's mostly naked date was picking skittles from our drug tree and eating them. Her face and body partly lit by the glow of EAT MORE ACID. Some guy I didn't know groped her breasts from behind. There were several others standing around watching. I causally wondered if she was going to fuck one or all of them then decided I didn't care.

"Suck my dick! *Somebody please suck my dick*!"

She didn't look away from the candy. Frank struggled against our arms, still trying to get back to her. The guys didn't look away from her breasts.

Frank couldn't be trusted. You can't trust drugs. The occasional person can be trusted, but people in a group and drugs in specific – never. We didn't want him in the party out of his head like he was, but we didn't want to leave him alone on the second floor where the bedroom windows were.

Gideon led us through the kitchen and out the back door. We dumped Frank on the back lawn where he continued to roll around in the frosted grass and beg someone, anyone, for fellatio. It took about four hours for Frank to scream his throat raw and pass out. He had some minor frostbite on his nose and ears but that's better than spreading his brains all over the driveway, and my new car.

Lysergic acid diethylamide is not a drug that we took causally. We didn't go into it looking for a trip or to have a good time. LSD doesn't work like that. Gideon had taken it every day for a seven-year period as a younger man. He was legally insane and used marijuana to keep himself even. It's why he smoked so much. LSD is a good way to quickly get in touch with the music.

Frank didn't really know what he was getting into. He thought that he'd be able to manage the trip. You don't manage LSD, it manages you, and it will do with you whatever it wants to. Manic joy converts to catatonic despair faster than you can snap your fingers. One minute you're awed by the miracle of fingers. The next minute finds you bursting into tears about how bad you are to your parents, the next, screaming for blow jobs in the yard.

A prepared mind can use those radical paradigm shifts to move closer to the music. We never did it without plans to play music all day. You can't take something like LSD if you have something you need to do later. You need a good eighteen hours to work the chemical out of your system and you need something for the chemical to do besides fuck with you. I'll never know how Gideon took as much as he did without his brains leaking out his ears.

George Lucas called it the Force. That's as good a name as any. LSD can take you far enough away from yourself that you learn how to let that force flow through you. It's scary. At the same time, it can be amazing. But you must have something to keep you occupied. You need to remain engaged to keep your brain from completely rebelling under the onslaught of this terrible drug.

The first time I took it was for music. The last time I took it was for the music. Gideon said we'd accelerate my training with a little chemical stimulant one Saturday afternoon. Right after the paper hit my tongue Gideon decided we needed snacks. There was a corner store less than a block from the band house. Gideon and I hopped in his truck to go get some chips, drinks, and cigarettes.

I felt fine, nothing out of the ordinary. I got some Doritos and a bag of Funyuns. I had my giant cup of Citra at the band house but I decided to get a giant Pepsi as well. As I filled the five gallon bucket the gas station sold as a large drink I noticed something. The Pepsi machine was breathing, it's sides expanding in and out. The backlit Pepsi sign across the front of the machine would bubble out then shrink back.

In and out. In and out.

The fucking machine was breathing. I slowly backed away from the machine, not letting it out of my sight, and found Gideon staring at candy bars.

"Did you ever notice the writing on a Watchamacallit looks like a slide? We should see where it goes." Gideon casually said to me.

"I don't know about that, but the fucking Pepsi machine is breathing. And I think the guy at the counter knows we're high. We need to leave. Now. Before the Pepsi machine decides to follow us down the slide." I said taking the candy from his hand and tossing it back on the shelf.

"You learn to whisper in a sawmill?" Gideon asked, picking the Watchamacallit back up. Apparently, I was talking much louder than I thought. He continued like I hadn't spoken, "You might be right. We should go. And the Pepsi machine is fine. I'm fine. You're fine. That dude is fine. It's fine."

We took our stuff to the counter and paid. I kept the machine in sight the entire time. Probably a good thing as that kept my back to the clerk so he couldn't see my eyes and how completely wrecked I was. Stoner logic. We couldn't have been more obvious if we had neon signs above our heads flashing the word, "Tripping!" I don't think he would have called the police, it wasn't that kind of neighborhood, but fuck it, why take the chance? Gideon slowly drove us back to the band house.

Nothing unusual took place on the trip back. I was freaked out about the breathing Pepsi machine. I told Chadwick about it, and he smiled and told me, "Hang on man, don't fight it, just hang on." That is some of the best advice I've ever received.

I hung on.

Then the three of us were getting ready to play. Chadwick ran the drum track back, so we'd have drums. Bruce and the Shawns were a no show. Gideon called to let them know what was happening and they decided to stay away. It didn't matter. We had guitar, phenomenal, amazing guitar, bass, a drum track, and a keyboard player completely out of his skull.

That's when magic happens. You get away from yourself in order to find out what it is you're really capable of. All the doubts, the "I can't", the negative thoughts fell away. There was only music. If mistakes were made, they were loud, but they didn't matter. The music came in and took over.

The lessons I learned in that state of mind stay with me. It is possible to do all kinds of things one might never have thought possible. We drifted as the music dictated. After that day I lost all interest in people who say things can't be done. I'm not saying I became the master of the piano thanks to one trip. I learned about possibility and potential, how to open myself to the Force.

Improvisational creativity can't be taught. The doorway must be opened, which is the role LSD played, and then the courage to walk through it must be found. On the other side of the door is where you learn there wasn't much to be afraid of. Failure was only a means to success. Success was only a means to a greater achievement. Some things worked. Some things didn't. It wasn't good or bad. Experimentation has no real consequence. There was only the courage to do it and the satisfaction of having ventured out. Success became relative.

I didn't want to imagine firing that arrow without a target. Frank found out the hard way that LSD wasn't a great choice for recreational idle drug use. Gideon had to smoke marijuana to keep balanced because of all the acid he ate. I got far enough out where I touched the infinite. I never did it without a direction in mind.

A few days after the party Gideon, Chadwick, Sean, Shawn, Bruce, Vito, and I were sitting around the computer smoking cigarettes. Sean had brought his current girlfriend, Mina or Tina, I'm not sure, over. She looked suspiciously like Franks date from the party but with her clothes on it was hard to tell. She was eating a bag of skittles from the drug tree and rubbing on Sean's leg.

We had a new editing program and Vito was walking us through some of the high points. She must have got bored with the tech talk and went for more candy off the tree. She had been gone for a few minutes when we heard a gunshot followed immediately by screaming.

I stopped just inside the doorway. The walls and carpet in the front room were covered in blood. Blood was pooling on the floor and arterial spray had peppered the area like a grizzly Jackson Pollock painting. Mina or Tina lay on her side in the middle of a spreading puddle. From my vantage at the doorway I saw she had a dime sized hole in the front of her thigh and a fist sized hole in the back. Sean took off his belt and tied a tourniquet where her leg met her groin.

Mina or Tina lay screaming like an air raid siren. Ear splitting then fading off to a moan. Again, and again. She was holding her leg one hand in front, one in back, like she was trying to keep the blood from running out. The gunshot burnt her jeans and the skin around the hole was puckered and blistered. What happened?

Mina or Tina decided to stay in the front room because it was closer to the candy. Gideon's jacket was casually thrown on the small loveseat beside the tree. She had moved the jacket not knowing that Gideon carried a .357. That thing was enormous. It was a hand cannon with a nine-inch barrel and loaded with hollow point rounds. It had fallen out of Gideon's jacket when she moved it. Normally you could drop that thing all day long and it would have never gone off.

This one time, this one perfect time, it fell at a million to one angle and landed perfectly on the hammer. The impact was enough for the hammer to push the firing pin and detonate the round which blasted into Mina or

Tina at better than nine hundred miles per hour. The burnt powder left her with second and third degree burns around the entrance wound. The round exited her leg, which barely slowed it down, impacted the wall halfway up the stairs and departed the house continuing into the stratosphere.

Unsure of what I could to do help, I called 911. I felt useless standing there staring at her.

The paramedics arrived ahead of the police. A self-inflicted gunshot victim was a big going on for the overpaid and underworked police force of our small town. I think all of them showed up. We had town police, county sheriff deputies, and even state troopers on scene. There were ambulances lined up beside fire trucks even though the victim had been taken to the hospital by first responders. It was the first responders who caused all the fuss for additional law enforcement.

As the paramedics were stabilizing Sean's date for transport, I looked at the first police on the scene who were standing on the porch looking in the front door, staring at our humble Christmas tree, now spattered with gore, with their jaws hanging open.

"Yeah, dispatch, we're gonna need some back up here."

Fortunately for us we didn't have anything in the house all those fine upstanding officers would be interested in. Despite their best efforts and the best effort of a large scary German Shepard drug dog which left the house unable to stop sneezing. Our carpet was foul. We were lucky. The remaining police did the walk of shame down the porch steps. No arrests were made. Gideon's weapon was legal. He had the paperwork proving it.

Following that little incident, we were a little more careful about what we did and much more selective about who we allowed in the band house. We had dodged a bullet, no pun intended, even if Sean's lady hadn't, and we felt now more than ever before that fate was watching out for us. It felt good having destiny guiding us along, safe. We all felt we could do no wrong, but we were still careful. More careful than we had been. Gotta start somewhere, right?

I spent winter furiously contacting mutual friends, music professionals, friends, and friends of family, to help get our music shipped up and down the East Coast. We shipped music to New York, both city and state, and to shops down in Florida. We also had music in stores as far away as Texas.

I had also been doing what I could to get our album on homegrown radio shows in areas that also carried our CD.

Spring brought the end of bitter, unholy, ungodly, ass wrenching, ball shrinking cold. Spring also signaled it was time to take our show on the road. Touring is an expensive, terrifying prospect. If no one comes to see you then you can easily end your tour early, broke, a complete failure. I was determined it wasn't going to happen to us.

Is there any more despicable slimy creature in all creation than the DJ in charge of putting local music on the radio? If there is a slimier variant of slug vomit oozing from the deepest pits on the bottom of the ocean I haven't seen it. I detested dealing with DJ's. Far too many would be happy to put my stuff on air so long as I shoved coke up their nose. Or they'd be happy to play our stuff if we got their little dinkies wet. Small cash donation to the scum fuck retirement fund? Sure. I'd fucking love to. Quid pro quo baby, it's a tough old world out there.

Now if you were already a success had a manager, a major label, or both push your music dealing with this fuckery isn't necessary. A small band, scratching its way inch by inch, well, dues must be paid. And why these douche bags were the gatekeepers we needed to pay was beyond me. If their program had a decent following, then you could be sure it was going to be a nightmare getting their attention.

If nothing else, I was faithful and steadfast. I persevered.

I managed to get enough guys blown, paid, high or laid to get us on the air. And our test tour started with a bit of a buzz to it. People who saw us at one spot told people in another about the lights, the music, and the general awesomeness of what we did. We were not the typical bar band banging around for beer money. Cream rises. The word got out. Slowly, so slowly, the word got out.

The initial tour had four dates. We booked shows in New York, West Virginia which was Gideon's doing, Charlotte, and would wrap up in sunny Volusia County Florida. Starting off in Yankee country and working down to the Orlando area sounded like a fair piece of work. We believed in ourselves but didn't have the first clue how the wider world was going to take us. Always a little niggling of doubt worming its way into our heads. Imposter syndrome. Ugh.

The time had come to stop dreaming, start chasing and turn sorrows into gold. We started the trip with an amazing sense of purpose. Young hearts set free on the highways. We had the majority of the equipment in a box truck I borrowed from the family business. Dad wasn't thrilled but I played him psychological convincing him it was easy advertising. Gideon and I took turns driving as this truck had our gear and sound system, the heart and soul of our show.

We had another smaller box truck for the remainder of the lighting and stage equipment. If something happened to this truck, break down or wreck, we could still play. And the funky living room carpets, all rolled up, were waiting to share their own wonderful toxicity with the rest of America. Chadwick and Vito drove thas truck. I can only imagine the conversations. Both were serious techies and could talk for hours about gear, software, voltage, effects, or exotic technology we happened to need. They spoke expert tech but sometimes forgot the rest of us spoke English. I'm sure they thought most of the world was populated by morons. The Shawns and Bruce were followed in another car.

We weren't at a point where we had much of a crew. We would get there eventually but for now we had to heft and tote on our own. Embrace the cabinet hand. The trip to New York was uneventful. We had clear skies and easy traffic. It was a straight shot up Interstate 81 to 78 east right into New York.

The bar was called the Crow's Nest. We had a good crowd. We rocked them. The club owner was a decent guy who appreciated the work we put in to build a little hype beforehand. He paid us accordingly. And I think that is the thing which stands out the most to me; there are good people in the world.

My cut after our expenses was more than I made in a month working for my folks. I made more money for one show in a tiny club than I did in a month. It bears repeating. It was incredible. Nothing pays like the entertainment industry. I'm sure that's why everyone wants to be a rock god. I had never seen so much money in one shot. And it was our first show away from home! Damn! We left New York on a high feeling like the next time we played New York it would be in Madison Square Garden. What did I know?

West Virginia was a different animal. Gideon booked a show at a place called Skye. I became nervous as we pulled into the lot at one in the afternoon and there was a line of Harley Davidson motorcycles parked in front. Nothing BUT Harley Davidson motorcycles. As Gideon and I were getting out of the cab we were approached by a rough looking man in a leather vest.

Dude looked mean. He looked hard. He was also a fully patched member of the Devils motorcycle club. The

Devils were a tough group of guys you didn't want to notice you. If you were driving down the highway and noticed a group in the rear-view, you got the hell out of the way. Devils were a big deal in Summit Valley. They had a reputation for everything from murder, dealing, human trafficking, to racketeering. My balls drew all the way up into my throat.

"You the band?" he growled at us.

"Yes, we are," I replied and amazingly didn't sound like complete chicken shit.

"Well, y'all better be good or I know what we're doing tonight." He turned his back, the Devil on his patch leering at us, and strutted inside the bar. He didn't elaborate then or ever as to what might happen if we weren't any good.

"You're fucking kidding me, right?" I grabbed Gideon's arm and pulled him aside. "A Devil den? Are you out of your damn mind? You're going to get us killed!" I shook my head. I couldn't believe he booked a biker bar. Not only were we going to take an epic beat down, but our equipment would also be taken from us, the trucks would be scrapped, and we were well and truly fucked. Thanks, Gideon, for ending us before we could even get started.

"Chill man," Gideon seemed unconcerned about our imminent demise, "these are good people. They're giving us a shot. It'll be fine."

"Yeah, they're going to give us a shot. In the face. With a .44."

"Relax, let's go rock and roll the hole."

No one else had even gotten out of their vehicles. They were watching Gideon and I argue, waiting on which one of us would win. Gideon walked toward the bar, and I motioned to the crew we should go see where we needed to set up.

The interior of the bar was every bit as scary as I thought it would be. It belonged to an outlaw 1%er motorcycle club and bikers were everywhere. Full patched members were drinking beer or playing pool or sitting at tables smoking cigarettes and looking to me like the end of the world. Never had I seen a crowd of people who scared me as much as this one did. My thighs were tense and jittery. I felt my heart pounding in my throat, and I felt slightly nauseous but was too scared to throw up. Who knows what they'd do to me if I puked in the floor?

Denim and leather prevailed in smoky neon gloom. There was the occasional glint of metal from a wallet chain. The stage, directly across from the door, was surprisingly nice. It was elevated four feet above the main floor and the space itself was large enough that we could make use of our full PA system. There were also three offshoots from the stage where brass poles were fitted. All during our show we had topless women dancing on stage with us. Another first for me.

The guy who met us in the parking lot was talking to the barman and ignoring us. Above the bar was a large mirror with that grinning Devil painted on. The high quality spoke of how much money must have gone into that mirror. If it wasn't for all the big scary men, the club would have been a nice spot to grab a drink. The furniture was all quality wood, padded leather barstools, and the bar itself was a deep mahogany with brass fittings. The pool tables were well maintained, the felt brushed and thick. Everywhere I looked spoke of quality and care.

Must be good to be a Devil.

The largest human being I have ever seen before or since approached me. Well over seven feet tall and covered in thick hard muscle. He asked how much stuff we had and informed me they would be helping us unload. They wanted us to hurry up so they could see the sound check. He set his hand on my shoulder and his fingers stretched down to the middle of my chest.

I'm not a short man. I'm almost six feet tall but this man made me feel like a child standing next to daddy. I had no doubt he could have picked me up and flung me across the room. But he didn't. He told me his name was Tiny. *Of* course, his name was Tiny. What else could it possibly have been?

Tiny moved three speaker cabinets in the time Bruce and I had teamed up to move one. He took that cabinet too before we could get inside the building. Tiny was stupid, ridiculous, comic book strong. Maybe it came from the yellow sun.

Tiny brought with him several hang arounds, want to be Devils, and they were moving equipment into the club and setting it up faster than we could have imagined. Tiny said he liked making sure the band kept their hands rested so they weren't too stiff or sore to play. The man understood cabinet hand.

We ended up standing around watching as they set our stuff up with the speed and precision of practiced professionals. I was shocked. I felt the need to hover but quickly discovered it was unwarranted, unnecessary, and unappreciated. I backed off. They had our stage complete, from the effect lighting down to the rugs, in less than forty-five minutes. Those guys were good. Really good. The patched members continued to ignore us until we got on stage to test out the sound. Then guys started paying attention.

That was scary. It wasn't being watched that was bad, I was used to being watched, but being watched by these men who I thought would kill me as soon as speak to me I found frightening. Vito dialed in our sound almost as quickly as the Devils had set up our gear. Vito even had his own seat and spot for the board isolated from the crowd.

The Devils seemed to approve of the initial checks and turned back to whatever it was they had been doing prior to our sound check. We decided it was probably a good idea to drop all the ballads. We needed to hit these guys with good old-fashioned rock and roll as ferocious and unrelenting as they were. We were terrified of slowing things down. They didn't seem like sensitive, sentimental, or introspective deep thinkers. We were ignorant of how those guys really operated.

Respect was not a buzz word to men like this. You were respectful and you were treated with respect. If you were rude you could expect to spend the evening picking your teeth off the ground. We didn't understand that then. We were just hoping not to get beaten and robbed. Or worse.

Showtime found the bar packed. There were more bikers with full patches but there were also a surprising number of civilians. A majority of who were women. I asked one of the ladies before the show why there were such a disproportional number of women here. It seemed like all the ladies in the county had decided to party with the Devils. She explained this was the safest place for a lady to have a good time. Nobody would try to harm one of them, or take advantage, on Devil property.

Apparently, the Devils were a chivalrous group of outlaw bikers. Who knew? The lady explained anyone trying to force a woman to do anything she didn't want to was likely to have to fight off the entire club. And since the bartender was a Devil, there wasn't much chance of someone spiking a drink. Not with a whole club full of bikers looking to protect their reputation in their home club. I looked over at Tiny who dominated the bar with his massive frame. It made sense. I wouldn't want to have to fight any one of these guys much less that mountain of meat.

We took the stage and gave them everything we had. It was enough. During our first intermission someone in the crowd yelled out, "SOMEONE TELL THAT GAWD DAMN PI-ANNY PLAYER TO PLAY THAT GAWD DAMN PI-ANNY!" Instead of a cigarette break I improvised some pi-anny music. During the second intermission the piano lover hollered again for the pi-anny player to play.

"Aw Mick SHUT THE FUCK UP AND LET THE MAN HAVE A CIGARETTE!" Tiny bellowed from the bar. Mick wisely decided discretion was the better part of valor and life would continue if the pi-anny player was allowed to have a cigarette. I had two.

We ended up playing through two encores and ending up with Voodoo Chile. I thought they might tear the house down. I was out in the crowd, by the bar, and guys kept clapping me on the back. Telling me how much they enjoyed it. One guy asked me to come back to his house and have sex with his wife. She smiled and said she loved rock stars. Jesus.

I politely declined.

Tiny saved me by pushing into the group.

"He don't want none of that worn out snatch. Get the fuck out of the way, Sarge wants to meet 'em."

Being a mountain has its advantages. Dude didn't argue. His wife pouted in a sexy manner but didn't say anything. I was grateful for the escape. Sarge turned out to be their sergeant at arms. Sarge was a senior in the highly structured Devil motorcycle club, a man used to getting his way. He had Tiny stepping and fetching so I made sure to be on my best behavior. I needn't have worried because all he wanted to tell me was they enjoyed the show and wanted us to come back. He also paid me. I tried to give some back for the help with the set up and the labor they'd promised for tear down.

He asked if I was trying to piss him off. I felt my face get hot, I blush easily, and he started laughing. He clapped my back. I would have a bruise between my shoulder blades the next day. He gave me more money and told me it was a deposit for our next appearance. I signed a receipt and then I signed a stack of CD's. It was a great night. At the end of the evening, I swallowed my pride and apologized to Gideon.

"You were right, man, it was all good."

Gideon smiled, nudging me with his elbow, "See? They're good people."

I learned a lesson about not judging books and all that.

Down the road in Charlotte, Dad would say, "a might further then where we was at", brought us to what became one of my favorite places to play. Viridescent. Through the blacked-out glass of the main door you had a choice of three directions. The lighting in the entryway and halls was a rich jungle green. Three doors were highlighted with a slightly brighter shade of green. If you chose left, you ended up in a strip club with male dancers. Right took you into a club with female entertainers. Continuing straight led to a cavernous dance club with a nice wide stage. Both major acts and local boys were welcome on that stage. If you had talent, Viridescent would showcase it. Great for the resume and booking bigger gigs.

No signs indicated which door led where. If you didn't have the owner giving you the tour, we did, it was a matter of trial and error. First timers to the club were in for a shock as they explored. I wondered how many people found something new they liked. The thought still makes me smile.

The building occupied a whole city block. An entire city block dedicated to sin and debauchery. People think the South is conservative. Ha!

Through a miracle of soundproofing none of the PA systems interfered in any way with the sound systems of the other clubs. The main dance area already had an impressive array of effect lighting. We made it that much more impressive.

There were three main bars, one for each section, as well as several smaller bars where you could still get the basics – beer, shots, whatever. There were prep rooms backstage for the bands. Viridescent went all out to make sure performers felt appreciated. We did. I couldn't believe they opened the doors for us, much less decided to pay us. Viridescent was a dream.

It was our best paying gig. One date at Viridescent easily paid for the rest of the tour. Our radio campaign in Charlotte had been successful thanks to an escort named Angel and an eight ball. The radio play generated interest in our music. People were talking about this new group, requesting our songs on the radio. As much as I hated DJ's I have to admit their power was worth the purchase.

Viridescent's reputation for good times and quality bands combined with the radio buzz resulted in a crowd waiting outside to see us. We also had the respective strip clubs relatively empty. People came to see us. The dance club was packed. There were over a thousand people in the building. I don't think the fire code allowed for that, but hey, I'm just the pi-anny player playing my gawd damn pi-anny.

I saw a few of the Devils followed us from West Virginia and I was glad to see Tiny among them. After the show they approached us and wanted to know why we hadn't played any of the ballads at Skye we played in Charlotte. I told them it was because we thought they just wanted to rock, and we had no idea there would be so many women. Next time I assured them we'd play the whole show.

Two days later saw us in Volusia County playing a much smaller venue. The crowd was still respectable given the size of the place but after the first few shows it felt like a kind of a disappointment. We had adopted a mindset wherein we thought that there would always be crowds of adoring fans waiting on us. Musicians' ego is a terrible thing. Reality slapped us in the face reminding us we were still small fish in a giant pond.

We were also without our Devils escort. And I must admit I liked having them around. The Rolling Stones felt something similar when they had the Hells Angels doing security work for them, I bet, but even they hadn't had a Tiny.

Fuck it. The drinks were cold, and the women were hot. We still blew that bar out and then we went to Disneyworld. I got a blow job from Cinderella in the tunnels underneath Space Mountain. Disney truly is the Happiest Place on Earth. We came to rock and roll the hole and that's exactly what we did.

The initial tour was a complete success.

I was a couple thousand dollars to the good and decided I was working much too hard. I quit my job to focus on music full time. I also decided a rock god had no use for a Bachelor of Arts degree in English, so I dropped out of school. What did it matter? I was on my way. *We* were on our way and nothing was going to stop us.

The tour and the subsequent boon to my bank account was proof of that. My father wasn't terribly pleased with my decision, but life is full of little disappointments, and he couldn't deny the money. Young, single, and indestructible I knew better than anyone and I doubt God himself could have told me differently.

Dad wanted me to stay in school at least so I'd have a degree "to fall back on." Pass. What he was really saying was we weren't going to make any money. Well, he wasn't there. What did he know? Gideon quit his job servicing prison phone networks. Chadwick kept on with his job but in a more limited capacity. He was the only one though. Everyone else was completely sold on *the band*.

Our music was being requested for airplay, by people NOT dating us or our friends, and the cokehead DJs had no choice, yielding to our growing popularity. We had club owners seeking us out as often as Gideon and I sought them out. People looked for us. We were wanted.

Our reality was changing, by our own hands, and the gratification of seeing all that hard work bearing fruit was beyond compare. There was also a certain smug satisfaction in proving doubters wrong. The neener

neener factor. Juvenile? Yes. Petty? Without doubt. Satisfying? Beyond measure.

We had to hire more help. We picked a permanent light guy to work beside Vito. We also approved each of them to hire as many as five people each depending on how large the show. Some shows required more hands for no other reason than to help watch the gear. We also had a following of Devils trailing us whenever we were in the mid-Atlantic region. Devils had also begun to show up when we played Complaints.

We didn't play there as often because we were pressed for time. Also, the owner was a dick. Yes, he gave us a start, but he was still a dick. I've always tried to distance myself from as much dick as possible. There was enough dick to deal with daily, so I didn't see the reason behind searching out more. I was doing the dick a favor. The Devils scared his clientele.

I was having a cigarette during intermission at Complaints. A kid from the college came up to me and wanted to chat. I was tired and didn't really feel like being social. The kid was a fan and I appreciate fans, so I was talking to him. Tiny walked up beside me and put that monster hand on my shoulder.

"This dude bothering you Anny?" Tiny growled at the kid. Anny har har har. I had been Anny to them since the night we met. Awesome. The color drained from the kid's face. It wouldn't surprise me if the poor guy had to change his drawers.

"No Tiny. It's cool. He's cool, just a curious fan."

"Yeah, well how about you fuck off anyway. Leave Anny alone, let him smoke in peace."

The college kid fucked off like his feet were on fire and his ass was catching.

Even today, I miss Tiny. He was a big man with a big heart. The more I got to know him, the better I liked him. He was a chill guy. He didn't fight often but with as big as he was, he didn't have to. He liked art, and he liked music. Tiny had a thing for small animals and small children. He was father to nine children, five boys and four girls ranging from two years old up to fourteen, with the same woman. He loved anything small.

I felt bad for boys who would eventually come to try and date his daughters. Those girls were going to be virgins forever.

He wasn't a gentle giant. He was a Devil who earned his patch. He would not hesitate to wade into a fight. He had a fist like a cinderblock on the end of a pneumatic piston. A bone crushing blow to face delivered by Tiny wasn't something you would quickly get over. One night I saw

him get angry and send four men to the hospital. But he
was always kind to me, and he was always quick to help.

Speaking of bone crushing blows to the face, we needed
security. Crowds coming to see us could sometimes
become unruly and on occasion we needed someone who
could do more than keep an eye on the gear. The Devils
weren't around for every show so after an asshole stole
a small stage monitor by cutting the wire and walking it
right off the stage, we decided we needed a guy.

I put out an ad and the first person who answered was
named Dexter. Dexter was tall, almost six and a half feet
tall, and skinny. Wiry. Dexter kept his head shaved and
wore thick Buddy Holly style glasses. He certainly wasn't
scary. The guy didn't exactly radiate confidence. I asked
him if he understood what we were asking for. He smiled
and said he did. I had my reservations and told him so.

Crowds can be rough. People will do things in a crowd
they might never do otherwise. The pack can make a small
animal dangerous. He told me he had spent some time in
the military. I didn't understand the relevance. I told him
so.

Dexter kept smiling his goofy smile. I was about to end
the interview and send this goofy bastard on his way when
he asked if I would take some crew and step outside with
him. Gideon, the Sean's, two of Vito's roadies, and yours

truly went outside with Dexter. He told us to attack him, consider it sparring, let him prove himself.

I'd never been in a fight during a job interview. What the fuck, run amok, let's do it. We came at him one at a time at first. It quickly became apparent if we wanted to take him down, we'd have to rush him in a group. The job interview ended with the six of us on our backs bleeding from various cuts and scrapes. One of Vito's roadies had an eye swollen almost completely shut. I don't remember Dexter ever actually hitting any of us.

He got the job.

Dexter spent several years in the Army. He told us his job title was classified but he was technically an anti-personnel asset. Dexter was dropped off in a jungle and told to kill everything on two legs from drop off to extraction. He worked for years doing ugly for king and country. Then he was turned loose on society with a thanks-for-all-your-good-work and a small shitty pension, blood still warm on his hands. Dexter was lethal with anything or with just his hands. Was it overkill for a rock and roll band to have a guy who could bitch slap Rambo working security? Possibly, but it sure was rock and roll.

Besides, what harm from an ex-soldier whose battle stress was off the charts monitoring a group of long hair drug addicts? Surely, he could keep them safe not just from fans but from themselves in the chaos of live entertainment.

Several more clubs were added to a newer and longer tour. All our previous stops were included along with another dozen venues. Despite the new stops to play and new places to go our strongest bastion of support was still right here in our hometown area of Summit Valley. We did what we could to keep it that way. Complaints didn't get much business from us, but we could now play anywhere we wanted to in our immediate local area.

Everyone in southwest Virginia wanted us to come play. We took some losses in our pay to keep community support high. We agreed to play frat parties even though they ended up costing us money. Sometimes you must pay to play. The local Greek organizations didn't have enough room for all our gear so we would show up with our monitors and a bare bones light show. And the carpets. Even doing the bare bones shows the frats couldn't afford us. But there were always alternative compensations.

Gideon's wife hated us playing frat parties. She complained bitterly. More than one practice happened with Gideon storming in, almost too angry to speak, after fighting with her about the band. Too many young women that would absolutely throw themselves at anyone *in the band* and they didn't seem to mind if he was married or not. Gideon didn't seem to either. I didn't have a significant other so I took as much advantage as I could. There were times I took a girl to the back of the truck only to find Gideon had beaten me there. It was another part of the life. We were all so very rock and roll.

Sometimes I'd find one or both Sean's or Bruce. Many naughty things happened in the back of that truck. Inhibitions dropped away as often as panties hit that dirty wooden planking. There was plenty of alcohol if a crew member felt like getting fired. There was also plenty of weed if he didn't. Those of us *in the band* didn't drink more than the occasional beer but we smoked and fucked like champs.

Kappa Sigma contracted us to play a party at Virginia Tech. Their house was a sprawling two story Craftsman with a large wrap around porch. Situated on a private three acers, a rare thing for a fraternity, of rolling Virginia hills farmland they had money and space for us to put on a decent show. We set up on the wrap around porch on the rear of the property. The lighting trusses were set up facing the house and throughout the evening shadows danced and swayed across the back of the house. A view of the Appalachian Mountains provided natural ambiance to an already fine evening.

Dexter did a fair job of keeping people away from the stacks of speakers, and more importantly, away from our instruments. We weren't take the stage until it was good and dark. In early summer Virginia that can be as late as eight or nine pm. The fireflies were out doing their thing, but it was too breezy for mosquitos. Warm pre summer air was scented by honeysuckle and kissed by enough of a cool breeze to keep from being balmy. Nights like that made me wish they would never end. It's as close to heaven as we get to come until we get there.

The students started out in a good mood and were enjoying the show. The property sat far enough away from the neighbors to avoid noise complaints. Vito did his best to manage our sound, not an easy task in an outdoor venue. The acoustics play hell with the sound, but Vito had a professional ear and was adjusting levels as required.

We brought a couple of guys I didn't know, and honestly, I didn't bother to learn their names, to help heft and tote and run wire. Those guys were flirting with a couple of girls that weren't quite pretty enough to hook up with someone *in the band* but would fuck a member of the crew to meet one of us. I already had sex with a brunette over a cabinet in the back of the truck while Gideon was being serviced on the other side. Sex with an audience can make it so much hotter. Maybe that's just my kink. I had another blonde staring at me during the first set and I was thinking of taking her to the truck during intermission.

It was shaping up to be a fine night.

I decided to take that blonde to the truck, and was on my way to chat her up, when I saw a guy out of the corner of my come stumbling toward me. Frat Boy was obviously very drunk, a large vacant smile on his face. I didn't understand the threat Dexter thought he represented but apparently Frat Boy had death and chaos behind his empty grin. He staggered a couple of steps toward one of the cabinetry stacks when Dexter intervened. Dexter had a way of appearing wherever he wanted to be like a genie set free from the bottle. The guy could have given a master ninja lessons on moving swift and silent. One second the guy was smiling up at the bald string bean that had just materialized in his path, the next second this poor kid was flying upside down through the large picture window on the back of the house. His poor body made a terrible crash as it smashed butt first through two thousand dollars' worth of glass. Girls screamed and beer spilled, and the blonde ran away.

I shouted, "Jesus Dexter! What the fuck man!"

Calm as always Dexter answered, "Oh sorry. I thought he was going to stagger into the stack."

"Fucking shit man even if he had he wouldn't have hurt anything!"

Dexter shrugged. "Maybe. I guess we'll never know."

I didn't see how Dexter threw him with so much force. He grabbed the kids' hand and twisted and the kid was airborne. I've talked to various martial art experts in the years since and none of them has any idea how Dexter did it. What I know is we had to pay for that window and then we had to pay for 47 stitches to close 4 different cuts. He had one on the scalp, two serious gashes over the right side of his ribcage which required the most stitches, and one nasty gouge from glass impaling him in the right buttock.

After putting our pay toward the hospital bill and replacing the window at the frat house we ended up spending twenty-five hundred dollars to play the show. That signaled an end to several things. Never again would we play at a venue that small. Also, we would never pay to play again. We weren't invited back, and I never did get with that blonde. Life is full of little disappointments.

The new tour schedule was tentative at best. Two serious issues needed to be addressed before any of us felt comfortable going on the road. The first issue was with

Sean and Shawn. They had been cutting practice short when they showed up at all and were acting flaky in general. On the first tour they always showed up on time, prepared, and ready to rock. Those two were giving off a strange vibe.

On a Saturday afternoon the Seans departed early. We told them nothing of the new tour schedule. I didn't want to share information with people that weren't as serious as the rest of us. Gideon said he heard they were playing with another band. That would have been fine had they been honest about it.

We were selling CD's. We couldn't keep them in stores. I was refilling the stores that sold local music at least twice a week. We would take thirty CD's in at a time. Sixty CD's a week at ten dollars a CD. After paying the store their cut we were bringing in four hundred and fifty dollars a week in CD sales. Not too bad for a local outfit. I didn't know of another group as hot in our area as we were.

Not to mention anytime we played out in the world, be it our community or another, the shows were always packed. Always. We had struggled through to the point where we were beginning to make a decent living playing music. The Seans fought through the hard part. Jumping ship made zero sense. Zero. No other local band, and we knew them all, had anywhere near the level of success we were experiencing. Other bands were calling Gideon hoping to go on our next tour. They wanted to open it for us. Why the fuck would you want to give that up?

But the Seans were always hard to read. Friends since high school, sometimes it seemed they spoke their own language only they understood. And the choices they made didn't always make the most sense. Like any good creative they possessed a self-destructive streak made worse when together. They were always together. I recognized my own.

We waited fifteen minutes after they left practice and Gideon and I rode over to the house where the other band practiced. We saw Sean's car sitting in the driveway outside. I got out of the truck and walked up to the side of the house where I could hear if anyone was banging around on an instrument. They were bringing shame to a MegaDeth cover. Possibly Symphony of Destruction but it was hard to tell. I don't have an issue with MegaDeth but who does MegaDeth better than MegaDeth? And how far can you go playing someone else's music?

I walked back to the truck and told Gideon what I heard. They cut my practice short to go play this bottom rung bar band bullshit. I was angry, but more than that, I was offended. Deeply offended. We had been passed over for what? So they might get some free beers and maybe a hand job on Friday night? Trading steak for hamburger was bad business but that was their choice to make. I didn't want to play a rock star one night a week. I wanted that fucking job full time.

We got back to the band house, and I told Chadwick and Vito what happened. Bruce had gone home after the Seans left. Their faces dropped and Vito began to cuss the pair. Chadwick immediately suggested replacing them. Fairly extreme for him. But that's what it was, a betrayal. They had lied to us about family issues so they could bang out cover tunes with their old high school buddies. They hadn't been the same since Sean's girlfriend had blown a hole in her leg.

I thought they were hanging on to us in case we caught the notice of a major label. We were well on track to doing that from the strength of our album sales alone. High school bonds run deep I suppose. Certainly, they ran deeper than the loyalty shown to the group of guys who had stopped dreaming about it and started being about it. We had gotten off our collective asses, quit jobs, and worked like slaves to make this thing go. And it WAS going! If that's what they wanted, then the general conscience with us was they could have it. They weren't adding a thing Gideon, and I couldn't cover. It would be fine.

I called them from Gideon's house later that night. I told them they were out. They wanted to know why. I told them. Sean's ego kicked in and he started to puff up. He told me he didn't appreciate being followed and I better hope he didn't see me around town. I told him he wasn't being followed around. We wanted to see if we were being lied to and it turns out we were. Who uses a sick mother as an excuse anyway?

I then told him my address even though he already knew it. There was nothing between us except air and opportunity and I hoped he would be smarter than what he was currently showing. I didn't grow up in this area. I grew up poor in a large city where Irish boys were a minority. There wasn't a single area in Summit Valley, not even the "high crime" areas, which inspired any kind of fear in me. I'd make jokes that if they paid me enough, I would walk around those areas naked with hundred-dollar bills taped to my body. I was young and invincible. And stupid.

Sean didn't intimidate me. I understood his wounded ego made him lash out. He wasn't coming to hurt me. I wasn't going to hurt him. I was going on to bigger, better things and he could say he knew me when. Being successful is always the best revenge. I never found out why they chose to start over again. There was never the opportunity to talk about it. When we hung up the connection we shared severed.

The second problem we had to address was much more serious. Bruce played the music much too fast. We couldn't take him on tour if his excitement sped up his drumming to the point it cut the show by half an hour. Without keeping the proper time, we were also unable to do many of the subtle nuances which gave the music character. The music was too good to let it slide. It felt disrespectful not to do justice to the songs.

We tried talking to him first. Bruce was a good guy and we all liked him. He fit in. We wanted it to work out. I bought him a metronome to help him keep proper timing. We broke the songs down, let him listen while I ran a drum machine, and generally exhausted every avenue to get him back up to speed. Pun intended.

Nothing worked. Bruce couldn't keep time. Or he wouldn't keep time. He would start off fine but then he'd get carried away and play faster and faster. We were having trouble keeping up at all. The more we tried to fix things, the worse they got. Bruce was our friend. We all liked him. We needed someone else who could keep time. Without a drummer who could stay on beat, there would be no growth for us as musicians and as artists. It was fucking tragic.

We took out another ad. I dreaded interviewing more drummers. I foresaw having to deal with more kids that couldn't keep time with a clock. Besides the hash and trash we'd have to sift through, there was the fact that Bruce had good chemistry with the group. Finding someone like him, who fit in that well, who we liked as much as we liked him, was not going to happen.

Putting in the ad hurt. It hurt a lot. I was angry at Bruce for making us replace him. We maintained a sense of secrecy about the ad that didn't sit well with me. I didn't want to go behind his back. But I was outvoted. Gideon, Vito, and Chadwick said they thought it was better Bruce know nothing until we had his replacement trained. It felt a little too corporate America for my tastes. I thought Bruce deserved the right to know what we were doing and why. He'd earned the privilege.

He was a good guy. He would understand. There wouldn't be any ugliness like there had been with the Seans, right? Right? He wasn't a petty liar like the Seans. He was trying to improve, I thought he was trying. I believed in him, wanted him to pull through. I went to his house with my keyboard to help him one on one. Bruce earned the benefit of the doubt from me. Plus, how fucked up is it to know after the fact that you trained your replacement? I didn't want chicken shit underhanded behavior to be part of us or what we did. It tainted everything. I was outvoted. *The band* remained a democratic entity.

The first guy to answer the ad was a self-employed house painter named Raven. He claimed distant Apache heritage, but the guy looked white as cottage cheese to me. He was balding. A severe widows peak started at the top of his head. He wore paint splattered t-shirts and paint spotted jeans. There was always a faint chemical smell about him even after he stopped painting houses. It was as if the paint worked into his pores and decided to stay.

He was a good enough guy. He was easy-going but had some of the odd personality quirks I have associated with drummers over the years. He was always vibrating. There was always a foot tapping or fingers subtly drumming on a wall or tabletop. Sometimes you would hear him talking out a beat under his breath, "bop – bop-tsss-b-bop POP!"

Not often, but often enough to make you laugh at his embarrassment over being caught. He came to the first practice without his gear under the guise of being friends with Vito. Bruce didn't take much notice. He did his usual speed run through the music. Vito had picked Raven up from his house in a neighboring town so he would have time to listen to some of our music. It turned out that Raven already bought our CD.

We pretended to finish practice for the evening, and we waited for Bruce to go home. Then we lit another joint, passed it around, and let Raven do his interview on Bruce's kit. The first song we played with him so impressed us we asked if he wanted to do more. He wanted to run through the show. He seemed vaguely offended when I offered him use of the metronome we bought for Bruce.

"No thanks. I don't need it. It's all up here," he said tapping his temple with his fore finger. Alright dude. We'll go with that.

I watched him a little as we played. We would play a small sample of the song from the CD and then we would do it live. Raven would pay attention to what we were telling him and while we played, he not only kept time but added his own flourishes to the music. For the first time, the drums came alive.

Character like this from the drums was something we didn't even know we'd been lacking until Raven. He sat behind another guys' drum set and worked it better than the owner ever had. Bruce also didn't have the number and styles of drums that Raven brought with him. Raven brought bongos, chimes, triangles, snares, bass drums, and a large and varied kit that he could work in any style we requested.

Raven knew the difference between a salsa beat and a rhumba. He could play distinct styles of rock or blues. He had flair for Latin styles of drumming which brought high energy and new attitude to the music. He was strange in the manner all drummers I've met are strange but that wasn't a bad thing. We were a group of misfits and freaks who didn't belong anywhere if we didn't belong with each other. I worried Raven would have trouble fitting in. My fear was there wouldn't be the same chemistry that there was with Bruce. And there wasn't. Raven wasn't Bruce. They were different people.

Raven fit in but he did it on his terms. It was hard not to like the guy. We timed it out on one of those early practices with him and he added twenty-five minutes to the show. Twenty-five minutes just by playing the proper tempo. Gideon and I were ecstatic. We were able to do things we heretofore couldn't. We were able to interweave melodies in ways impossible before Raven.

The music grew.

The guy clicked and no one denied it.

Raven fit so well it made firing Bruce so much worse. Bruce came to pick up his kit. We moved it to the spot where the Christmas tree had been. We had wanted him to show up on a day we weren't practicing but Bruce knew our schedule. He showed up to see who replaced him. His face clearly showed surprise and hurt at seeing Raven set up where he used to be.

"Guess your friend decided to stay huh?" Bruce asked Vito.

Vito looked away shamefaced and mumbled something about he guessed so.

His sad little kit looked so pathetic contrasted with Raven's collection. He wanted to stay and listen to one more jam session. Gideon didn't think it was a good idea and told him maybe when the hurt feelings died down, he could come back. Bruce looked to Chadwick for support. He looked away. He looked at me. I couldn't stand the desperation and hurt I saw there. I looked away. I felt like a coward. We helped Bruce carry his stuff to the car. We pretended not to notice his tears.

After Bruce left nobody really felt like playing. Personally, I didn't feel we deserved to touch the music after the sneaky backstabbing way we treated Bruce. I still feel like he deserved to know who Raven was at the start and why he was there. Bruce had put in enough hours with us that he deserved an honorable exit. I don't know how we could have arranged it so Bruce could have left feeling like it was his idea instead of ours, but we should have figured something out. We should have put in the effort. Last I heard Bruce had quit playing music and moved to Savannah Georgia. I hope he finds his peace. He deserved better than he received.

Raven brought an entirely new dimension to the music. He felt like the missing piece we needed. There was a small issue with him though because life will never give something good without accompanying it with something as proportionally bad. For all the good Raven brought us and brought the music, he also brought his wife, Jody. What a vicious unforgiving bossy know it all heifer.

She controlled every aspect of Raven's life and there was immediate conflict when she found out her authority didn't carry over to *the band*. She wasn't *in the band* so nobody except Raven gave much of a fuck what she thought about anything. And she was a woman who was used to men giving a fuck what she thought. She wasn't super attractive, Raven wasn't with a model, or an actress, but nevertheless possessed a grossly inflated sense of her

own self-importance. Someone along the course of her
life had told her having a vagina made her opinions more
relevant. Not only did she have a vagina, but she had the
golden snatch which made her superior to every person she
encountered.

Jody was an ex-hippie turned shop owner. She ran
a moderately successful head shop near the college. I
don't have an MBA. I'm not an expert in business but
I don't think you need to be Steve Jobs to sell bongs
to college students. In the right location they practically
sell themselves. She believed she possessed a superhuman
business acumen and any business decision we made as a
band must be run by, and get the approval of, her expertise.

Gideon and I didn't care if she pulled on Raven's dick,
but she damn sure wasn't going to pull on ours. When
it came to *band* matters there was a short list of people
with decision-making privileges. And she wasn't on that
list. When she decided to pick up an instrument and prove
herself worthy of being *in the band* then she would be
entitled to voice her opinion on *band* affairs. Raven might
step and fetch for her, I didn't. Her golden vagina meant
fuck all to me.

Raven was often caught in the uncomfortable position
of having to mediate between me, Gideon, and Jody.
The fighting got so bad we had to make practices *band*

only. There was much groaning and grumbling about that decision, but it was the only way we could practice in peace. I liked to bring the occasional girl by the band house. Sometimes it got me laid. Raven's wife fucked that up for everyone. *Band* only is *band* only.

Her main issue was a point I had to give her. She was right, but so damn abrasive. Instead of looking at things from a budgeted, and time conscious position, she argued we were lazy. We weren't doing enough, trying hard enough. There was only so much money available to buy coke or hookers for DJ's. People had lives outside the band. Wrangling everyone into freeing a block of time, all together, is akin to working magic.

Her people skills were zero. I couldn't agree just on general principles. Ravens wife wanted us pushing harder on the tours and doing more to get more airplay. I happened to agree but I had to deal with the general pace the majority set. I loved touring. Touring is where the money came from, really. I wanted success. We all did.

She wanted it right now. She thought we should already be a top forty band doing arena tours. Nothing wrong there, it would be amazing, but we didn't have the album sales major labels notice. I read somewhere, and I won't vouch for the truth of it, Hootie and the Blowfish sold over a hundred thousand copies of their album Cracked Rear View in the Charlotte area alone before they were signed.

We weren't anywhere near those kinds of numbers. Yes, things were progressing, and progressing nicely, but we still had to keep grinding. We weren't even close to being able to walk into a major label and tell them we'd sold a hundred thousand albums without any help so what were they going to do for us? If we went to a label with our numbers, great for a small-time band but nowhere near the big leagues, we'd get laughed out the door.

Unless they happen to catch us live. Live we're a whole different animal.

But labels, especially major ones, are big businesses. And big businesses are in business to make money. They don't give a single shit about soul or feeling. The artistry is nice, but it doesn't pay the bills. OR the stockholders. To a label, bands are a commodity, a product, and nothing more. The blood, sweat, and dreams that go into giving life to the music means exactly dick. What they want is a product to sell. Have a product or fuck right off.

If you're a small-time group of losers like we were then you have even less of a shot unless you can prove you are profitable. Album sales and ticket sales are one way that you can prove their interest in you is going to be worth their time and money. Someone with the business sense Raven's old lady claimed to possess should have understood.

It takes time to build a fan base. It takes time to organize the tours and build the demand. This was an ongoing process when she made the scene, and she immediately began to berate the people that were making things happen. I didn't know what I was doing. I was too young to be effective. Gideon wasn't aggressive enough. He needed to take a larger hand in making the *band* a success.

Gideon was writing songs. Playing guitar. Singing. Gideon's hands were full without booking jobs, hiring, firing, expanding the show, researching new technologies we could adapt, and making sure all the book work was correct, so the taxman didn't take anyone to jail. I had taken on most of those jobs in addition to playing *in the band* and I was doing a damn good job of it. None of us appreciated her rough assault of our business practices. And all of us felt sorry for Raven for having to put up with such an epic bitch.

She might have made a great manager with how much she liked to fight but she was such an asshole. She would ruin the good rapport we had with our business contacts within five minutes. She described herself when we first met her as "brutally honest" which is code for I'm really an asshole, but I don't want to admit it.

I wanted to get out on the road too. I wanted to push our album sales. Her intent was good, but she was too aggressive and rough in her treatment of people. There were so many times I wanted to sit on her chest, and scream in her face, "SAME TEAM BITCH! SAME FUCKIN TEAM!"

I liked Raven and we had wronged a friend to have him. Karma certainly made us pay for him. And pay. And pay. And pay.

Bringing Raven up to speed on the show was easy. The guy was a natural and he understood showmanship. He was also a fan of our music, which was a plus. Being a fan and then being *in the band* was a dream come true for him. Finding out we valued his opinion on which direction to sail the ship was probably a novel experience for him.

I was comfortable taking him out on the road. Gideon was comfortable with it too. Raven's wife was rabid about it. I wondered since she wasn't going with us if she had a boyfriend. Gideon and I made so many jokes about the hard dick waiting to move into Raven's house. Who would volunteer for that job? I couldn't have been paid to fuck her with someone else's dick. We never said anything to Raven's face but in private we had our fun.

We had crew who quit their day jobs to tour full time with us. Dexter wanted to continue in his role as G.I. Security Terminator for hire. Dex had a government pension, so he really had nothing but time. After making sure the booking dates were solid, I went to his farm with Gideon to give him our tentative itinerary. He asked us to walk with him while he checked the animal traps around his property. We had no idea how large his property was, so we agreed to go with him. Dexter walked us across the lawn to the wood line. We walked into the woods and the temperature dropped ten degrees. The trees were thick crowding right up beside the trail. The shade was cool and most welcome after the afternoon sun. A thick blanket of last year's leaves crunched companionably underfoot as Gideon talked about the larger scope of this tour.

Dexter was unusually silent, and I turned around to see if he was still following the conversation or if he had drifted off. Dexter wasn't there. He wasn't behind us anymore. He wasn't anywhere I could see. The woods were silent and empty except for the two of us. I stopped Gideon mid-sentence, controlling my rising panic. Gideon sensed as I did the immediate danger we were both in.

It wasn't always obvious if Dexter was with us, on Earth, or if he'd traveled back in time to fight the enemy again. Had Dexter said or done anything flashback-y? I didn't remember but the silence made my butt pucker.

We were in the woods with a trained killer who occasionally thought the people around him were Vietcong. Dexter was a man turned into a living weapon with the express purpose of ending lives. We were in the woods on the home territory of Officially Classified as Antipersonnel. Antipersonnel. He was silent and neither Gideon nor I or even both of us together was anything even close to a match for him. We were on his property and no one else knew we had taken this trip out here. I don't think any other members of the *band* even knew where this place was.

I hoped Dexter wasn't currently in the grips of a flashback. Gideon looked as scared as I felt. His face was pale, and he had a fine line of sweat beaded on his upper lip. His eyes were darting left and right trying to look at everything at once. I understood the feeling. Every tree hid a thousand different horrors. Death lurked in every shadow.

"Hey, uh, you uh wanna go back to the car?" I asked. I hoped I didn't sound as scared as I felt.

"Y-Yeah," Gideon's voice broke a little and he softly cleared his throat, "Let's get the fuck out of these woods."

Gideon walked back along the trail silently. There was no sign of Dexter. We couldn't say exactly when it was Dexter split. One minute he was there and the next gone! Poof! With anyone else it might have been funny, or if not funny then at least cause for wonder. Dexter was terrifying when you weren't sure where his mental state lay. He'd tossed a kid through a plate glass window for stumbling, leaving him bloody and hurt, with barely a thought.

It's disgraceful how we as a country treat our Veterans. There is so much demanded of our soldiers, their time, their family lives, their blood, and sometimes their lives. Veterans should never have to pay taxes again. They should have access to all the free health care they need, be it mental, dental, or just the random checkup. Our country should honor their wounded warriors. Instead, we leave them homeless, destitute, and unable to work normal jobs or fit in with society. Broken minds, broken bodies, and broken souls. Twenty-three veterans commit suicide a day. Nearly one an hour.

Dexter grasping his troubled way back to civilization touched something in me. My father was ex -military, and a combat veteran, as was his father before him, an island hopper in World War II. I looked at Dexter and saw the struggles of my own family. I wanted him to succeed, and I wanted to be a part of his return to a semblance of normal life. It wasn't fair to him for me to project like I did, but I couldn't help it.

Dexter was an extreme example of a farm boy who believed murder in the name of country was a just and patriotic thing. He allowed himself to be turned into a weapon. A killer. He became Death, lethal, a coiled spring always ready to react. He couldn't relax because he couldn't get rid of the paranoia that had kept him alive in the jungles. His constant state of readiness, useful for killing in the green hells of southeast Asia, wasn't as useful in southwest Virginia. Fear and stress had broken him. And what did the government do? Nothing.

They gave him a shitty pension and shut the door. Rehabilitation? What rehabilitation? His youth and his ability to trust were taken in the name of duty. What he got in trade was a lifetime of guilt and nightmares and fear. No gradual reintroduction to society. All he had was a DD-214 stating his honorable discharge and they turned him loose on the world.

Poor guy was destined to fail. It's absurd to think he could ever hope to regain some kind of normal life. A wife? What woman could put up with the screaming night terrors or the slips back in time to when he was fighting for his life. Kids? Family? Forget it. No way. Children bring all manners of chaos into the house. Anything can happen anytime with children and chaos is exactly the wrong thing Dexter needed.

We took him on, not really understanding what we were dealing with. If Dexter was having a flashback, there was a very real possibility we weren't going to get out of those woods. We wouldn't even be able to fight him off. Maybe we'd get lucky but with Dexter counting on luck was a bad idea. Luck didn't keep him alive in the jungle.

Gideon and I walked slowly back to the car trying to stay in the middle of the trail away from all those crowding trees. Both of us breathed a sigh of relief when we cleared the wood line and were back in the open acreage around the farmhouse. At the car we lit up cigarettes with shaky hands. I exhaled the first drag when Gideon pointed toward the far edge of the clearing. Coming out of the woods a half mile from where we were was Dexter carrying half a dozen animals he cleared from traps around his property.

In the time Gideon and I noticed his absence to the time we saw him coming out of the woods on the far side from where he entered it Dexter cleared and reset all the traps.

The round trip was probably close to three or four miles and Dexter had silently left us and cleared them all. We weren't moving fast enough? Maybe he was protecting us from witnessing the carnage of the traps. We were civilians, soft, in Dexter's eyes. I think in his own weird way he was trying to protect us? Respect our time? Figuring out why Dex did whatever he did was one of the great mysteries of our time. He set the pile of animals by the side of the house to skin later and smiled his Dexter smile and told us when we were ready to go on tour just let him know. He'd keep us safe. Unbelievable.

We had been pushing cocaine up the noses of DJs in the areas where we were going to play. There were dancers and escorts aplenty who were sent to give blowjobs or hand jobs or whatever odd jobs might be necessary. Any means we could employ - straight or not - were used. All for the music. Anything for the music.

We pushed hard to get our names and our music known in those communities. If the area was a six-hour drive Gideon and I would often take weekends and walk the club scenes doing our brand of homegrown promoting.

This second tour needed to be a success. Pressure to succeed leaned heavily on our minds.

We started our second tour with Gideon, Chadwick, Raven and me. We had Vito and he decided until he found someone he was comfortable with, he would run lights as well as sound. When Vito made up his mind about a thing it was best to move and watch him go. Dude was stubborn as all hell. He also decided without the Sean's around he would use a portion of what would have been their cut to hire a couple of strong backs and weak minds to heft and tote cabinets.

Dexter showed up with a nice surprise for us. He was driving a VW microbus *the band* could ride in while Vito and the roadies drove the truck. We still had to take three vehicles at a minimum for the gear and personnel and that meant gas for three vehicles and food and lodging for the people but those are the breaks.

Driving in upstate New York when we decided to stop for gas and snacky snacks. A Mountain Dew to hold off on the munchies until we got somewhere I could get dinner sounded fine. One of our road crew didn't want to wait and grabbed a can of Chef Boyardee SpaghettiOs from the gas station. Judging from the dust I bet they'd been sitting on that shelf since sometime after World War II.

Vito asked if I'd spell him in the truck for the last sprint to the hotel. Gideon spent the last two hours farting in the van. I think any of those guys would have happily taken the truck to get away from the mad gas attack.

"Hey man, I don't think you should eat those. "I told him climbing behind the trucks steering wheel.

"Nah man, I'm starving. It's cool."

"We can hit a drive through if you aren't going to make it. Really, don't eat those."

"No reason to spend the money or the time. I'm cool."

"Dude, at least heat them up in the microwave." I pleaded as he had popped the top and was eating cold SpaghettiOs out of the can. The stink of that cold jellied tomato sauce is best left undescribed.

"Nah man, they're good like this. You don't need to heat 'em, they're good just like this, right out of the can. It's cool."

My father always said, "them that can't listen let 'em feel." I abandoned trying to help the guy. If he wanted to destroy his gastrointestinal tract with ancient pseudo-pasta, then that was his business.

We left the gas station, and the roadie pitched his now empty can in the trash between the pumps as we left the lot. He grinned and told me again how it was cool to eat cold Spaghetti-o's out of the can. He had an iron stomach.

It's cool, it was all so very cool. I shook my head and concentrated on the road.

An hour or so down the road Iron Gut looked a little green. Said he wasn't feeling so good. What a surprise. There was nothing for it. I couldn't stop, we were so close to the hotel and an end for the night. He told me he was going to puke. I told him if he puked in my van, I would have Dexter make sure he ate every last drop.

Threating people with Dexter got things done. He rolled down the window, leaned out, and distributed the contents of his stomach along the interstate at seventy miles an hour. He hung out the window for a good fifteen minutes puking and finally stopped as we exited the highway. In the hotel parking lot ol' Iron Gut told me he was feeling much better and was ready for dinner.

I stared at him for a moment, at the flecks of used SpaghettiOs on his face and in his hair, then got out without responding. The next morning Gideon pointed out our van had an orange stripe splattered down the passenger side.

"That's cool man. Where'd that come from? Why don't we match the other side?"

I looked at the stripe. Iron Gut found something extremely interesting about his shoes.

"I don't want to talk about it."

Touring this time around didn't have near the surprises the first time had. When we played for the Devils again, we played the entire show without worries. They managed to get us to stay for back-to-back nights on a Friday and again on Saturday. We didn't have to be anywhere until the middle of the following week and that was to finalize preparations for an outdoor festival in our hometown before heading south. Dragging out the schedule made us more money and built more goodwill. Goodwill is an important commodity when dealing with an outlaw motorcycle club.

Dexter surprised me by asking if he could ride with me when I went to sign contracts for the Summit County Fair. He never asked to be included so I supposed he was getting comfortable with me. Maybe he was lonely. Goodwill is important dealing with Dexter as well. I knew he would watch my back, not that there was much of a chance of being attacked while signing contracts, so why not?

He picked me up at home in his VW and drove over to the fairgrounds. He waited quietly while I signed the contract and then collected our check. Paid in advance was nice, we didn't usually do things that way. The promoters seemed anxious to secure us. I fought to keep my ego in check but right after I singned they told me the band they had scheduled for our spot canceled and they were taking a chance on us. It was our dumb luck we were available to play the date at such short notice. So much for ego.

We booked Saturday afternoon leading up to their headliner later that night. We weren't the lead act, but we'd play on the main stage. Playing for an estimated crowd of five thousand people or more was going to be a whole new challenge for us. Dexter and I went to the main stage area, currently unoccupied, and security allowed us to check out the backstage area. We played clubs smaller than backstage.

I looked to where the crowd was going to be. It would be a sea of faces. A decent size crowd wandered around the carnival attractions and various food vendors. I had never seen so many people. This was going to be intense.

I left the stage and Dexter and I decided to walk around the fairgrounds a little. The main stage was located at the north end of a street lined with vendors, food booths, and games of chance. Roasted corn and fried dough scented the air along with the yeasty undercurrent of beer. At the southern end was the entrance to the carnival rides and the two smaller stages which flanked either side of the ride area. A Ferris Wheel silhouetted against a flawless blue sky and a wild mouse drew screams from riders as cars clacked along the tracks dipping and turning. There were swings and one of those god-awful boat rides that rock back and forth and look like a Viking ship. For whatever reason I can't stand those. If the boat goes upside down, I can deal, no worries. Otherwise, they're terrifying. The rocking back and forth scares the hell out of me. The one at the fair didn't go upside down, I'd be avoiding it. I turned away from the Viking ship, continuing down the throughfare. More crowd than I was comfortable with pushed in around me. A merry go round blasted its merry, slightly psychotic music, drowning out conversations of anyone who happened to pass by. Bored parents stood next to squealing wide-eyed children while frozen horses with insane expressions chased each other in an infinite circle.

Multiple food vendors caused my inner fat kid to rejoice at the variety. Booths offering barbecue sandwiches, corn, popcorn, popsicles, ice cream, funnel cakes, fried coke, fried butter, fried shrimp, fried okra, fried fish with French fries. There were chocolate dipped fruit kabobs, cotton candy, and all manner of desserts on a stick. So much greasy goodness everywhere I looked.

Local restaurants set up booths as well. Dexter and I made our way by people sampling actual meals and wines from local restaurants and wineries, beers from local breweries. Alcohol should go great with all of the spinning rides. I envisioned cascades of slightly used beer and onion rings with a dash of freshly chewed corn dog flying off of the wild mouse, or spinning swings, showering the crowd underneath. County fairs are always fun.

In addition to the restaurants various other businesses paid for tents and booths. Everything from livestock, head shops, fad diets, and martial arts were represented. I stopped outside an open sided tent where a guy was putting on a martial arts display. Not surprisingly Dexter reappeared at my side. I had no idea when he had rejoined me. I was almost used to it. Almost. The sign on the tent read Flying Dragon Dojo – MMA, Karate, Jiu Jitsu, Krav Maga, Mui Thai Boxing! Never feel afraid again! Walk the dangerous streets with confidence!

I had never thought of the streets around Summit Valley as dangerous. A guy wearing a white gi, loose pants and a loose jacket secured with a black belt, stood in the center of the tent whipping a pair of nun chucks around. On the back of his shirt a snarling Chinese dragon bared its teeth. I guess it was his business. He was wearing a crisp white gi tied at the waist with a black belt. The head instructor, I assumed. He told the onlookers he could teach them to do everything he was doing. The nun chucks flew around in a blur of speed. He could make a warrior out of anyone.

Dexter pushed up to the front of the crowd and smiled at the guy.

To look at Dexter you wouldn't think the man was as deadly as he was. In fact, he looked like the kid that got pushed around on the playground all grown up. There was nothing intimidating about his string bean build and there certainly wasn't anything intimidating about those military style Buddy Holly glasses Dexter wore.

Dexter smiled and subtly shook his head. My balls drew up.

"That guy doesn't know about being a warrior. He'd get you killed." Dexter none too subtly whispered. He whispered like he was in a sawmill guaranteeing nun chucks would hear him. The guy looked over, already irritated when he saw the tall doofus who'd been smiling at him was the source of the comment.

Maybe the instructor decided he was going to teach Dexter a lesson. Humble the upstart in the crowd. Earn a little more business. Maybe he thought whirling those nun chucks right up in Dexter's face would scare him off. Dumb decision. Dexter didn't move as the guy approached the nun chucks missing Dexter's face by mere inches. And maybe the guy thought Dexter was too scared to move. Dexter was neither humbled nor intimidated. Faster than I could follow Dexter snatched the nun chucks away from the guy and hit him in the forehead with his own weapon.

Dexter hit him hard enough the instructor went from standing to sitting. He looked confused as to why he was now seated. Dexter leaned down and handed the nun chucks back to him. The surrounding crowd uttered a collective, "OOOOOH!" at the flat clap of wood against skull. Dude snatched his weapon back, apparently deciding Dexter had gotten lucky, got back to his feet and set the nun chucks spinning in Dexter's face again, possibly hit him back.

Dexter had no intention of being hit and took them away, again, and hit the instructor in the same spot on his forehead. A large purple egg was starting to form. Once again Dexter handed the weapon back. The goofy smile never left Dexter's face.

The crowd was shouting things like, "don't do it!" and "dude's faster than you, deal!" and "better leave that nerd alone before he kills you!" Sound advice. Martial art master ego must be as bad as the musician ego. He wouldn't let it go. He couldn't accept this dorky string bean was faster, better, and making him look silly.

I expected the police to arrive any moment.

Neither Dexter nor the master spoke a word during this exchange. The guy tried twice more to the exact same result. The last time Dexter hung the chucks around the guy's neck. Shouldn't martial arts teach humility? Isn't that the point of having a "master"? I wouldn't need four nasty shots to the nugget with my own weapon before I concluded maybe, just maybe, this guy wasn't really worth the pain. Maybe I'm a big pussy but it wouldn't take that many knocks to my noggin for me to get the message.

The ugly goose egg on the man's forehead split open and blood was freely flowing down his face. He didn't seem to know where he was. I thought I should get Dexter away from the tent before he either killed the master or got arrested. Checking the fairway we were still clear of police. Regular folks strolled unaware by the tent, sipping ices and munching Lions Club corn dogs.

Dexter's hands moved faster than my eyes could follow. The poor dude trying to promote his dojo never had a chance. I dragged Dexter away hoping the master would stay home Saturday. Let his head heal. The crowd was quickly shifting from awed to angry and I was hearing murmurs of unnecessary beatings, but no one was brave enough to confront us. Yet.

Everyone has heard the urban legends about Bruce Lee's superhuman speed. Bruce caught a striking cobra, played ping pong with roundhouse kicks, and the fabled one-inch punch. Some of it might even be true. Dexter's speed, his hand eye coordination, would have put a serious whuppin' on Bruce. I have never seen hands move that fast. He didn't even seem to try. Fuckin' Dexter. What the fuck were we thinking taking this guy on?

When people think about a rock and roll tour, they don't imagine the reality of being on the road. Ask someone what they believe a tour is, and you'll hear variations of debaucheries and self-abuses. Alcohol, sex parties in hotels, drugs, and other insanities. I'm not saying these things didn't happen but never to the extent you might hope for. I've never been to a sex party. Not that I'm opposed to such a thing, I've had sex in the same room while other guys were having sex. I'm certainly no prude. I'm down for group sex. The thought of a mass of bodies all sweaty and rubbing around on each other, well, yeah, that's pretty hot. But I've never been to one and I doubt I ever will.

We didn't really go wild with drugs either. We smoked more weed than anything else. more to take the edge off or help get us in the mood to play than a desire to get fucked up. Nobody I knew trusted man-made drugs like meth or cocaine or even prescription drugs. We had a saying, "Beware the dread coke beast."

That was a mantra we took seriously. Besides, we were all too broke to afford a coke habit. Cocaine is expensive, a rich man's habit. I always associated cocaine with big money. You need to keep a serious influx of scratch to afford two thousand dollars a week or more for a fucking habit. That's successful actor, investment banker, trust fund kind of money. We were all small-town kids with small town bank accounts who had no business in big city drugs.

We all valued our brains too much. I know, what about the LSD? Acid is a tool. Using acid was a way to accelerate the learning processes. We used acid to take away the fear. Inhibitions were absolutely destroyed and without them it's possible to explore in ways you never believed possible in a straight mindset. Not a recreational thing. A teaching thing. Most people don't need this kind of teacher. Most don't fear their abilities will never unlock. Artists fight fear above everything else.

There is fear of failure. Fear of being thought a fraud. Crippling self-doubt can keep an artist, even the greatest of them, from ever putting their work forth. Artists give themselves to the uncomfortable if they are to grow in their chosen medium. Acid short circuits those fears, shortening the learning curve dramatically. This will build self-confidence. If you don't understand the difference

between a tool and recreation, don't fuck around with
LSD.

By most rock standards we were fairly tame. Touring
is hardly glamorous. Sometimes we slept in the vans.
Sometimes we went without meals. And sometimes we ran
out of money through no fault of our own.

We were in South Carolina headed south after a
successful week in Charlotte. There were shows in Myrtle
Beach and all of us were looking forward to rocking the
bars and watching bikinis. We stopped at a small motel
on the outskirts of Myrtle, the kind of place tourists avoid
in favor of the larger and nicer condos with ocean views.
Within budget, quiet, and little chance anyone from a
show might find us, the place had its charms. We might
have to fumigate the luggage for fleas or bedbugs, but it
was within budget, and we could crash there.

The motel was a two-story building built in a U shape.
The office was located at the center point of the U and
the rooms stretched off to either side. A scummy pool sat
between the arms of the U surrounded by tired looking
plastic and in some cases moldy lawn furniture. A few
stubby palmettos and more than a few cigarette butts

dotted the cracked landscape of the parking lot. The wind had blown random garbage around the base of some of the trees.

The place had seen its heyday forty years before we got there.

One nice feature the place had, besides cheap rooms, was a large stucco painting of a seascape at the far end of the left branch of the U. It looked recent, a fresh painting and the texture of the wall lent a depth which granted a striking realism. The theme was simple, cliché even; a brigantine fighting its way through a storm. A pirate ship like I imagined Captain Kidd or Blackbeard might Captain. You could almost hear the groan of the wood beams, the flapping of the torn sails, the sting of the windblown ocean as the ship battled a storm that surely would sink it.

I almost expected whitecaps to spill over onto the ice machine soaking anyone foolish enough to stand there. Lightning ripped an angry sky, but the boat struggled on. Courageous. Defiant. I stood there staring until Gideon made a joke about me either opening our door or moving so he could. I opened the door a little shamefaced, I had been sucked in. It was so out of place in this seedy motel. I couldn't imagine why the artist would allow it where almost nobody saw or appreciated it.

Putting the boat and its struggles out of my mind, I left to go relax by the pool. It was more of a mosquito breeding ground than swimming pool. I picked a chair that wasn't too cracked, missing too much plastic or too moldy, not an easy task, and angled it where I could look at the seascape. We spent the evening hanging out around the pool. Vito and Dexter hit up a drive thru and brought back a couple bags of burgers, another glamorous aspect of being on the road. The diet inevitably sucks, and I almost always end up constipated. Man was not meant to live on French fries and burgers alone.

The first week or two we try to be good. We try to take care of ourselves and eat vegetables, usually from cafeteria style restaurants, but a couple of weeks in everyone is too tired. All we wanted was get something quick and go to sleep or get something quick and set up the show or get something quick and get on the road. Nobody wanted extra hassle. We grabbed a quick meal so we could relax and maybe do a little touristy something before the gig.

The next morning, I woke to the manager screaming outside the door. Gideon looked at me, I shrugged, and we went out to see what the ruckus was. During the night one of Vito's crew had gotten really drunk. I checked out what made the manager so upset. That magnificent painting had melted, the stucco ran in goopy rivers down the wall to pool under the ice machine. The painting on the stucco was destroyed.

During the night our roadie had taken a roll of paper towels from the public bathroom and filled the ice bucket from his room with water. He tore off one sheet at a time, soaked it in the bucket, rolled it up in a ball and launched the wet mess at the painting. There were literally hundreds of paper towels stuck to the wall, the ice machine, and bunched up on the floor. The stucco melted and ruined the painting. The roadie had passed out in the watery mess by the ice machine. He still had a big stupid grin on his face, probably still drunk, when we woke him with the irate motel manager.

The roadie apologized over and over. I wanted Dexter to punch the guy through a palmetto or hold him under that mosquito breeding ground until the bubbles stopped. And with the excellent relationship I had with Dexter he probably would have done it. Shameful a beautiful work of art like that was ruined by a drunken moron. Worse still, that drunken moron was associated with the *band*. He wasn't *in the band,* but he was without doubt with *the band*. We didn't make the guy pay for the damages because Gideon felt there wouldn't have been any damage if that idiot hadn't been with us. It made zero fucking sense. Gideon acted like it was our fault, like bad karma finally caught up. I thought dude bro should own the consequences of his actions. His drunken stupidity had nothing to do with me or mine.

The manager was furious, screaming about damages, vandalism, lawsuits and sending people to jail. He hadn't called the police and Gideon and I tried to soothe him before he went to pick up a phone. He insisted we pay for the damages. What we should have done is fire the roadie on the spot, packed up, and left him to deal with the manager as well as find his own way back to Virginia. What we did was pay the manager most of the money we earned in Charlotte leaving us with enough cash to fill up the trucks and get us to the show in Myrtle.

In the interest of presenting a united front, and compromise, I agreed to stop arguing and Gideon paid the manager way more than the painting was worth. He could have that stucco replaced five times over with the amount of money Gideon shelled out. Gideon didn't want the cops involved and I didn't either. The manager sensed our reluctance for police involvement and hustled us. I don't really blame a dirt bag manager of a dirt bag motel for doing dirt bag things to dirt bags that had damaged his dirt bag property. It's a mean old world out there. Everyone wants to get paid.

We left the roadie standing in the parking lot of the motel to find his way back to Virginia, the second part of the compromise between Gideon and me. No, I don't feel the least bit bad about it either. I didn't want to look at a moron who spent all our money with a bucket of water and a roll of paper towels. We didn't eat an actual meal for two days. The group existed on chips, peanuts, jerky, skittles, and beer until we got paid again. We slept in the van which wasn't as bad as usual because we parked down by the ocean and the crashing waves lulled us to sleep.

We were a little wobbly after the show because we all needed to eat. One of the benefits of being in a tourist trap is there was no shortage of good places to eat open late. We took a handful of newly acquired cash and went out to find some vegetables. When I woke the next morning, I walked from the van over to the public restroom and had a nice long uninterrupted poop to the sound of the ocean. It felt great being back on track again.

We spent the next two years working in a series of clubs from New York down to Florida and as far west as Texas. We made money. We sold CD's and I was feeling like this whole rock star thing would come to pass through sheer force of my will. It was an incredible feeling.

Fucking fleas were everywhere. The band house needed a bug bomb, bigtime. Chadwick took in a neighborhood stray cat. The cat came and went as it pleased, as cats tend to do, but most of the time it stayed in or near the band house. We never knew who owned the cat but Chadwick fed it and kept fresh water out for it and let it come in out of the rain or cold. It was a female and every so often it would get pregnant.

The pregnant cat disappeared, had her litter and showed back up with no clue as to the whereabouts of her kittens. Sold, eaten, in someone's house, we had no idea what she did. Nor did we care. Gideon started calling her Slutcat because we didn't know the cat's name and really, it fit. The name stuck.

After a year and three litters of us not knowing where she went to have her kittens, Slutcat had a litter on the porch of the band house, specifically under the porch steps. Chadwick kept food out for her but didn't take any further steps to help her or the kittens. I don't blame him; it wasn't my cat, and I wasn't spending any money on it either.

I offered to bring my Boston Terrier over and let her handle the kitten problem with her Boston brand of extreme prejudice, but Boston would have taken care of Slutcat too. Boston was mean. If she had been a big dog

I would have had problems with her. Along with getting rid of moles in my mother's basement, Boston was also requested to get rid of a group of stray cats and their litter at the bed and breakfast my family owned. She performed with vigor and enthusiasm. Boston wasn't big, but she was tough. If you asked me to place a bet on who would win in a fair fight between a twenty-pound dog and a twenty-pound cat my money would be on the cat every time, unless the dog in the fight was Boston. Always bet on Boston.

Chadwick knew Boston's reputation and declined my offer of her varmint purging services. I couldn't blame him for being human. Chadwick brought the kittens out from under the porch and put them in a box in the band house. Slutcat seemed alright with it and would lay in the box and nurse. Then she would get bored and leave.

The kittens quickly discovered how to climb out of the box and were running wild around the house in no time. It wasn't uncommon to be practicing and feel something clawing its fuzzy way up my pant leg. Or to look up and see a kitten climbing the soundproofing on the walls or working their way up a microphone stand. They got particularly frisky when Slutcat was out working the streets. With mama there they stayed in the box but when she left, they raised fuzzy blue hell everywhere. Maybe they were lonely.

Along with having six wild fur balls with claws rampaging around the house the kittens all picked up fleas. Maybe Slutcat brought in the first ones, but the infestation quickly reached biblical proportions. I was terrified of bringing them home to my two dogs because I knew what a nightmare it was getting rid of fleas. Killing fleas requires a different Trinity than Get High, Play Music, Get Paid. This one is Bathe, Bomb, Blitz.

Flea collars are a scam. Complete garbage. Flea collars are only good for putting into a vacuum bag or tank if your vacuum is fancy. Used properly a flea collar will kill all the eggs you can suck up off your carpets or furniture. On an animal, flea collars only kill the fleas underneath the collar so that leaves ninety eight percent of the animal a flea carnival.

The only way to get rid of an infestation is to spend a day committed to a total killing blitz in the house and yard. First thing is to bathe the animals in some type of flea killer shampoo. I preferred Adams as it did a good job killing and smelled nice afterward. It also did a good job conditioning and protecting the fur for the three days until you could apply drops, like Frontline or Advantix, to the neck of Barney or Biscuit or Boston.

After the dog or cat has had their bath, the next step is to get them out of the house for at least four hours while you set off a metric fuckton of bug bombs in the house. Before detonation of the chemical death, bag up all the laundry and bedding in plastic garbage bags, and take that mess to a laundry mat where you can wash it all at once. Make sure your food is covered or in the fridge but otherwise leave the cabinets open so creeping insect Armageddon can find its way into all of the cracks and crevices of the house.

Once the laundry is loaded and the house is nice and smoky with poison then you must blitz the yard with more bug killer. You can no longer get the toxic stuff, I was a big fan of Spectracide 5000, a biblical, Old Testament, wrath of the Gods blanket killer, as was my father, but that turned out bad for the hummingbirds or fish or some such. After using a blanket killer nothing moves in the yard except the wind through the grass. There are still some environmentally friendly varieties you can find to treat the yard, but there isn't anything on the market anymore with the pure killing power of Spectracide 5000.

Everything must be done the same day. There can't be any place for the fleas to go and hide so they can regroup and attack the house later. There must be total and complete annihilation of any and everywhere they can go. Fuck them and their eggs too. I knew Chadwick wasn't going to go through those steps even if he had help from the rest of the *band*. There were people who would help him out just to see the place where the music came to life. I told him to take advantage, but Chadwick was an extreme introvert. How he managed to go in front of hundreds of people and rock that bass like he did will go down in history as one of the great mysteries of the ages. Okay, probably not, but it was still damn peculiar.

In order to avoid bringing Slutcats fleas' home to my animals and then having to do the ritual of insect death I needed to keep the fleas off of me and my things. Before I went into the house, I would coat myself, paying close attention to my legs and shoes, with Deep Woods Off. With my chemical shielding set to maximum, I could do my thing secure I wasn't bringing home parasites to my fur babies.

The flea problem at the band house got bad. I could see them crawling up Gideon's legs like a plague while he tried to play. Nothing will break your concentration like being attacked by a swarm of blood sucking parasitic insects. I also sprayed down my area. My chair, the stands, the area around my keyboards all received a coating of Off. Every time. Gideon was frustrated with Chadwick's seeming indifference to the flea problem. He started meeting me outside the house, always making sure he was there before me, and using my Off on his legs and feet. Before the pre practice joint there would be a ten-minute bitch session about the fleas.

He started bringing his own Off. Before every practice, new time had to be dedicated to spraying down the area with repellant. Raven quickly followed our example and was soon spraying himself and his kit with Off. The room would fill with a noxious miasma of Off, cigarette smoke, marijuana, ash, Chadwick's grilled hamburger, and dirty cat.

We finally had enough and forced Chadwick to get rid of the kittens. While he was taking the kittens to the shelter we snuck in and set off bug bombs in the band house. They might still be in the yard and Slutcat still came and went but the departure of the kittens signaled a gradual end of the infestation. I wanted to go back on tour for no other reason that I could play music without having to smell pine funk all night.

Chadwick came home to Gideon, Vito, Raven, and me standing on the porch. We told him he couldn't go inside because we were fumigating the house. Nobody could deal with the fleas anymore and if he wasn't going to address the problem then we would. In typical Chadwick fashion he wasn't upset he couldn't go in his house, neither was he grateful for help with the bug problem.

We took Chadwick to a movie then we went out to eat Chinese. Chadwick seemed mildly offended he had to pay for a meal, but too bad, tough shit. I ate a plate of General Tso's chicken and sticky rice. I've lived all over the world and one of the best Chinese restaurants I've ever been to is in a tiny town in southwest Virginia. Funny that.

After dinner Raven went home to his bitch wife. The rest of us went to Gideon's house for an after-dinner smoke and strategy session. I was still pushing to get back on the road. We made money despite the cost of touring. I had made more contacts and lined up several new venues for us to play. We had been invited back to the festival despite Dexter's shenanigans and this time we were promised the main stage headlining act but on an off night. That was fine. Playing for several thousand people was still playing for several thousand people.

\There was a large club in Florida, actually several clubs together linked by swimming pools and outdoor bars which wanted us to rock. The owner of the club had a brother who was an active member of the Devils and because of him I got the phone call.

There were some big names who played there but those big names were typically in the rap or hip-hop market. We didn't do rap and hip hop. I wasn't sure the crowd would appreciate the type of music we did but a paying gig is a paying gig. If we could prove crossover appeal it would only strengthen our resume when the time came to actively start shopping for a major label.

I thought it was time to start looking but Gideon thought we needed more seasoning. He was alright with touring if he approved of the places, but he didn't want to start pimping us out to labels. I booked the jobs, and I did it if Gideon approved or not. If it made him feel better to think he was the final word on what jobs we did, it was no sweat off my sack. He was still going to play what I booked. Gideon's approval mattered not at all to me.

Chadwick and Vito were growing increasingly nervous about the growing power struggle. Gideon and I were both stubborn and headstrong and there were times we were going to butt heads. Things hadn't gotten ugly so far and I had no reason to think they would. Gideon would puff up, I'd puff up, we'd argue, and then I'd get my way. Gideon was a straight-ahead type of narrow thinker. Things were black or white for him. The guy had no talent for subtlety, and I could usually direct him to wherever it was I needed him to be.

Gideon would think he'd won an argument and not realize until days or weeks later that I'd manipulated him. By the time he figured out he'd been led by the nose the deal was usually done and we were on to other things.

Our system might not be the most efficient, but it was our system. I could work within it to keep my little ducks in a row.

Any band or artist that travels will tell you traveling all over the country is not glamorous. Nothing ever is, but traveling in a band, hustling from show to show, there is a certain romantic appeal. Despite what everyone thinks, the life is too dirty to be romantic.

Miles drag by so slowly. Staring out the windshield as whole world reduced to the waterborne paint dividing the highway. Yellow and white, solid, or broken, mile after mile. Time slows down and I felt like the van was standing still and the country was rolling by us. Sugar maple and cherry gave way to live oak and palmetto only to turn back around again. The food sucks and the conversation grow stale. I always wanted a shower.

Sometimes there isn't anything more to say. You've heard all the stories and laughed at all the jokes and really all you want is for everyone to take some time to shut the fuck up. The mornings weren't too bad, wake up, and everyone is moving around getting ready to do some traveling. I rousted any stragglers who maybe partied a little too hard and couldn't get up with the clock.

One morning in Daytona, right at the tail end of Spring Break, I went to wake Raven. His beds were undisturbed and instead I found him in the bathtub buried underneath two naked coeds. When I die that's how I want to go, naked in the bathtub buried underneath two beautiful nude women. Raven woke with his cheeks red and a surprisingly large hard on. I couldn't help with the boner, but I wouldn't bust him out to his old lady.

Why would I? I'd been caught having sex by pretty much every member of the *band* and most of the crew. Shyness has never been a concern of mine. I freely admit to being a pervert as long as I'm in the proper company. Some folks get it, some don't. I'm fine either way. I'm still barking up that threesome tree.

Hope springs eternal.

Gideon had complained to us Ashley was boring in bed. He said she laid there like a plastic doll and took it. She would do what he wanted, didn't tell him no, but there wasn't any passion. Gideon said she had nice tits, absolutely true, but she didn't know how to work her body. Completely disturbingly unequivocally false. The man had no idea what his own wife was capable of

With the exception of Chadwick, the ultimate in introvert technology, and Vito, who was Vito, everybody cheated. We were members of a traveling rock and roll band. A partner would have to be spectacularly stupid to think we didn't fuck around on the road. I didn't even think of it as cheating, none of us did. We were there, they were horny, hard dick has no conscious. I've made countless women feel good, they made me feel good, and that's all good.

Gideon invited me over, nothing unusual, since I hung out with him most of the time anyway. I grabbed a Dr. Pepper from my fridge and headed over. I should have gone anywhere else. Things were about to go completely sideways. Sitting in his living room, passing the bong back and forth, he approached me with the idea of working the camera for some new angles while he fucked his wife. What the fuck run amok?

I told them I didn't have an issue with that, and I'd run a camera if they wanted me to. Ashley said it wasn't right I got to check her out, so she wanted me to be naked too. It was only fair. I shrugged and said it sounded like a deal. Part of me didn't think he was serious. Girls on the road were one thing, but Ashley was his wife. In my mind that made a big difference. Gideon brought the conversation back around a couple of hours later saying if I was going to be there and I was going to be naked it wasn't right to me to send me home with blue balls, so I might as well join in.

We'd gone from work the camera to fuck my wife. Whatever, she was cute, and I'd be lying if I said I never thought about her. Gold panties flashed through my mind. She smiled like I didn't know what the evening had been about. I would have fucked her when I got there but they seemed to need to work up to asking me. Gideon continued to escalate telling me I should bring a partner.

Now things were making sense. His wife had told him she wanted to fuck me, so he agreed if he got to fuck another girl. And since I was going to fuck his wife, he wanted one of my girlfriends. None of the ladies in my life wanted to have sex with Gideon. They weren't plastic fuck dolls I could leave at someone's house and pick up later. They were grown women with thoughts and opinions and control over who they let inside their vaginas.

All I could do was ask if they were interested in maybe getting a little freaky in a foursome. I wanted to see another woman going wild with Ashley. I'd even have it preserved digitally for those long lonely cold nights on the road. Unfortunately, I couldn't get another woman interested.

Ashley still wanted to do it without another woman involved but Gideon wasn't about to let me have sex with his wife, or her with me, without compensation. Ashley's gratitude wasn't reward enough for Gideon. She'd indulge him, but it had to be on her terms. She wanted me and said as much.

I picked her up from work the next morning. Gideon slept in and didn't answer the phone. He hadn't heard the alarm clock either, Ashley was stuck at her job as an overnight nurse at an old folk's home. The retirement village was across from the hospital and about five minutes from our apartment complex. I answered and went to pick her up.

She asked me to take her back to my apartment. I was a little leery, but I was still fuzzy from waking up. Yes, I was a little horny; I'm always a little horny. Too often I let my dick do my thinking. Back at my house we went inside, and she sat down on the couch. She asked me if I thought less of her because she wanted to do this.

I told her of course I didn't think less of her. I didn't and still don't. I admire someone confident enough to experiment with their sexuality. There is a degree of bravery involved in trying something new. I told her I was safe. I was her friend. She told me if I was going to get into the mix, I should know what I was getting into.

Turning on her phone, she showed me a video of her having sex with Gideon and Chadwick. I wondered if it was a recent video. An older one she carried around with

her? You never know when you might need video proof
of yourself having sex with multiple partners. On screen
she was taking directions from Gideon. On my couch she
was lightly, discreetly, rubbing her nipples through her
nursing scrubs with her forearms. Ashley leaned into me.
She smelled fantastic. Her scent, sweat and juniper, made
me light headed. The blood left my brain in a rush headed
for parts south.

Her cheeks flushed, breathing heavily through slightly
parted lips, her hand furthest from me now blatantly
rubbed her breast. Subtlety be damned. I don't know
if she thought I couldn't see what she was doing or
if she was trying to seduce me, or if she was turned
on watching her video with me. Thought was difficult.
Whatever her reasoning it was hot. The situation was
wrong, Gideon's wife was on my couch while he slept. She
was watching homemade pornography with a man not her
husband, rubbing herself and beginning to softly moan.
The wrongness of it increased the tension making the act
seem inevitable. We'd spiraled out of control. I pretended
not to notice what she was doing.

We watched her performance with Chadwick.
Chadwick without pants was odd. His legs were pale and
skinny dotted with age spots. His chest was pale and
sunken with only a slight darkening of the skin on his

forearms where his t-shirt failed to cover. He was so stiff, in every way, but he didn't seem to be enjoying what Ashley was doing. His head was back, mouth open and if I didn't know better, I'd think he was about to die. His hands were stiff at his sides and balled into fists. He didn't look like a man who was receiving oral attention from a good-looking woman. It looked like it felt good to me. Gideon's voice, low and thick, continued to encourage her.

She turned to me saying she hadn't been able to read Chadwick. He wasn't telling her to do anything differently, but he didn't seem to be engaged either. Then she pointed out how he was immediately pounding away inside her. No build up. She liked to work with the body and build up to the pace Chadwick started at. She was telling me how to fuck her. Not trusting my response, I didn't say anything, my eyes drifted from her phone. I wanted her. My head spun; the moment surreal, thick with sexual tension. I was hard, my jeans preventing my member from standing properly, pressure making the erection worse. Her cheeks flushed as she leaned further into me.

And she was right, Chadwick jumped on her, immediately pounding as hard as he could. Did he want it over? He didn't last long. He came on her back in less than three minutes. Gideon handed off the camera to

Chadwick and came into frame his member at attention. Ten inches at least and thicker than a Snicker. I'd seen his cock before, so it wasn't a surprise. Gideon had a big dick. Ashley watched me instead of the screen. Our eyes locked and the desire passing between us made my heart pound. My cock throbbed, hard at the wrong angle, aching for release. Her eyes dropped to my lap and the obvious bulge in my pants. She licked her lips. It was a subtle gesture, unconscious, but sexy as hell.

She made eye contact again, her naked want plain on her face. Then calmly for how heavy she was breathing she took off her shirt and unhooked her bra. She kissed me. Hard. My hand found her gorgeous breasts and I rolled her nipple between thumb and the knuckle of my forefinger. She moaned into my mouth and ground her hips against my leg. My other hand was down her pants to find her soaking wet, slippery. Her upper thighs were also wet as she ground herself against my hand. If her ferocity was anything to judge by, Gideon hadn't turned her on like that in years.

I took her on the couch and then again in the bedroom and once more in the kitchen when she offered to make lunch. She said Gideon would sleep into the afternoon left undisturbed. Let him sleep. I couldn't get enough of her. She came eight times I counted but she may have had more silently. Women keep their secrets. I came three times, fair trade.

She went home later in the afternoon barely able to walk. I didn't feel anything after betraying Gideon. She wasn't his property and hadn't been properly fucked in a long time. She had sought me out. I wanted her, too. Not for Gideon's entertainment, and not because I loved her, we were both lonely. I knew she didn't love me. We were friends, I spent so much time at her house, and there was the mutual attraction which boiled over. It didn't feel like a betrayal to either of us. We both wanted it. For some reason sneaking felt more like private time rather than a betrayal of a friend and wrecking of a marriage.

We continued the affair. I picked her up in the morning, Gideon thought it was his idea since he initially asked me to, and I'd take her back to my place. Sometimes we'd cook breakfast and other times we'd stop for a sausage biscuit. We'd eat our food naked, we hung out naked, mornings through early afternoon spent in random love play. There was the thrill of knowing Gideon slept right across the hall heightened everything we did and we knew all kinds of ways to make each other feel good.

We'd hang out, smoke, talk, sometimes put on a movie, but mostly we'd fuck. She was an amazing lover. All she needed was someone who would take the time to let her warmup. Once she got hot, she got all the way hot and there wasn't much she wasn't willing to do or have done to her. Plus, she had a wild imagination and when she was comfortable, she would let her creativity go.

She was one of the best lays I'd ever had; generous, passionate, uninhibited, and she reveled in her femininity. It was sad she didn't bring that heat to their marriage bed. Worse than sad, it was absolute proof to me their marriage was falling apart. I told myself it was another reason I felt no guilt every time we were together.

The three of us sat in Gideon's living room, watched The Delicate Sound of Thunder, a Pink Floyd concert video, and got high. Ashley on one end of the couch with her feet on Gideon. Gideon sat at the other end and we talked about lighting effect ideas we could steal from Floyd. I sat in my usual armchair, Ashley between us. As the evening got late, Gideon passed out over the side of the couch. I'd been nodding and woke as Ashley stood. She held her finger to her lips and crept over to me. She'd removed her underwear wearing only a t-shirt. Gideon slept. No idea it was going on.

"What are you doing? I asked both terrified and turned on.

"You know what I'm doing." She smiled as she pulled my hardening cock out of my pants. Ashley and I had sex in his favorite chair while Gideon passed out on the couch mere feet away. The fear of getting caught combined with the delicious friction of her grinding hips caused me to cum so hard I bit my lip bloody in order not to cry out. Her orgasm left deep claw marks on my back and shoulders. She also bit into my neck hard enough to leave a violent purple bruise.

Afterwards she lay back against me, her lips just brushing my neck, and said, "I don't love him anymore." I didn't know how to respond. While I wanted her, I needed him. She didn't make me choose. She stood and went to clean up and go to bed. I went back across the hall, locking the door behind me.

The *band* made jokes about how I needed to calm down my kinky sex habits before one of my girlfriends killed me. I didn't have the heart to tell Gideon his wife did it as I made her cum like he never could...while he slept not three feet from us.

Ashley said she didn't love Gideon anymore, but they had the little one and she stayed for the sake of their child. She didn't want him growing up in a broken home. She grew up in a home without a father and always felt she was missing something. I couldn't tell her what that thing was. I had a father who rarely spoke to me except to get a job. What was the big deal? Life wasn't always all hugs and backyard barbecues. Was indifference, or mild disapproval, better than absence?

Gideon had taken advantage of her daddy issues. She was much younger than he was and attracted to dominant males. Once she found one, she would give everything of herself. I thought she needed something other than a child to keep her occupied and she agreed. She had me. Then she began kissing around my soft parts which quickly became hard parts. She continued to distract me and by the time she was finished I couldn't remember what we'd been talking about in the first place. Woman was hard to argue with.

My mornings I spent with Ashley, and I was with Gideon in the evening. Or I was with Gideon and the rest of the *band*. We were in the process of recording our third album. We had recorded close to five albums worth of music in our tenure together. So many songs to choose from.

Evenings we didn't practice were spent arguing over which songs should go on the third album. We also fought about which songs we should push for airplay. The cover art for the second album was in dispute as well. I put it down to growing pains. Any organization with more than one chief must go through this. I didn't mind sharing ideas with the *band,* but I think Gideon argued with me simply for the sake of arguing.

Right is good if that moves things forward for us as a band and as a business but most of Gideon's ideas were straight out of 1982. As out of date as the mullet on top of his head. What's worse, he didn't get it. He fought every suggestion like a personal attack. I didn't have any girlfriends willing to swing with him hurting his ego, and Ashley telling him she wanted me injured his ego further. What a pain. It wasn't my fault his wife found me attractive.

Ashley said Gideon was completely obsessed with the idea of trading women with me. Said he talked about it all the time. He had this idea in his head of him doing naughty things to both her and my girlfriend. I guess I was out of action behind a camera. I didn't have a steady girlfriend at the time, girls came, and girls went.

I couldn't tell him, but I scratched that itch for her every morning. It was a highlight of my day, unlike fussing with him. The constant arguing wore me down.

I brought in a design for the second album. Originally a picture of an iris from a top-down perspective I worked some digital magic on it, running it through a few filters. The flower became a swirling vortex of color sprouting up on a background of stars. A fitting picture for an album entitled Duende which contained more of the artsy songs we had recorded. There were influences from our usual inspirations of Pink Floyd and Dream Theater to a trilogy of songs influenced by Yanni.

Yanni had done a series of concerts for PBS that Gideon had become enamored with. For a time, those concerts ran nonstop on Gideon's television. I think if his Yanni fixation continued on one more day Ashley would stab him. The music he wrote during this period, while not bad, were obvious attempts to copy a style that wasn't ours. There was no way we would ever do any of these tracks live without an orchestra so putting them on a spacey album like Duende seemed a natural choice.

Gideon thought the flower was too feminine.

Gideon fervently believed the second album cover should be his exclusive domain. After all I hired the artist for the first album so by rights the second was his. It made no sense. I brought the artist around because he was a friend of mine, not to do the cover art. He was drawing a picture while we practiced and the *band* as a collective liked it so much, we decided to make it the cover of our debut. Gideon forgot, glossed over, that minor detail.

His idea for the second album was less conceptual. Our four faces, half in shadow, on a black background with nothing to suggest the legitimacy of the music within. Nothing to draw the eye or the interest. Four ugly mugs trying to appear mysterious. Pathetic.

We looked like uninspired unimaginative douche bags. The pictures sucked individually, and they sucked even more collectively. If you saw an album cover like it you might doubt the music if so little effort went into the cover? If you thought anything about it at all. Then you'd pass it on by.

Queen and Tears for Fears both did it better. The former being the classic album The Miracle and the latter belonging to Songs from the Big Chair, and they were both stylish, interesting, and drew the eye. Those musicians weren't ugly as fuck either. The concept was almost a direct rip off the cover of Kiss's album Dynasty with the minor exception of we didn't wear face paint. Make up, by default, made the Kiss picture a better one. I wanted to scream

The constant arguing took a toll on everyone. Chadwick and Vito argued over minor board changes or tweaks to the lighting program. Raven argued with Gideon over drum accents to the new songs. Gideon argued with me over any and everything no matter how insignificant. No one argued with Dexter. I considered hiring a hooker to pose as my girlfriend so he could move past this. The problem was the women who might legitimately pass as my girlfriend were out of my price range. Never mind Summit Valley isn't exactly a hotbed of sin and prostitution.

The affordable ones...well, I don't think would have fooled him. Toothless dirty meth heads and truck stop lot lizards weren't exactly my thing.

I had even contemplated trying my luck on the college campuses. Maybe I could trade tickets, CD's, backstage passes, lunch with the *band*, or *anything* else to get a coed to pretend to be my girlfriend and have sex with Gideon. *Would I want my daughter or my sister treated like that?* I thought. No. There had to be a way to get his ego settled and his head back in the game where we needed him.

Ashley and I were naked in the kitchen, defrosting spicy sausage to go with pancaked when she offered a possible solution. She had a girlfriend who might play the role of girlfriend for me. The only issue she said, hand working industriously, was she wasn't totally confident Gideon didn't know her.

The reward was worth the risk. A threesome might get him out of this bitchy streak before someone, probably me, choked him to death. As I worked on breakfast, and she worked on me she also asked if I'd seen anything about the Star Search competition coming to our area? According to the ad, first place was a recording deal with a producer at a major label.

There was an entire list of famous people this producer worked with from Madonna to Sting. I thought the ad a bit optimistic, but it was within our territory and well within our ability. There wasn't another group of local yokels around doing it as big as we were.

At a minimum it would give Gideon something new to think about other than my nonexistent girlfriend's cooter, which, ironically, didn't exist. The only vagina I had access to right then belonged to Ashley.

I didn't think we'd have any problems winning the contest, but was it worth our time to do so? We were an up-and-coming act, certainly. Another certainty, we were doing bigger and bigger shows making more and more money. Being rich didn't seem like such a far off impossibility.

I would have loved the exposure, been all about it, really, but I wondered what this producer could do for us we weren't already doing for ourselves. In the entertainment industry a sure point of fact, a constant, is: It's all bullshit until you start getting paid. Once you sign your name and start getting money, the bullshit stops. Ashley caused me to burn the sausage, but the pancakes turned out great. Only two hours cold when we finally got to eat them.

Time came to do another tour, or run as we now called it, along our circuit of the east coast. We finished a show in Orlando the night before and I was now enjoying the variety of observable delights on any of Florida's beautiful public beaches. Me new job had amazing perks. Why wasn't everyone doing this? Why had I ever thought to do anything else? I relaxed under a large multicolored umbrella belonging to the condominium behind me. The place was too rich for us. Luckily, we met some girls after the show who insisted we check out their condo. Daddy's money paid for an impressive place. All palms, oceanfront, and private gates.

And why did rich men leave their daughters unsupervised access to places like this? Was their daughter's virtue atonement for whatever sins they had committed becoming rich? A sacrificial balancing of the scales, but out of sight where they didn't have to think about it? No fucking way I'd let my daughter run wild unsupervised at a Florida condo.

Could be I was overthinking it.

I had a sweaty Corona and lime in one hand, not my favorite beer but it seemed appropriate, and was digging my toes into warm sand. There were a few too many tiny, crushed shells for my taste, I prefer sand to be smooth and soft, but the price was right, and the view was fine. Who was I to complain?

One of the lovelies coated my back in a coconut lotion with a SPF somewhere around lead. I have fair skin some might even call pale. Apparently, I was born without the ability to produce melanin and I do not tan no matter how much time I spend outdoors. When exposed to the sun I burn. Dad had the tan gene, but he didn't pass it on to me. Dad could walk through a bright room and come out golden on the other side. I got pale skin and shitty enamel. Thanks. After a burn, next comes manic itching. I would rather do anything than itch. Burn, bleed, pain, whatever it is must be better than itching. I freak right the fuck out when I itch.

After the itching passes and the crazy scratching subsides, I peel, and the underlying skin is just as creamy as what I started with. There might be a few more freckles. Thank you, no. It's not worth the aggravation. Better to avoid the whole sloppy mess, cover up, and use sunscreen from the start. And even better is when my sunscreen is being lovingly applied by beautiful young women in barely there swimsuits.

Raven and Vito approached from poolside where they'd been swimming and sat on either side of me. Raven, just as pale as I am, swam in a black t-shirt and swimsuit. Smears of sunscreen that hadn't been rubbed in collected tiny grains of sand along his forehead and nose.

Vito was the only one of us with any kind of color. Years working construction outdoors had given him a deep tan and years smoking made his skin almost leathery. Both had sweethearts following them around which they dismissed back to the water. They looked serious and wanted to speak with me for a moment. I'm awesome, but I'm nowhere near as awesome as young flesh in wet bikini. They must be serious. I was intrigued.

Did Raven have an STD? Had Vito been arrested? What could be going on? And why did they think I could help?

All I wanted was to help myself to another beer and then a little more of the vapid cutie rubbing my back. Then maybe some time in the hot tub and a little more cutie.

"HEY! YOU LADIES WANT SOMETHING TO EAT?" Vito bellowed interrupting my chain of thought.

The cutie behind me answered, "Oh my God yes! I could so go for some Chinese! Couldn't you go for some Chinese? God I could die!"

There seemed to be a consensus among the women that yes, they wanted Chinese food and yes, they could die. Vito volunteered us to go and waved Dexter off. . Dexter sat back down, the wind tossing his short hair around, his eyes already losing focus on the ocean. Begrudgingly I got up, put on a shirt, slipped my feet into my flops, and headed toward the van. The heels of my flops happily slapping the heels of my feet in the staccato beat of Florida tourists since there were Florida tourists. Hopefully the ladies would survive until we returned.

Raven's own flip flops added their voice to mine as we walked around the condo to the underground garage. Flop-FLOP flop FLOP echoed through a mostly empty garage. Empty of people anyway, the BMW's seemed to be breeding. Fucking things were everywhere. How much money do you need to make to have a home you visit only a couple of times a year? Underneath that home is a car that you only drive a couple weeks out of the year. I've never made that kind of money.

I knew if the *band* was the kind of success it was shaping up to be maybe I'd find out. I'd spend more time here than just the summer months

Raven keyed open the door and then leaned across to let me into the front passenger seat. Vito slid open the side door and hopped into the middle of the bench seat where he could speak to both of us up front. He pulled a small apple out of his pocket and began to munch. Raven sat behind the wheel, hand on the ignition, but he hadn't turned the motor over.

He looked at me, as earnest as I've ever seen him, and said," Dude you know how much I love this fuckin group. We've done more than any group I've ever played with."

Not quite sure where this was going, I answered hesitantly, "Yeah. You're a bad ass drummer dude. Wouldn't be the same without you."

Raven started the motor and started out into the Florida sunshine. He stopped for a moment, the glare of the sun particularly harsh after the cool shadow of the parking garage. He had forgotten his sunglasses at the beach, hopefully they'd still be there when we got back. Vito took another crunch out of his apple.

"Glad you said that. Listen, the arguing has to stop."

"I'm with you brother. I'm fucking sick of it too."

"Are you fucking Ashley?" Bam! Out of nowhere. I felt gut punched.

Vito didn't say a word. He sat back there chewing and not talking. Neither Raven nor Vito had ever shown the slightest interest in who I romped around with. A cold chill flitted up my back as I wondered if Gideon was as oblivious as we'd thought. We hadn't carried on at practice and when I saw her in the evenings with Gideon, she was always warm but distant. She was the picture of a southern hostess, and I did my part as a respectable house guest.

No. I don't think he knew, but then why the question?

Raven turned right on Highway 1. There was a chain of restaurants right off the road in Palm Bay and I assumed that's where we were going.

"Ashley?" Best to feign offense, I tensed up, raising my voice, "Gideon's Ashley? Why the hell would you ask me that?"

"Dude I'm not trying to start shit, but the only reason we could think of as to why Gideon's been so bitchy is someone, you, has been back dooring him."

"Fuck man. Don't you know him at all? If I was fucking Ashley, Gideon would go completely sideways. There wouldn't be an issue of am I doing it, there'd only be the question of keeping him cool enough not to kill anyone. How'd you feel if someone was boning your old lady?"

"Man, I'd probably thank the guy for taking the bitch off my hands."

I turned in my seat a little to see what Vito had to say. He looked at me and took another bite of his apple. Vito wasn't eating an apple; he was sitting in the back seat eating a gigantic damn peyote bud. I don't even know where he could have gotten the thing but I knew in about twenty minutes we were going to have a raving lunatic on our hands. Vito looked at me with a huge shit eating grin on his face.

Raven brought my attention back to the front seat, "I'm glad to hear it. This fighting needs to stop. We got a real shot here. I've never thought about any of the other guys I've played with before, but I feel it here. It's like it's supposed to happen, you know? Feels like destiny, magic, or some shit."

"I know what you mean brother,"

"Because if you were fucking someone's wife, even if she came on to you, that would be so bad. Look at what Yoko did to the Beatles."

The comparison wasn't exactly apt, but I appreciated his point. Nothing can break up a group of guys faster than a female. Wars are fought over them, yeah, I got it. I didn't want to go war for Ashley. She was a nice way to start the day. For her I guess I was a nice way to end one.

"I'm not fucking Ashley." I watched the scenery roll by. Tourists, traffic, palm trees, and run down businesses lined the street.

"Yeah, but if you were, I mean, I understand, she's fucking hot, but, like, don't. It'd be bad."

"I know it'd be bad. That's why I'm not fucking her." Raven was starting to get on my nerves. Vito sat in the back silently chewing his bud, watching, not talking.

Raven pulled into the parking lot of a Chinese place about a mile from the condo. The heat baking off the asphalt stole my breath as I opened the door. I could see the condo shimmering in the distance. I thought about another beer and my little cutie. I thought about being the cause of the *band* breaking up. Heat all around me, leaning on me, my own fault. Radiant heat pushing up through the soles of my flops filling my lungs with hot, hard to breathe air. Pleasant enough filtered through the soles of my shoes but it would quickly blister my feet without protection. I thought about lime in beer and orange in chicken and how fruit had surrounded me.

I liked the sweet tang of lime against the bitter hops of beer. A sweet orange sauce, sticky and refreshing, on small chunks of fried tempura chicken. I thought about the obvious parallel of my own Forbidden Fruit, so sweet, and so dangerous. I didn't want to give her up. I don't know if I could. I thought about being burned if I wasn't careful. Vito crunched his apple. I followed Raven into the restaurant to pick up the order the girls had placed during our drive over. Vito sat in the van with the sliding door open. I prayed no police would happen by.

Coming out with the food we saw Vito still sitting where we'd left him.

A couple of egg rolls on rice rockets buzzed somewhere down the highway, their motorcycles screaming like swarming insects. The air over the parking lot hung heavy. Where was the ocean breeze? Storms seemed to hit the Florida coast everyday around five o'clock and I could see those clouds pushing in from the ocean. Fifteen, possibly twenty more minutes until the clouds over the ocean took all they could take and dumped the day's humidity back down on the shore. Every day the five o'clock storms emptied beaches and rendered the superheated air cool and breathable again. The hour before the storms was miserable.

Mercifully, when we started the van after piling in again, the AC started up cold. Raven wanted peach tea and the girls didn't have any. He drove toward the Big Top across from the condo. Big Top was a chain of grocery stores located mostly across the South. They must have done a thriving business in Florida judging by the number of them. It seemed there were Big Top grocery stores on every corner. Big Tops were across the street from Big Tops, surely a sign of end times. Raven either hadn't noticed what Vito had been eating or, like me, assumed it was an apple. He didn't show near the level of concern that I did our soundman was beginning to murmur and vibrate.

The three of us braved the stagnant oven like air, pregnant with humidity, smelling of fish and asphalt and faintly of garbage, hanging over the parking lot and hurried into the blessedly cool store. Summer humidity is an absolute treat in the South. We have a particular brand of heat super saturated with as much humidity as physically possible without rain. So much moisture in the air completely defeats the body's natural defenses to overheating. All sweating does is make you sticky.

Raven kept up his interrogation, determined to get me to admit, yes, I was fucking Gideon's wife. He'd have to ask from now until next Christmas if he thought he was going to get anything other than a "nope, sorry" from me. Raven was not the guy to break me, not today, not ever. Raven was into his role as interrogator, and I had all but tuned him out. I grunted negatively every once in a while, so he'd think I was still listening.

"Dude, because if you were, you know, doing her, none of us would really blame you. We all wanted a piece of that at one time or another." Raven said as we wandered through stacks of fresh produce. An old woman pushing an empty cart heard and shot us a disapproving glance. I ignored her too.

Gideon might blame me, I thought. Out loud I mumbled something like, "Nah, uh uh. No way," now I'd worked past the initial shock, this was getting boring.

Ignoring Raven was getting me nowhere. If indifference wouldn't bring back the blessed silence then I might as well try anger. I'm good at anger.

Moving through the vegetables we'd found the drink aisle. Juices on one side faced cases of beer behind sliding glass doors like a cartoon decision to sin, angel on one side, devil on the other. The chill radiating off the aisle felt delicious against my sweaty skin. I got a little loud and turned with a sharp right face that put me about four inches from the tip Raven's nose. I'd seen my father use this technique when he was the executive officer for a basic training squadron in the Air Force.

"Look man! I'm getting fucking sick of the third degree here! I didn't fuck her but if I had she would have loved it! Now accept it or don't but please SHUT THE FUCK UP ABOUT IT!"

Raven took a couple of involuntary steps backward and bumped his head on the beer coolers. An old couple at the end of the aisle stopped to stare at us. A mother with a child who had been arguing about fruit punch was stunned to silence. The mother put the juice in her cart and walked quickly away from us. The kid flashed me a smile as he followed his mom away from the belligerent longhairs arguing in the beer aisle. I tipped him a wink. Glad I could help the kid.

Raven hadn't noticed any of it. He was completely freaked out at my rapid change in demeanor. I'm good at anger. My Irish ancestry combined with a natural resting bitch face keeps folks at distance. He was backed up against the cooler and I was kissing distance close to him. Silently thanking my dad for the drill sergeant routine, I gave Raven my best I'm-going-to-cook-you-and-fucking-eat-you stare. I'm also a good five inches taller than Raven. The effect was a complete and instantaneous cessation of interrogation.

"Oh-Okay man. Chill. I'm just wor-" Raven stammered out at me. Looking around I noticed that among the various curious stares we were getting, Vito's not among them.

"ZIP IT! Where the fuck is Vito?"

I backed away a few steps and allowed Raven to collect his manhood. I walked around the aisle, away from the delightful chill of the fresh juices and adult beverages and began to sand march back through the store. I looked for Vito down each aisle I passed.

Raven caught up with his peach teas in hand. "What's the deal man? Vito is a big boy."

"Yeah, Vito IS a big boy," I growled back, "He's a big boy that ate a peyote bud the size of an apple on the way over here."

Raven stopped, "That was a fuckin' peyote bud?!"

"What the fuck did I just say? Is there a reason you don't believe anything that comes out of my mouth? Did I stop speaking English? Yes, Raven, that was a great big fucking peyote bud, and we need to find Vito and get him out of here before he turns into a wild animal."

We found Vito in produce. He was bent at the waist, nose to nose, and engaged in a heated, albeit quiet, debate with a large watermelon. The watermelon wasn't taking him seriously because as we got to him Vito was beginning to get loud.

"Vito, what's happening man?" I asked casually like he wasn't arguing with a melon.

He stood up suddenly and looked at me. I could see the madman nearing surface depth in his eyes. We didn't have long until the insanity got intense.

"Where did you go? Fuck it, I don't care. Raven got your tea? Grown man drinking fruit juice, fucking sad, like a grown man in a Miata, fuck it, let's get the fuck out of here. This is the dumbest fucking melon I've ever seen. You won't believe the ignorant shit I've been listening to. There's only so much stupid I can put up with, you know?" Vito's voice grew in volume as he spoke, eyes wild, body vibrating.

"Yeah Vito. I get it. Stupid ass watermelons couldn't find their asses with both hands and a map. Let's go." I began herding him toward the door. Raven left us to go pay in order to expedite this little trip. Cashier 9. Good idea. We walked over where the girl was bagging up Raven's bottles of tea. Condensation caused the plastic to become translucent and stick obscenely to the bottles.

The girl had been watching the Vito show and was now warily eye balling the three of us. Never one to miss an opportunity to make an impression Vito leaned in. She recoiled dramatically, hard enough to make the lighted 9 above her wobble. At the top of his lungs Vito screamed, "ALL HAIL THE GREAT SUN GOD MESCALITO!"

He spun on his heel and left the store, head up, shoulders
back, and without another word.

The trip back to the condo was quiet. The great sun god
Mescalito seemed content watching the rain, which had
finally begun to fall, run down the windows. The rain had
broken the heat if only temporarily and I was enjoying
the silence. Raven was driving the van which smelled like
grease and orange sauce from the stained brown bags of
Chinese food in the floorboards. At least the food would
be warm when we finally got to eat.

I spent the remainder of the evening with the kittens at
the condo. Raven didn't say anything else, but it seemed
to me Chadwick and Gideon were doing what they could
to remain either away from me or apart from the group.
It was hard to tell. Dexter sat where he could observe the
room and Vito spent the night talking about resistances
to the waves and the crabs. Could it be that Ashley and
I weren't as careful as we'd thought? Gideon's issue
came from my women not wanting to fuck him while
his wanted to fuck me. Through no fault of my own I'd
hurt him and now everything I did was like a personal
challenge.

Ugh.

All I wanted was to get us off the ground. I wanted to enter the Great Cycle so the rest of our lives there would always be something to look forward to. I wanted my morning love. I'd have to walk a razors edge to keep Gideon from finding out what happened. If he knew, it would ruin everything we'd built. Without the *band* what was I supposed to do? What were any of us supposed to do? Going back to a straight job was going to be a near impossibility after tasting the near freedom and money of entertainment.

Where else were any of us going to have a group of rich girls take us back to a condo, feed us, and fuck us all silly? Most guys I knew would pay for girls like this and still not get with them. What life was there if the music broke up? There was no going back. No. Losing the *band* wasn't an option. Raven was right, we needed to knuckle up and get through this...whatever...and get back to the place where we were most comfortable, making music.

Gideon had forgotten the reason we started the *band* in the first place. It wasn't about who the boss was or who called the shots. We started this as a group, made decisions as a group, had success as a group, and as a group we needed to recover the mindset that had carried us this far. Raven was right. This was something special and we needed to protect it. Together we had created a monster that was beginning to take on a life of its own. And not only was it beginning to live it was starting to RUN! If only we could hang on.

Ashley mentioned a competition. She was right. It was time for us to take the next step as a group and see where it might lead. I gathered up the boys and told them about the competition. It wasn't a battle of the bands. Those were more about smoking weed in whatever venue while band after band performed on the same equipment with the same soundman. Those types of competitions could be fun but weren't going to do us any good.

We'd dominate a battle of the bands. There weren't any groups out, on the east coast anyway, hitting it like we were. We had a state-of-the-art light and laser show to go with a completely original line-up of amazing songs guaranteed to touch the hearts of anyone. From motorcycle heavies to frat boys, little sex kittens to housewives, businessmen to factory workers, they all were taken away on our flavor train. Working class to upper class we had rocked them all. We destroyed small venues and shut down large outdoor concerts with over five thousand people in attendance. This was going to be an actual Star Search competition with only a couple of bands, comedians, and whatever variety acts entered. Lambs to the slaughter I thought. We were going to kill it! And Star Search was a national competition!

Back in my own bed, almost alone, Boston against my thigh, and my Sheperd asleep on the floor, I thought about everything we'd done. Pride, excitement, and satisfaction warred with shame. Things were going so well and now I'd stepped in a steaming pile. Smack dab in the middle of a marriage not my own where I had zero business being. But I didn't want to lose Ashley.

CD's were selling almost as fast as we could stock them. Stocking remained a chore we took care of ourselves. But to me it was a labor of love. I enjoyed taking stacks of CD's to record stores. The location was inconsequential. I always ended up signing a bunch for people who grabbed them off the shelves as soon as the stores checked them in. We had a growing website and a social media following that was downright respectable.

We had undertaken all of this on our own without a famous mommy or daddy to pave our way. We worked as a team, kick, scratch, and claw. That's how life is for guys like us. None of us ever had anything handed to us. We worked, and worked hard, not only to keep our dreams alive but to keep believing in each other when no one else did. Pushing our art when the world believed we'd fail.

I flopped over on my side earning an irritated grunt from Boston.

Now people were taking notice. We couldn't implode. Not now. It made no sense Gideon needed someone to fuck other than Ashley. There were tons of women on the road. Not enough. He'd become a local celebrity with all the perks. Not enough. He needed something belonging to me. Why? Ego? Some alpha male bullshit? If that's what he needed, then I'd find something we could say was mine he could stick his dick into. Whatever. The music was too important. Without Gideon it didn't work. He wrote songs, sang lead, and played lead guitar. Without me it couldn't happen. I was the glue holding us all together. Annie – The Keeper of the Faith. Anyone else, and I mean no conceit, could be replaced. Not Gideon. And not me.

Gideon did a lot for the *band*. We thought of our frontman as the deep soul of our group. I was the beating heart which kept the thing alive. I kept the faith that kept the group. The dream of a better day was the lifeblood holding us all together and moving us steadily onward.

Without Gideon the soul was gone. Without me the group couldn't hold together. We made each major decision together often before presenting it to the group.

In the beginning, our first winter, sitting in his den, dreaming and smoking we started a thing. And we, together, held onto the thing when there wasn't a single soul who believed the trash we were talking was even possible. Those early frozen months we shrugged off condescending looks and patronizing talk *never* allowing people to take away our hope.

I kept the faith. I believed in Gideon's guitar. I had spent hours before we'd even met listening to the music haunt the hall between our apartments. I believed in that music. Gideon and I had to get right if we were to survive. This was the last thing any of us had. It had to work.

Now we had proof. Now we possessed evidence not only would it work but it *was* succeeding. The music transported the crowd every night to the heartbreak and yearning of our first winter. The music dragged us along every time, only we knew the destination, we'd lived it. And it took us every single time we sat down to our instruments together. People followed us and talked about us. We lifted this thing out of the dirt and given it wings of sound and it would take flight with all of us if we didn't crash it on the runway.

Back from the latest run I gathered the *band* at the band house. Coming off a successful tour made everyone feel good. We had money in our pockets and more importantly our energy was recharged. We felt rejuvenated. The money being good was worldly proof we were doing something valueable. Anyone who doubted us could be jealous of the money we made. Anyone who supported us felt pride in our success, like they knew it all the time.

We didn't need Vito or Dexter or any of the random road crew because we had everything set up back in the house. Vito knew the settings for the studio without being told. He set up our sound system without the need for any of the rest of us to make noise. Vito's opinion was valued. He brought more than just soundman to our group. He was both friend and mentor.

No crowds to control in the band house so Dexter was back at his farm killing small furry animals. Raven's wife, Jody, brought along a girlfriend who wanted to meet the *band* and possibly get some autographs. That was fine. The post tour vibe was strong, and we were feeling generous.

Her name was Chianti. Maybe that's what her parents had been drinking when she was conceived. I don't know. I wasn't there. She walked in the door with nearly a quarter pound of marijuana. After we all autographed her CD, and a *band* t-shirt, she pulled a monster brick of weed out of her purse.

"I bet you guys can't smoke all this." She said, cocky. but grossly misinformed. We were dedicated professionals here. Vito busted a pack of rolling papers out from somewhere and was thumbing out the first paper, "Roll 'em."

Most of her stash ended up as a haze in the studio. Vito and Gideon were rolling and lighting joints like machines. Raven, Chadwick, Ashley, Ravens wife, Chianti, and I began to smoke and pass like it was our job. I was so high I couldn't get off the floor. Gideon looked at me, also from the floor, and asked me to get his guitar. If I could get him his guitar he could play it. He just couldn't move.

"Sorry brother, I can't do it." I said. If I got to my keyboard, I'd play, but that wasn't happening either.

Raven bet me a hundred dollars I couldn't walk out to my car and back. I don't know why people were trying to get me to go places. My body didn't seem to function either. I was glad I had my giant cup within arm's reach loaded with ice and Citra which complimented the piney taste of weed perfectly. I had a half a pack of Newports in my shirt pocket and an unopened pack behind that. I was all set for the days' practice with the necessary supplies to keep me on this side of the ragged edge.

The guys gave me crap about smoking Newports. I told them I had soul, and then I quoted Langston Hughes, "my soul has grown deep like rivers." This was met with a smile and a good-natured rolling of the eyes. I liked the menthol bite Newports have, alive with pleasure indeed. They also tasted better with weed. More than one of those guys bummed cigarettes, even when they had their own, despite the shit they gave me.

We didn't get much practice done. Chianti scuttled out the door with Jody while she still had something to smoke, amazed we'd burned through so much. I was more amazed we hadn't smoked it all. Also somewhat miraculous, we were still, as a group, upright and taking oxygen. True we were scattered around the practice room, somehow, I'd made it to my chair although I don't remember when or how. Maybe we weren't moving well but that was ok. I decided to bring up the competition.

"So, any of you fuckers want to be on Star Search?"

That's how we, as a group, took the next step. Together.

I researched Ashley's tip. It was a legitimate talent competition sponsored by the company once fronted by Ed McMahon. Now Ed was walking with Jesus, and I didn't recognize the host of the show. It didn't matter. What mattered was the prize in our category was a recording contract with a subsidiary of Virgin records. We'd record an album for the subsidiary and then Virgin would maintain the right to sign us directly if they liked what they heard.

We were already a record executive's wet dream. With industry professionals the music could reach people all over the world instead of up and down the east coast. All we needed was a shot to the right ear and we'd be on our way.

I'd never seen anyone yet deny us. People who didn't necessarily like rock music became fans of ours after seeing and more importantly hearing us live. A record producer looking for his next big act could do much worse than taking us on. Gideon thought there wasn't anything else out quite like what we were doing a weakness. He was mistaken. That was one of our biggest strengths.

We could be the next Seattle Grunge era that came about on the heels of 80's hair metal, when people finally tired of the glam rock scene. The two sounds couldn't have been more different. When groups from Seattle began to tour,

Nirvana, Soundgarden, Pearl Jam, and Alice in Chains, people loved the new raw edgy angsty music. When NWA burst on the scene in the 80s there was literally nothing out anything like it. I was a white suburban kid at the time and everyone I knew had a copy of Straight Outta Compton. Gideon didn't need to be afraid there wasn't anything out there like us. I was counting on our uniqueness alone drawing people to us. We would bring the pendulum crashing back to real music, artistry, and musicianship like the Grunge era had done so many years before.

I knew it. And I think the rest of the guys knew it too. It's a scary thing to stand on the edge of the abyss. Looking down you don't know if the next step will be the one that sets you flying or plummeting. With luck, our lives were about to radically change if we hung on a little longer. We needed a producer's ear for five to seven minutes and then we could write our own ticket. We'd take flight.

From my perch behind the keyboards, I surveyed the room, tried to gauge reactions. Raven was excited, vibrating like a child in the way drummers do, behind his kit. Vito was skeptical. I understood. It's all bullshit until you start getting paid. After registering for the show, there were three other bands, Vito became more excited and more anxious the closer the day came. Gideon and Chadwick were excited but skeptical. The excitement was infectious. Hell, I had my doubts too, but what if? Just what if?

I'd researched the producer's name and both he and his company were on the up and up. They even had good reviews in the Better Business Bureau. He worked with major acts but what exactly his work entailed I didn't know as yet. I figured I could ask him over lunch once we blew the competition out of the water.

We would be allowed to set up the stage our way, with our people, and play our equipment. This was another aspect that I think set the guys at ease. We were going to be playing on our gear and we were going to have a guy in the crowd who knew our sound. We'd have our carpets. Things were looking better and better! Advantages like this were going to be tough for the competition to overcome.

The day of the competition, Friday, it rained. The storm blew in dropping record breaking amounts of rain. It was an hour ride from Summit Valley to the hotel where the competition was being held. The rain began Thursday night. In true southwest Virginia fashion, it rained steadily for the next three days. The Dan, the Roanoke, and the New Rivers all overflowed their banks and rampaged small town main streets all over the southern part of the state. Monday would see the area patiently waiting for flood waters to recede and for the power to come back on. Businesses and homes near the rivers were evacuated. Flood insurance claims filed.

This wasn't an uncommon thing. Rain during the warmer months here can last for days and might be the only rain until autumn. The rivers hadn't begun to flood although they were rising alarmingly as we loaded the trucks in chilly morning drizzle. They lined the street outside the band house waiting for the truck to move. Once it did, they fell into line behind us, our caravan of faithful. The intensity of the storm picked up as we drove down Interstate 81 to the hotel. At one point the rain was so heavy in combination with the water being thrown from the tires of other cars visibility was reduced to a scant few feet past the hood of the truck. The world vanished in a white misty haze.

For most of the drive my balls were drawn up into my throat. We were in a heavy truck, and I was taking it slow, but I saw more than one car pass too quickly only to hydroplane into the ditch. I didn't stop to help. If they're dumb enough to speed with the weather the way it was, they deserve to stand on the side of the road in the wet for a few hours and cool off. Besides, they were much less of a danger on the side of the road than whipping back and forth in heavy traffic. The tow trucks, working both sides of the highway, battled desperately to keep up with the tide of idiots in ditches.

There wasn't much wind either and the rain fell in flat heavy sheets my wipers had trouble keeping up with. Even with the weather trouble and the awful conditions on the roads spirits were high, and we had a serious convoy following us down the road. We had an escort of Devils that had been tipped off we were going to compete. I thought their presence alone might inspire the judges to vote for us. On occasion the rain would break enough for me to recognize Tiny's massive frame atop his Harley. He rode like the weather didn't touch him at all, like it wouldn't dare. His hair was soaked flying out behind him, a Viking charging to war.

Behind us were several cars being driven by various crew that helped out here and there. Guys who'd run wire and cable, carried cabinets, worked security, restrung guitars, or did whatever odd job we needed, had shown up in support.

We filled the hotel parking lot with a chain of vehicles stretching a quarter mile down the street. It was fucking amazing. The valet asked if we were the *band* and told us there were already people waiting to see us. It looked to him like every seat in the house was going to be taken by fans of the *band*. "You guys shouldn't bother with this.

You've already got it won. You should just head over to the Civic Center and do your normal show."

My jaw fell open. I knew this area contained our largest base of support, but it hadn't occurred to me how popular we had become. We filled the hotel with our fans! Tough break for the other bands competing against us but I wanted to win. I wanted a record deal.

The competition consisted of various categories. Adult Vocalist, not us, Teen Vocalist, also not us, Model/Dance, sexy as I am this wasn't for us either, and Group Vocals. Bands were entered into the Group Vocal category and when I went to talk to the producer who was busy organizing the acts she told me one of the bands dropped out. That left us and one other group of local boys competing for the Group Vocalist title.

There were Adult Vocalists and more than a few of the Teen variety. I saw several dance groups. Sadly, I didn't see many models. I had been looking forward to that part. Models and guys in bands go together like peanut butter and jelly. I was hoping for a sandwich. I comforted my broken heart by directing the personnel to set up where we had been instructed to.

There were three competition stages. Only one of the three was being used at any one time so the other two were always being broken down and set up again behind the scenes. With one of the bands dropping, we were allowed to set up and our gear was left alone until showtime. We were given seven minutes once the curtains drew back, more than enough time to rock this place out.

I seated myself behind my stacks of keyboards. I was nervous, sweaty, guts fluttering, and cotton mouthed, because this one mattered. A sea of faces, although not the biggest crowd we'd ever played, watched us take the stage. It was a small relief there were so many friendly faces. Good natured cheering and whistling, and a roar of clapping hands wrapped around my like a warm blanket, sheltering from the cold and doubt. I hadn't felt pressure like this since we auditioned for Vito. We needed this to happen and every one of us felt it. If we failed our task here what would happen? A devil whispered in my ear. We would keep gigging around for a couple more years always lamenting the missed opportunity before the whole damn thing fell apart. People would slowly start drifting away, getting day jobs, CD sales would slow down, and radio play would disappear no matter how much coke disappeared up the DJ's nose.

People would say they knew there was no way local boys could ever do anything. We had been fooling ourselves, thinking we were more than what we were. We'd gotten uppity. And what we were was nothing but local boys too sorry to get real jobs. Damn shame they were such an embarrassment to their families. We were nothing from nothing and would always be nothing. Maybe we had a shot, but fuck ups that we were, we blew it.

I saw myself in raggedy jeans with greasy hair and a faded, stained flannel working some factory job, pretending my life wasn't that bad. I was ok. I hadn't really wasted my life or my talent on a pipe dream. I wasn't really buried under crushing debt and broken dreams living weekend to weekend. It's alright. Life is debt, sorrow, depression, failure, and maybe a brief flash of sunshine but only enough to illuminate the regret. And I know after those thoughts comes the suicidal ideations. Those midnight thoughts which hide in the dark corners and tiptoe out at night to gnaw and gnaw and gnaw. Finally, the regret would become too much, and I would put a pistol in my mouth. My wife and kids would cry and ask why.

But they would know. Everyone would know. Go away devil. Go away.

"Well fuck it, TIME TO ROCK AND ROLL THE HOLE!" Raven popped up out of nowhere, hopped behind his kit, and hollering the same war cry he hollered before every show. All the doubt fell away.

It was time to rock and roll the hole. That's what we did and that's what we were going to do here. We weren't going to fail. We were going to blow this mother fucker out. The judges weren't going to know what hit them.

Our seven minutes started off with a three-minute piano piece I pruned down to a minute and forty five seconds and bled into a slow grinding hard rocking piece we always used to get the crowd hopping. We practiced it and had our time down to six minutes and fifty four seconds-ish. I was nervous there was so much riding on this but with one sentence Raven threw those fears away. The curtains were drawn back and the *band* was announced to thunderous applause. We four warriors took the stage to do battle.

And we rocked the room.

That brief glimpse of our show, our sound, our lights and our bond were enough to overshadow everyone else. We won. We knew it. When we finished the room was going wild with people screaming and chanting for more. All three judges gave us five stars, a perfect score.

We were the last act to go on and I doubt that was by chance. There wasn't anyone going to follow us. Hell, people backstage, performers, were cheering for more. The producer came to me and asked if we had any more material. The crowd wanted more, he said, and the hotel was worried about the crowd turning ugly. Even as she asked, she had to shout over the chants of, "ENCORE! ENCORE! ENCORE! ENCORE!"

Gideon and I grinned at each other.

"Should we do it?" He asked.

"They'll probably burn the place down if we don't." I answered.

"Do you mind?"

"Not a bit."

I couldn't wait to get out there and soak it up. The curtain pulled back again, and Gideon, Chadwick, and Raven cut loose with a fifteen-minute version of Voodoo Chile. I slipped out to let Vito know what was coming. He already knew and had the lights cued up waiting.

While Gideon was up on stage soothing the crowd with the dulcet tones of Jimi Hendrix I was approached by the record producer. He was portly, grey in his hair and in his neatly trimmed beard. He wore a blue silk shirt underneath a grey suit that probably cost more than the truck we drove here in. The guy looked like an understated success to me. He looked exactly like I wanted him to. He looked like money. He gave me another card, a direct line to his assistant. Why I would want the assistant when I had the attention of the man was silly. Behind his glasses, his eyes were sharp and shrewd.

He introduced himself as Bob and said we needed to speak. He told me he loved the act. Of course he did, everybody liked the act. He asked how much material we had available to record. He also told me we needn't bother going any further in Star Search. We had won his attention, and his attention was worth more than any more competitions would provide. Granted the competition would get us exposure to new areas of the country but Bob said he was planning on making that happen anyway.

Even as he was talking to me he kept getting distracted by the show. I was able to tell him what we had been doing, funneling a percentage of the profits from the shows we played back into buying newer and better equipment, selling albums as hard as we could, and some of the basic promotional things I was doing. I swear I could see the dollar signs in his eyes. I could use more dollar signs in my life. He wouldn't speak to any of the other vocalists and didn't acknowledge the other band at all. I watched him walk right by without even looking at them. The same guy that shook my hands a half dozen times at least didn't even look at the other acts. Cool, I thought, time to get to work.

The local news rag ran a story about our victory in Monday's paper. The headline on the front page was of course the floods and the damage caused but on the inside front page was a story about a local *band* winning the Star Search competition in Roanoke. The article listed the winners of the other categories but the main focus was about the group who collected a perfect score from the judges. The article said we were a high energy talent. Pink Floyd for the next generation.

The article quoted Bob as saying he thought we were one of the best musical acts he'd been privileged to witness in thirty years in the music business. He said with proper guidance, meaning him I suppose, we would be something special that Southwest Virginia could always be proud of. High praise from an industry veteran and I said a silent thank you to Ashley for bringing the idea up in the first place.

I picked up Ashley from work Monday morning telling Gideon it wouldn't be an issue, to enjoy the win and sleep in. I told him I wanted to go rub my dad's nose in the success of both the contest victory and the praise in the article. I wanted to do no such thing but if he thought I was with my parents he probably wouldn't call to check up, assuming he was awake to do so. Better safe. I thought of some celebratory activities with Ashley. She should be properly thanked after all. And then thanked again.

Practice that night was more party than anything else. Chadwick and Vito were their elitist selves staying close to and talking mainly with each other. Gideon was telling stories and jokes and looking like he was enjoying all the adulation while Ashley played hostess even though it wasn't her house. She flitted from group to group bringing drinks, cleaning up, chatty and charming, and directing people to the snacks she'd prepared in the kitchen.

Dexter was hiding upstairs with Chadwick's son, Jack, a teenager I'd rarely seen. The two of them were playing an old copy of Mortal Kombat 3 Ultimate. Jack was frustrated Dexter won round after round. I heard him through the door, "Seriously man! How do you keep doing that? I should be doing that to you!" Jack didn't know when Dexter wasn't with us, or killing furry things, he spent his evening murdering rivals in a digital universe. Even on the road you could always count on a good round of Mortal Kombat in Dexter's room.

Raven was downstairs, behind his kit, arguing with two road crew Hulk could beat Superman in a fight. I stood in the doorway and rolled my eyes at them. It was obvious Hulk would win. The more Hulk fights, the angrier he gets, the angrier he gets the stronger he becomes. Hulk's power increases exponentially while Supes has limits. Everyone knows this. Duh.

I wandered throughout the house floating on air from room to room. Friends, family, *band*, girlfriends, friends of friends, and general hangers on gossiped as I moved through the crowd. From the practice room I moved toward thinner populations in the kitchen. Most parties end up in the kitchen, but not in Chadwick's house. First, there wasn't much space. A rectangular kitchen table painted white but now yellowed with age, cigarette smoke, or both, dominated the space. A small path, large enough for two to pass if they didn't mind rubbing into each other, led to the back door or around to the sink. A window looked out on rampant overgrowth. The ghost of burgers' past and dirty dishes ensured nobody stayed for long.

There were rumors flying everywhere and the article in the paper only served to inflame the speculation. I had another crew member who wanted to engage me in a debate over who was the better band. Rush or Tool? Another silly argument, probably inspired by the heated comic book debate in the practice room, but for completely different reasons. Not wanting to remain in the kitchen, I begged off this conversation, moving through the practice room through to the front room, the former location of the drug tree.

I like Rush. Getty Lee's voice is kind of annoying, but they are undoubtedly one of rock and roll's classic bands. Neal Peart is an amazing drummer, and his work is mainly what I found interesting. Tool is a completely different animal all together. This comparison was apples to rocket science. One you could enjoy with no thought at all, the other you had to study and think. I've always found Tool to be a more cerebral experience and that is what I like about them.

The melodies are complex, the rhythm is intricate, and the lyrics are deep and philosophical. I've never spent hours contemplating the meaning of a Rush song, even one I've enjoyed, but I have spent time listening to a particular guitar strain or lyrical stanza from Tool over and over trying to get every nuance from the music. Comparisons like this are completely subjective. No one will ever be right because no opinion is the correct one.

Maybe he thought I was being rude, but it didn't matter.

I've often seen difference of opinion arguments devolve into brawls which send someone to the hospital. No one wins. So why fight? I miss the civility of previous generations. There was a time when it was all right to agree to disagree and still be social. Now a dissenting opinion is a declaration of war. Every little thought isn't worth defending to the death. Every feeling I have and every time I get offended doesn't need to be broadcast to the world. No one cares anyway. Especially me. Have your opinions, think what you want, I'm not going to knuckle up if I don't agree with you.

I turned back, again, moving through the crowd, deciding I'd spend the evening being an elitist with Chadwick and Vito. I enjoyed the comfort of familiarity. I listened without need to justify myself or contribute. I sat back on the couch casually assessing the onscreen porn and listening to their tech talk. There is a time in the life of a party when the initial buzz wears off. This is a critical point in the lifecycle of parties because it is when people will either go home and the party dies or things ramp up and the party gets wild. One of the two always happens.

When we reached that point in our own little celebration, I gathered the *band* to sit them down and tell them everything I'd been talking to Bob about. They knew we won Star Search and they knew we weren't continuing on in the competition, but they didn't know why. The crew knew even less than the *band* did apart from maybe Vito. He was near me in the crowd when I was talking to Bob. The *band* had been rocking out Voodoo Chile so Vito was occupied with maintaining the board, but he was smart. The Great Sun God paid attention to the world around him.

"So, you guys know we dominated the competition." I started out.

Wild cheers and applause interrupted me. I hadn't moved from my spot on the couch and the party was doing what it could to crowd around in a kind of horseshoe. Vito and Chadwick stayed by the computer, but they were standing up now looking at me. I had a strange vacant space to my left and then I realized Dexter was leaning against the wall next to the couch. Everyone kept an instinctive bubble away from Dexter as it was usually better to remain out of arms reach.

I saw Gideon in the crowd, those aviator style glasses focused on me. Gideon knew what was going on because he and I spent so much time together. We already discussed in detail what this new opportunity meant for the *band*. Raven abandoned his spot behind his kit to a spot at the far end of the couch. His bitch wife behind him, one hand possessively on his shoulder, and staring at me like I was

on a menu. Ashley stood between me and Gideon, close
to both, next to neither.

Next to me on the couch was the artist, Turtle, that had
done the drawing for our first album. He knew the deal
and was the only person not *in the band* who knew the
inner workings. He stayed at my house frequently and was
a good friend of mine. He leaned into me with a hand on
my shoulder and said into my ear, "Really happy for you,
man." I gave him a quick sidearm hug.

The applause and cheering died down. My skin burned
with anticipation. I paused and lit a cigarette. I exhaled
the first puff and studied the glowing cherry for dramatic
effect. This was turning into so much fun. If felt like
the beginning of a show, all the pent up excitement,
except everyone waited on me. "We got a perfect score and
made history as the first act ever demanded for an encore
performance."

"WOOO YEAH! YOU FUCKIN RIGHT WE
WERE!" someone yelled from the back. There was more
applause and cheering. I smoked my cigarette patiently.
When the applause died down again and opportunity
reappeared, I took my time, drawing it out.

"I'm sure you all saw the article in the paper this
morning. Probably why you're all here on a Monday night
instead of at home being responsible." Laughter, slightly

forced but appreciated. "So, here's the truth of what's going on. The paper doesn't know half of it because they didn't interview me. Typical small-town reporting, but that's alright. Yes, we won, I've said it but what does that mean? Why aren't we going further if we won this one? Simple. We got the goody out of Star Search. They can't help us anymore. We're now on the next level.

Another drag and slow exhale.

We have the ear, no the attention, of Star Search's top prize. I have the personal phone number and have been talking with Mr. Bob Wingood. He is the record executive that founded MTM Music. MTM Music is owned by Virgin Atlantic records. Virgin Atlantic has the right to claim any artist that signs with MTM and contract them to Virgin. In short, we got the ear of the big boys."

Riotous applause followed. Raven's wife stood with her jaw hanging open. I think it was the first time she'd ever been rendered speechless. Raven mouthed "are you serious?" I took a drag on my now depleted cigarette and gave him a slow nod. Chadwick was stone faced as usual, but I think there was a hint of a smile there. Probably my imagination. Vito looked concerned and full of questions. I could count on a good three-hour interrogation from him once he was able to corner me. Or he'd just show up at my house if I managed to slip away. I mouthed the word later at him and he nodded. That seemed to soothe him for the moment.

The crowd, made up mainly of road crew and their significant others were cheering and clapping each other on the back. I heard various exclamations of victory from our people.

"We did it! We fuckin did it!"

"I knew it!"

"Only a matter of time."

My personal favorite, "Hopefully they won't fuck it up." but I wasn't able to determine who said it.

Ashley was in tears. Several of the women were but hers were the only ones I paid attention to. I wanted to hold her. Kiss the tears away.

I stood up from my spot on the couch and made a quiet down motion by slowly flapping my arms. I don't know why pretending to be a bird is the international symbol of shut the hell up, but it works.

"This is a good thing and it's something we've all been working toward," I continued when the noise died down, "but this doesn't change much for our day-to-day operations ok guys? We are still practicing, we are still playing shows, and we are still selling CD's and fighting for airtime. The only difference is now we have someone who is going to help us with that task. It's still going to be up to us, nothing new there. MTM Music, Virgin, none of them change what we started out to do. But hopefully they'll help us do it on a much larger scale. I'll be happy to answer any questions any of you have, but now you're going to have to excuse me. I'm going to get drunk like a *fuckin rock god*!" I raised my arms again, this time in a celebratory gesture, and felt myself bigger than everyone else in the room.

The crowd went completely sideways. Our party turned the corner and now was on its way to becoming a completely epic rager. As wild as the party was, I don't seem to remember the police showing up. I think they knew the local boys done good and were going to let us have our fun. Or maybe no one called them, and they didn't give a fuck. Maybe they showed up and partied with the *band*. I don't know.

I snuck out the door and went home alone. Sober.

I talked to Bob three times that week while pacing back and forth in my tiny apartment's kitchen.

"Annie! Bob here, how the hell are you?"

"Still walking on cloud nine."

Bob laughed, "Good. That's good. Let's talk about the plan. Where did we see yourselves in five years?"

"In five years, I'd like to be blowing out amphitheaters around the world."

"Nice, but that kind of thing comes with time. What do want to do with the music?"

"I'm not sure what you're asking. The music is part of us. We must do it, be it for you, for ourselves, for fans, or no one at all. We have to get it out there."

"Which is good," Bob said, "but not exactly what I'm talking about. A better question might be are you all willing to work as hard as necessary to do this thing?"

Of course we were. I thought the last few years of cd sales and gigging around proved it. Bob said the real work hadn't even begun.

Bob talked a lot about how hard it was to be successful in the music industry. The fans have short memories and its constant pressure to be the next thing. If you're lucky enough to be the next thing then you must work twice as hard to prove you're still relevant. The only thing people loved more than watching a star rise was watching one fall. He warned of the dangers of women and drugs and alcohol.

"I've seen hundreds of acts come and go." Bob said, "Some of them rose on to bigger and better things, most crashed and burned because people got into music for the wrong reasons. Let me guess, you people got into music thinking being a rock star was better than having a day job only to find out it was even harder to do this than it was to go to work every day. People become shocked, disillusioned with the amount of pressure applied at the higher levels."

The kitchen was growing dark. We'd been on the phone for several hours. I clicked the kitchen light switch and the room burst into light, forcing the growing shadows back.

I wondered when the last time was he had to make a choice between using the last of your money to buy gas, buy food, or keep the lights on. There wasn't enough to do all three and you had to pick. That was pressure. Making those kinds of choices when you have kids was even worse. I didn't have any kids at the time, I thought of my dogs as the closest to kids I'd ever come, but I'd had to make those kinds of decisions. Poor people make awful no-win decisions every day. Please give me the stress of being a rock star. I'd get a dog sitter and go rock and roll. Please please throw me in that briar patch.

Bob was concerned there wasn't a clear leader of the group. I acted like a spokesperson but we, in theory, made decisions as a group. He said successful groups had clearly defined leadership. Gideon and I made the decisions when it came down to it. I could manipulate Gideon if necessary, so I wasn't as worried about this as Bob was.

I had his address and I sent him copies of the three albums we had together. I told him only the first one was for sale in stores, and it was selling well. We had sold a few copies of our second album at shows for fans who asked about a particular song they'd liked but wasn't on the first album. The feedback from those little experiments was positive and Bob seemed impressed at our hustle.

He thought as long as we were willing to work like we'd been working we would do something amazing. He liked our sound, and he liked our first two albums, but he thought the third was a little weak. Alright, I thought the third album had some solid tunes on it but was a bit more artsy. On Friday we had a conversation about coming to Orlando.

"Annie, I'd like you boys to come to Orlando. It's important."

"What's going on in Orlando?" I asked.

"I'd like to fly *the band* down to play a show. It's an audition for a major label."Bob said. Not that he wanted us to come down and audition. Fly down. Fly us down specifically. I felt gut punched. I slid down the kitchen wall. "Really?" I asked not entirely sure I'd heard correctly.

We would be flown to Orlando, put into a hotel for a couple of nights, and go play a club where a major label was waiting to hear us. Major label could only mean Virgin-Atlantic. I kept trying to tell myself it didn't mean anything because we weren't getting paid. I didn't have any airline tickets in my hand. The situation had been discussed in generalities and generalities are cheap.

Still, I couldn't still the voice inside that wanted to scream *we did it we did it hot damn we fuckin did it!!* Hanging up the phone I wanted to run screaming through the streets. I wanted to sit on the chests and scream in the faces of everyone that had ever doubted us, doubted me, *"ahhhhhahahahaha! How you like that action?!? Suck it! Suck it! Suck it til your head caves in! neener neener mothergrabbin neener!!!"*

Instead, I picked myself off the floor, went to the bathroom, and threw up.

I turned on the bathroom sink and let cold water run over my flushed face. Unbelievable.

The sensation of finding success was unlike anything. It was righteous. I felt vindicated and justified in the sacrifices I'd made and with the bridges I'd burned, Bruce's face flashed in my mind. I headed to Saturday practice with a big smile on my face. It was all going to be worth it.

I saved the news of Orlando until we had run through the show. It was just the *band* and necessary crew and Dexter, because Dexter wanted to be there. I told them Bob was preparing an audition in Orlando, and the *band* should be expecting tickets for the ride down there. This was greeted with amazed silence.

"Damn, this is happening, isn't it?" Raven quietly asked no one in particular.

Gideon answered him, "What's he going to do for us that we aren't already doing for ourselves?"

"There's the small matter of flying us out for an audition for one," I answered Gideon slightly annoyed.

"I just don't see what he's going to do. We've played Orlando before."

"Not for someone with the power to make us a national or even international thing."

"We could book jobs in Europe without him. What's he doing for us?"

I couldn't understand Gideon's resistance.

"Let's do the audition and see what comes. He's paying for us to come down so why not go? We aren't out anything."

"Yeah, but we can go play Florida without him. We can do everything without him."

"What the fuck man? What's with all the static?"

"No static. I just don't see why we're all suddenly all for a guy we don't know."

"Because he is an industry professional in an industry we're trying to get into. You're the only one with a problem with him."

"Fuck it man, whatever. Do whatever. I just don't see what he's going to do for us that we aren't already doing. We're selling CD's. We're booking shows. Music is supporting all of us. All without magic man Bob. Now there's some dude that just comes along and you all act like he's Jesus Christ of Rock and Roll and he's going to save us all. Sure, let's give some guy a piece of the pie. Hallelujah! But we don't need saving. We're doing fine without him."

Gideon stomped out of the room. If the guy was legit, good for us if he wasn't, we weren't out anything. The rest of the *band*, including me, couldn't see anything but good stemming from a relationship with MTM. Maybe my confidence stemmed from the amount of time I'd spent in conversation with Bob. It wasn't a TON of time, but it was enough to make me comfortable.

The only holdup was Gideon who was having some type of crazy daddy issue. We needed him to be on board and he knew it. I would bring Gideon around, kicking and screaming if I had to. I followed him outside. I probably should have let him go but I was tired of the prima donna act and wanted him to unfuck himself before he ruined things for everyone.

"What the fuck man? You're cool when it's me and you but you freak the fuck out in there?"

Chadwick's back yard was silent, lit from the glow of the houselights. A quarter moon rising in the darkening sky.

He turned around with a look I had never seen. He looked, sorry.

"Man, I don't know. I'm scared, you know? This is the best thing in my life, and I don't want it ruined."

A picture of Ashley, laughing in my kitchen, skin glowing in the sun floated before my eyes. I wanted to punch him.

"If you don't want it ruined then why are you fighting the rest of us so hard? I don't get it; we don't lose anything."

"You ever have a fight with your best friend? Like a real fight?"

This change in direction caught me off guard.

"What, like, a fistfight? Or like what we've been doing for the past few months?"

"Like a fistfight. You just go at it and afterward you feel better, and everything is good again."

"No. I try not to have fistfights with people I care about."

"See? I didn't think you'd get it."

"What's there to get? I don't want to fight you Gideon. I want to play music with you, get high with you, get paid with you, and enter the cycle. Remember?"

"Yeah, I want that too, but" he left it hanging.

"Do you seriously want to fight me?"

"Yeah, kind of clear the air."

"This is so stupid."

"Let's do it anyway."

He set his drink down in the yard and emptied his pockets. Then, I guess before he could rethink it, he lunged at me. He left his wedding ring on and almost before I could react he swung that hand in a nasty left hook. I grew up in Texas where street fighting was a daily occurrence. I have scars all over my knuckles from fighting. I leaned back and his fist swung harmlessly by my nose. I stepped forward and quickly hit him twice in the solar plexus knocking the wind out of him. As he was bending over to catch his breath, I hit him again under the chin laying him out in the yard. One, two, three and done. Gideon was a tough country boy, but he never had a chance.

I was angry he'd tried to sucker punch me. I let the anger take over, wash over my common sense and drown my inhibitions in burning red bloodlust. I was holding him by the shirt, he'd gone almost completely limp, and was using the shirt to pull his face into my fist. Each time I hit him I asked him if he was done. He'd shake his head no and I'd hit him again. Enough? No? Whap!

That's how we were when Raven and Vito came out of the house. Vito ran over and jerked me by the collar separating us. I fell backwards in the grass but quickly gained my feet.

"He wanted it!" I tried to plead my innocence, but Vito and Raven just looked at me in this blank accusatory way I'll never forget. They already made up their minds. I was a bad guy. Gideon didn't deserve what was happening. Raven was helping Gideon to his feet.

Gideon was smiling at me in between wiping blood and snot from his face and spitting blood in the grass. He had a look on his face like he won. The crazy fucker looked like getting beat down really did make him feel better. Vito looked angry. I wondered if he wanted to pick up what Gideon dropped and continue with me. Fuck him too, it wouldn't work out differently.

I kept trying to plead my case. Raven looked tired and suddenly he looked old to me. He said, "Why don't you just go home? You've done enough. We'll sort this out Monday."

Gideon never said a word. He stood there and bled. As they went inside, Gideon turned flashing me a secret smile, there and gone, a quick flash of bloody teeth. Not once did he confirm what I'd been saying. Fighting was his idea. I had been against it. He was turning the group against me. In a way I admired the manipulation. He'd taken the beating, but he'd gotten control. It was going to be hard going for me to get anything accomplished in the group after this. I drove home angry.

I was angry I'd allowed him to manipulate me. I felt stupid which fed the anger. I was angry he had to make things so difficult. Mostly I was angry because I didn't know how Ashley was going to react to me beating the snot out of her husband. I didn't want to do it, but I doubted that was the version of events that she was going to hear. I was going to lose my morning love and that pissed me off. Fucking Gideon! Ugh! Fuck that guy!

When I got home, I let the dogs out, sat on my porch, and sulked. Ice from the freezer wrapped in a towel cooled the burning in my knuckles but did little to cool my shame. With a couple of careless acts, I had thrown away years of hard work. My stupid temper. My god damned angry heart. I had no idea what the rest of the *band* was going to think but I could imagine Gideon even now persuading them I had to go. Smoking and brooding weren't doing anything to improve my mood. I went to bed and stared at the ceiling for a long time before sleep claimed me.

Sunday wasn't any better. I felt like a fool and there wasn't anything I could do about it. All day I expected the phone to ring and hear I was out of the *band*. When it didn't happen, I almost wish it had. Nobody called me at all. I spent it either on the porch, smoking cigarettes, watching the dogs or in front of the television, smoking cigarettes, trying to get into a video game. I couldn't concentrate so the game was more frustrating than fun. My house stank of stale tobacco smoke and rather than open a window I would light another only adding to the problem. The dogs had bailed out for the relative funk-free air of the bedroom.

Monday morning was also spent alone. No morning pickup. No morning love. I made breakfast of half of a leftover Subway spicy Italian sandwich and Newports. I thought I might head over to the family business but quickly dismissed the idea. I didn't need my folks to tell me it was okay. Two years of work just blew up in my face because they knew it was only a phase I was going through. I couldn't deal with smarmy condescension this morning.

I waited until noon before I decided maybe I should let Bob know there were some internal issues in the *band* that needed sorting out before he sent any plane tickets our way. The phone rang twice before the man himself picked up.

"What do you want?" he asked. He sounded, well, angry. His tone threw me off my train of thought.

"Uh, yeah, Bob, I wanted to let you know that we have some internal issues we need to work out."

"I don't care what you have to work out. You guys are, you are some kind of arrogant. I will never work with people who act as unprofessional as you guys' act."

Unprofessional? Huh? My stomach dropped as my balls withdrew. My hands began to shake. The kitchen was suddenly too small, too claustrophobic. I didn't understand why the radical shift in his demeanor. On Friday he was talking about flying us out for an audition and two days later he was never going to work with us again? What happened there? I completely abandoned the plan and asked him what happened to cause his radical change of opinion.

Bob said Saturday afternoon he happened to be in the office when Gideon called him. Apparently, Gideon had stolen the number off of my kitchen table some time previously. He had come over the previous Wednesday before practice and I guess that must have been when he decided to fuck over all of us. Gideon called before the Saturday practice and knew it was already over with Bob before the fight. That explained why he was so dead set against further contact with Bob, but it didn't explain why he had made the call in the first place.

All of this flashed quickly through my head as Bob explained that Gideon called with a ridiculous list of demands. Gideon demanded a whole list of silliness if Bob really wanted our business. We were to be flown down to Orlando first class and we had to be picked up at the airport in a fully stocked limo. The limo was to drive us to the Ritz-Carlton Orlando Grande Lakes hotel where we were to have suites, as in a suite for each member of *the band*. The ballroom at the Ritz was to be reserved in case we decided to practice before the audition or party afterwards. The limousine needed to be available for our use anytime day or night. We were also to be ferried back and forth to the audition by this same limousine. Preferably the same driver but Gideon had graciously remained flexible on that point. The entire trip, including all room service, was to be paid for in its entirety by MTM Music and Bob Wingood.

I couldn't believe it.

I felt sick. My stomach dropped and I wasn't completely sure I wasn't going to throw up. We weren't going to Orlando. We weren't going to audition. We weren't going to take the next step in our careers. Bob finished his explanation, which he really didn't owe, and told me he thought I'd be better off away from Gideon. He then wished me good luck in my future endeavors and asked me not to contact him again.

I managed to mumble an apology and thanked him for the time he gifted me. My face felt hot and numb at the same time. I was and still am genuinely sorry things didn't work out better. Bob could have helped us become something more.

Gideon completely fucked us and didn't bother to tell us negotiations with MTM were now moot because of his little list of demands. Since I hadn't heard anything from the *band* over the weekend, I now had the distinct pleasure of letting the group know everything we had been working toward had burned to the ground. More than two years' worth of work and sweat, and tears thrown away with one selfish silly phone call. All our sacrifice had been for nothing.

There would never be another opportunity like this. This had been a once in a lifetime deal. We had taken our operation as far as it's possible for an amateur group to go without crossing over into the bigtime. We had attention, were knocking on the door of the majors, and then fucked it up like the good ol' bunch of Summit Valley boys we were. Everybody knew it was going to happen. Fuck.

I felt sick. People had quit their jobs. Vito sold his house and moved halfway across the country. There were people counting on us for their livelihood, but I doubted that mattered much to Gideon. We had a responsibility, hell an obligation, to the people who trusted us. We were supposed to keep things going so they could continue to feed their families. Now it was over. Gideon, in his rush to spite me, screwed over everyone who ever believed in us.

He *knew*. The thought wouldn't leave my head. He came into practice, started a fight, and all the while he *knew*. He looked us in the face and rather than tell us what he had done he pretended everything was the same. I don't know if he was cowardly or if he was such a sociopath, he was indifferent to all the hearts he had just broken. Even though it was wrong, I felt better about whipping his ass. He knew the whole time and said nothing. It's haunted me since and I'll never understand the why of it.

It was still several hours before practice was scheduled to start. I had a long wait, and the whole time I couldn't get my head around why he'd made that phone call. I spent the meantime trying to get my temper under control. I paced. I walked the dogs. I smoked a lot. I beat a stick against a tree until it snapped, and shrapnel popped me in the eye. I smoked some more. It wouldn't do to go into practice and beat his ass again as much as I wanted to. It was best if I maintained a clear head. The *band* deserved to hear everything in cold calm calculated detail. Emotions needed to be kept out of this for now because I was sure the *band* would be emotional enough once they heard the news. Never mind the crew who sacrificed so much because they believed in the music, those guys were going to be extremely emotional. Ashley's gold hair, the feel of her lips on my neck, brought goosebumps, and a shameful cooling of my anger.

I got to practice close to a half hour early. I couldn't stay in the house anymore. Vito, Chadwick, and Raven were already there. I thought the meeting was probably about Gideon and me but what did it matter now? The conversation died when I walked in the room, and they were all watching me. Tension in the air made my stomach flop, my hands shook slightly.

"You don't need to worry about me guys. But you do need to know what happened over the weekend."

"We need to know why you beat up Gideon. That was way out of line man." I was surprised Raven needed to ask, he picked Gideon up off the grass, but then I remembered

he wasn't outside for the conversation between Gideon
and me beforehand. I tried to explain that night, but no
one listened! What they saw was me leaving after Gideon
and then finding Gideon beat down on the grass. There
wasn't any context so they must assume I went outside
to attack him. Apparently, Gideon hadn't told them the
truth about that either.

I explained what had really happened but then I told
them it didn't matter. None of this mattered. I began to
unhook the effect lighting I had purchased. Vito wanted
to know what happened. Why didn't my fight matter?
I stopped unhooking the acid beam from the truss so I
could face them. I wanted to look them all in the eye.

"Gideon fucked us. It's over. We could continue gigging
on but gentlemen, the *band* is done. The audition is gone
and there will be no working with Bob. We'll have to sell
a billion CD's on our own before another label takes a
serious look at us."

"What do you mean? What happened Saturday?" Vito
looked as angry as I've ever seen anyone get. "I sold my
fuckin house! Don't tell me it's over!"

It broke my heart to tell them about my final
conversation with Bob. I was finishing the story when
Gideon walked through the door. He was about thirty
minutes late, something he never did. He was always

early to practice because, like me, playing music was the highlight of the day. It was the thing all of us looked forward to. Maybe he thought they were going to collectively fire me, and he wouldn't have to fess up to what he did. If I was gone there would only be his word as to what happened to our producer.

Chadwick sat down in front of the computer and put his head in his hands. Glowing images of naked women softly illuminated his skin. Raven looked at Gideon and asked, "Is it true?" and the expression on Gideon's face told more than a confession could.

"I believed you. I took your side." Raven looked like a child shocked a loving parent spanked him.

Gideon stood in the entry way to the practice room. He wore shorts and a muscle shirt with an island sunset and the *band* logo airbrushed on the front. He never denied what he'd done. He didn't say anything. He stood there, drinking cup in one hand, keys and cigarettes balanced in the other, looking from Raven to Chadwick to me. I turned my back and went back to unhooking equipment.

"That belongs to the *band*." Gideon tried lamely.

"Fuck yourself. I paid for it." Gideon didn't press it.

"Mother fuckerrrr! I sold my fuckin house! My home!" Vito screamed, grabbed Gideon's guitar, and swung it into Gideon's Marshall amplifier. The amplifier with guitar

firmly embedded flew into one of the forward stacks and the entire speaker tower crashed to the floor. The amplifier exploded with a POP! and a shower of sparks. Vito turned, knocked Gideon out of the way, and stomped out of the band house slamming the door behind him. It was the last time I saw Arizona Vito.

Raven and I removed our gear from the house in silence. Chadwick never moved from in front of the computer, even when the speaker tower fell, he didn't move. Raven took his kit apart while I took my keyboards, amplifier, stands, and chair and loaded them into my car. I had the effect lighting I'd paid for underneath the musical gear packed away neatly, ready for a run. My last run would be back to my house, the final run.

I stood by the car while Raven finished bringing his gear out. He loaded the car and walked over to me. I lit a cigarette. Raven lit one too.

"Sorry man. He told us you attacked him. We should have called you."

"It doesn't matter Raven," I exhaled a blue grey stream like my music career, so much smoke.

"It matters to me. We were wrong."

"Raven, it was good riding with you. I was fucking his wife. I couldn't help it. I'd pick her up in the mornings when she got off work and I'd fuck her until the early afternoons when he wakes up. Been fucking her for months."

"I knew it." Raven looked at me through the smoke. "I think we all knew it. She seemed happy."

Chadwick was standing outside the door looking up the hill. He lit a cigarette, watching us. He never spoke. The three of us stood there silently, each feeling the death of something we loved in our own way, smoking and saying a silent goodbye. Chadwick looked over, into the house, as I got to the end of my cigarette. Gideon stepped outside holding the pieces of his broken guitar. He looked up at me and said, "Go on then. We don't need you. We have everything here."

I had flicked the butt away and was getting in the car when the sound of his voice made me turn back to the house. I stood back up and faced him. Leaning on the inside of my car door I lit another cigarette, "Gideon, I've been fucking Ashley for months. She told me about Star Search while naked in my kitchen. She said I make her cum like you never could." I sat down, closed my door, and drove away. I guess I was no longer *in the band* but there wasn't a band to be a part of anymore. I drove home and unpacked my gear.

A neighbor called over from the Porch and asked me when the next show was.

"Never can tell, Jimmy," I answered. He raised his beer. I went inside wondering what was left. What was I going to do now? Never can tell, Jimmy. That's the fucking truth. Never can tell.

I woke up the next morning feeling like there was a hole in my chest. Something was missing and it was something I was never going to be able to recover. Like an amputee a part of me had been removed and what I had left were ghost feelings from a phantom piece no longer there. I was angry. I'd been robbed and now I had to figure out how to replace being a rock god.

The feeling of loss only got worse. Everywhere I went there were people who wanted to know when the next show was, what we were doing, when does the next album drop, and how were things with the *band*. Great, fine, things are just fucking fantastic.

I couldn't stay in Summit Valley. There were too many memories and too many people invested in us. I took my dogs over to my parent's house with their food, food and water dishes, and bedding. My parents weren't home, but they knew the dogs, watched them when I was on a run sometimes, and loved them almost as much as I did. Plus, they had land the dogs could run on.

I called Turtle to stay in my apartment. I didn't leave the dogs because Turtle could be flighty. I wanted to make sure the dogs were taken care of. Turtle would be around enough to make sure thieves wouldn't think it was open season on my stuff. He was grateful to get out of the dorms and asked if I minded if he brought his girlfriend over. What the fuck did I care? She wouldn't be the first, wash the sheets on occasion, brother.

I packed some clothes and threw the suitcase into the back of my car. I then got on I-77 South to see where it might take me. I had money, I had time, and I had nowhere in particular to be. I only knew I couldn't be here. I left.

I had been lost and then the music found me and now that was gone. I didn't have it in me to try and set up another band. I couldn't work that hard only to have someone I was supposed to count on sabotage me again.

I spent a week in Florida with a friend. He lived alone and was happy to let me stay. I could cook and he hadn't had many home cooked meals so that paid for my keep. In the evenings I would tell him I was going to move on the next day, and he would beg me to stay one more day. Poor guy, he must have been starving to want me to stay for that long. I taught him how to make some basic meals. Spaghetti, pancakes, burgers, steaks, macaroni and cheese, basic guy food, nothing too complex. My family owned a high-end bed and breakfast and did catering as well. Cooking was in my blood. The things I taught him weren't nearly as complicated as the things I cooked but it would keep him alive and out of restaurants.

That would save him a few bucks anyway.

He still didn't want me to leave and in truth I could have stayed longer. I liked Palm Coast, and it was just the two of us in a four-bedroom house. Jenkins was a childhood friend who moved to Florida to race motorcycles. He had been to a couple of the shows when we were in the area, and he was saddened to hear about the break up.

Being the good friend he was we didn't spend much time discussing it. We smoked weed in his garage and talked about racing. He would gleefully ask what I was planning for dinner that evening. Did I need anything from the store? Then we would go to the grocery store.

The afternoons were spent by his pool, drinking Fresca, or playing darts and smoking weed in the garage. He never broached the subject of the *band* unless I did but I was still so heartsick and tried not to. All I wanted to do was the nothing we usually got into. In the evenings I would cook, and Jenkins acted like a kid at Christmas. I've never seen anyone as excited about home cooked food. It felt good to make someone happy.

I loved him for the kindness he showed and for the enthusiasm he had for my cooking. I was grateful for a place to rest. But I was feeling like I wasn't quite far enough away. I had money in the bank and an intense desire to be off the east coast. I had never seen the Pacific Ocean, so I decided to head west once I left Jenkins.

Even as I had the car packed, he was asking me not to go. He didn't care how long I stayed. I told him he had a few meals to build his confidence and once he was comfortable, he would begin branching out and experimenting. He looked doubtful, like I was making it up so I could leave. I got in the car and drove west.

Florida, Alabama, Mississippi, and most of Louisiana disappeared without me really noticing. Driving has always been cathartic for me. I smoked a cigarette every hour to keep track of the time. The miles rolled out under the tires, and I thought, and I smoked. Paying attention to the road and the traffic around me kept things from turning into an introspective nightmare and deep pooling depression.

Drive. Smoke. Stop and eat or sleep when needed.

I spent some time with friends in Texas. I grew up there, so it was nice to see some of the old neighborhood and some of the old friends. We ate Tex Mex and laughed and didn't get too personal. When I felt like it was time to go, I didn't have to postpone. The people there loved me, but they weren't going to fall apart if I left. Out of San Antonio I entered the great nothing of West Texas desert.

My car had a CD player, but I didn't have any CD's other than the *band*. There are no radio stations and when I hit the search the dial spun and spun finding nothing. I rolled down the window and let the desert wind be my music. The land was mainly flat and there wasn't much to see. There were no towns. I stopped at a dusty gas station to fill up the car and empty my bladder. Sitting on the side of the toilet was a large tarantula. It turned toward me as I came through the door, drawing its legs in defensively. I didn't know if tarantulas jumped but thought it best not to find out. I pissed in the sink.

I left the gas station relieved I had made it out without being chewed on by a giant spider. The sand, spiders, and flat wide-open burn of West Texas led me into the American Southwest proper. Should I live long enough to retire, and if I can't afford to live by a beach, I'm coming back to New Mexico or Arizona. The beauty of the land made the wrong done to Vito somehow worse. He gave this up for us and then we gave up. Thousands of miles from Virginia and I still hadn't outrun the memories.

I pressed on further west and hooked north into Nevada. I was out here; I might as well see Vegas.

I approached Vegas from the southeast on Highway 93. Over the Hoover Dam which wasn't my intention but a happy accident. Passing through Boulder City, where they're dam builders and dam proud of it, I drove up a hill. At the top, the shining lights of Las Vegas below me. I almost stayed in Vegas. Nearly seduced by the lights and the noise, the frantic anonymity. Nobody there knew or cared that I had once been *in the band*. Manic oblivion held a certain appeal. Vegas was pure chaos. I wanted to lose myself in Vegas' wild, carefree, hard luck attitude.

Out of the noise of Vegas I drove into the peace and silence of the desert. I passed through Reno and over the mountain into California. The first time I saw Golden State it was snowing. The mountain passes were dealing with a late spring storm and as I got under the snowline the snow turned to rain which stayed steady and monotonous into Sacramento.

Having recently left a major urban area I didn't have much desire to get into another one. From Sacramento I headed north into Oregon and Washington State leaving the golden state behind me. As quickly as I could I made my way to the 101 and finally saw the Pacific Ocean for the first time. I found a place to park and walked to the end of the country. I sat down on the beach and let the ocean wash over my legs.

I'd put the entire width of America between me and the *band*. The future was still as unclear as it had been since hanging up the phone with Bob. I was no longer angry, too many days on the road, too tired, but the confusion which settled in anger's place was worse. When I was mad, I had a sense of direction even if my misguided direction was to beat the snot out of Gideon (again). There was an overwhelming feeling of now what? Expectation. And I didn't know for what.

Where was the sense of destiny? Where was my guiding hand? Had it swept me off to the side, forsaking me? How had everything changed so quickly? What was left now that the music was gone? I ran the same group of questions over and over in my head, smoking my Newports, and watching the sun disappear into the Pacific. I would have to move soon; the tide was coming in and the weather was getting cold. My t-shirt and shorts weren't cutting it. It also looked like the rain I'd left in Sacramento was about to find me again.

I felt a tap on my shoulder. Speaking to me was a beautiful redhead in a black bikini top and a green sarong. Goosebumps stood up on her arms.

"Excuse me, I know it's nice here and all, but you should probably leave. Cops like to roll through here just after sundown and roust homeless and teenagers. They are, like, really aggressive, you know?" She was smiling but was also watching down the beach. Maybe at those cops she was worried were going to roust me.

"There's a shelter not far from here, I can show you if you want."

She thought I was a bum. I smiled back and told her I had a car.

"Oh! Sorry! I thought-"

"I know what you thought. It's ok. Thank you for the heads up."

I asked if she had anywhere to be and if she knew a good place to eat. I would be happy to buy her dinner as a thank you. She agreed and we walked back to my car. She held a towel up and turned her back providing me with a screen while I changed my wet pants. She was beautiful. I said that already, but it does bear repeating.

She was originally traveling to Los Angeles when her boyfriend abandoned her at a hotel in Sacramento. She had family in North Carolina, but the relationship wasn't good, so she hadn't called them for any kind of help. She had been living on the generosity of people she met and moving from shelter to shelter always heading north away from the boyfriend.

Over dinner I asked her how long it had been since she had slept in a bed and had a hot shower. She started to get a little defensive, withdrawn. I realized I sounded like a complete creeper.

"No! No! No! Not like that! I'm not trying to imply anything!" I stopped cutting my steak, holding my hands up in a pacifying manner.

She still looked doubtful, but I couldn't blame her. There was no telling the number of perverts and creeps she dealt with since her douchebag boyfriend abandoned her. I liked her and felt a little White Knight syndrome for her. I wanted to help, and I enjoyed her company. I managed to convince her I wasn't propositioning her.

Her name was Rae and for whatever reason she decided to trust me. We stayed the night in a hotel room. I let her shower first then I did. She slept in the bed, and I piled some blankets on the floor. I locked my wallet and my valuables in the car and kept the keys on me. I wasn't a complete moron. I wasn't about to trust some chick I just met. There was something about her, a calm, a trustworthiness. In the morning, we had breakfast and Rae told me she was content to ride up to Astoria.

I wanted to see Astoria since I was a kid. I was a huge fan of the Goonies which had been filmed there. Kindergarten Cop had also filmed there and it looked like a beautiful place. The reality was somewhat different. It was a poor fishing town. I could see the houses that had so charmed me as a child stretching up forested hillsides, poking up amongst the evergreens. But instead of looking homey and inviting like they had in the movies they looked worn and dirty and sad.

Rae didn't say anything. She didn't have to. The disappointment on my face must have been plain. We got back in the car and left Astoria in the rear-view mirror. She suggested we hit I-5 and head back south to Portland. It was as good a plan as any. I got a room with two twin beds and while we were checking in the clerk told us how he was planning to move to Eugene. He said, "The people there are a lot more chill, you know, than people in Portland yeah? Fuckers here are way uptight, you know?"

I nodded like I knew. When in doubt, nod and smile. Chill people sounded good. I'd had my fill of uptight fuckers, so we decided to take him at his word. Rae didn't have anything else to do and we were getting to like each other so she came along.

After a pancake breakfast at the restaurant attached to the hotel Rae and I got back in the car. We stopped in

Creswell, just south of Eugene, and got another hotel room. Rae took ten dollars and walked over to a coffee stand and brought us back a pair of the tastiest white chocolate mochas I'd ever had. Coffee booths seemed to be on every street corner in Oregon.

There were booths across the street from booths. Worse than Big Tops in Florida. A plague of small wooden coffee booths here. You could drive through for coffee or walk up to the window. You could sit down in an upscale café or be served by girls in bikinis. The Breast Coffee in Oregon! There was coffee everywhere. I heard about how serious people in the Pacific Northwest were about their coffee consumption, but I had no idea. The booths were everywhere, and they were always busy.

On our fifth day together, Rae decided we probably only needed one bed. I didn't mind. She was amazing. I was falling in love with her. She was charm, and wit. Kindness and sex appeal. I didn't want to get clingy and chase her away, so I kept my feelings to myself. I hadn't told her much about the *band*, as that subject was still entirely too raw. She never pushed, giving me space where I needed it. We walked around the downtown Saturday market in Eugene when Rae turned to me and said she liked it here.

She said we should look for an apartment.

Being with her felt good and the last person who made me feel this good was another man's wife. It felt right. Already by that point if she told me she wanted to go back to North Carolina, I would have taken her. She wanted to get an apartment with me. She said we could get jobs and even if things were rough at first, she thought we could build a good life here. When we met, she thought I was a bum, a transient, and she didn't want the police to hurt me. Now she wanted to build a life with this bum.

I didn't tell her I had a sizeable bank account filled with the proceeds of the entertainment industry. I quietly paid cash for an apartment off the Beltway behind a WinCo Foods grocery store. WinCo was within walking distance of our place. I thought it was unique that we had to bag our own groceries. Sometimes we had to check ourselves out AND bag our own groceries. I'd never seen anything like it back on the east coast. The level of trust shown was astounding.

After renting the apartment she rode back to Virginia with me. I arranged to have the furniture moved and picked up the dogs. We headed back across the country again and made it to the apartment on the day before the furniture arrived. There was only one night spent sleeping on the floor but with Rae I didn't mind. If I was with her it didn't matter what we did.

Traveling back and forth across the country (three times!), setting up a new household, and keeping us fed while we looked for work took a bite out of my bank account. Rae managed to find work first as a salesgirl at a snobby furniture store. Her natural sweet disposition made her a successful salesperson, but her boss was a sleaze.

I couldn't blame her. Her boss was a sleaze, always trying to get her alone so he could come on to her. She hated it but she worked at it because we needed the money. Our downstairs neighbor came knocking one night. His name was Riley and he had knocked on our door late one night to ask if we were making the noise which had woken his infant daughter. The apartment across the stairway from us, and directly above him, was occupied by a prostitute. At least I hope she was getting paid for it as many men were in and out of there.

She was rude and nasty, took peoples assigned parking spaces where space was at a premium, blasted her electronics, had parties, and when she had sex she moaned like a porn queen. She had sex most every day and usually multiple times a day. Riley had a wife and a little girl, and they all went to bed early. This rude bitch knew it but didn't care. She acted like she was all alone in the universe and did as she pleased. She told Riley it wasn't her blasting the stereo but rather Rae and me. He said he knew it wasn't us but to be sure he knocked on our door anyway.

I told him that we didn't even have the television on, which was true, but if we were disturbing the baby please come knock on the door. I believe in good neighborly relationships, I'm a Southern Boy. The following morning, I met Riley as we were taking our trash to the dumpster. He told me we could get fined for not using the proper recyclable bins. This was something I'd never done in Virginia. I thanked him for the advice, and we separated out my trash together.

He would come to our apartment and play Mortal Kombat. I would steadily kill his best characters and through hundreds of Fatalities we became friends. It wasn't like playing Dexter, I won some rounds. Rae liked him well enough but thought he was a bit of a blowhard. Riley was a good guy but no matter what you've done he'd done it before. If you had something, he had a newer one. If you discovered a shampoo you liked he'd been using it for years. It wasn't anything too dramatic, but Rae had a point. He could be annoying.

He asked one night what I was doing for work. I told him I was currently looking for a job and was considering putting in an application at Blimpy's Subs in the WinCo parking lot. "Don't bother," he said. He told me he could offer me something that paid a lot more. He was a crew chief for a window washing company and he had an opening on his crew. It was entry level work, but the pay was good. It wasn't rock god good, but it would take the pressure off of our dwindling bank account.

I took the position. I didn't know anything about washing windows but during the summer months the job was pleasant enough. We mostly worked outside, and it was never too hot. Things could get a little spicy at the top of a thirty-foot ladder working a twenty foot pole to clean an eighteen inch transom when the wasps got curious. A person could get a little bit nervous.

During the fall the weather changes to its more permanent state in the Northwest. Rain. The local weatherman had at least fifteen ways to say it's going to rain tomorrow. Rain, rainfall, mist, mizzle, shower, spit, sprinkle, squall, thundershower, thunderstorm, cloudburst, downfall, downpour, flurry, and deluge were a few of the terms that translated to bring an umbrella and don't wear suede. Weathermen in the Northwest have the most boring job on earth. Nine months out of the year, it's raining. The other three, sunny. Most people I met in Eugene didn't carry umbrellas. They didn't notice moisture in the air until it was heavy enough to affect sight distance.

Once the sun went back into its nine-month hibernation the mostly outdoor job of washing windows began to lose its charm. There are few things as pointless as giving the outside windows a good scrub only to have them spot up again as soon as the soap is wiped off. It was a true exercise in futility and where I found the end of the road. I was outside, enjoying a nice mizzle, cleaning the windows at a local diner. I was working my way around the outside, racing Riley who was inside, when the thought occurred to me if I didn't take immediate drastic action this was going to be my life. I saw a reflection in the glass, me, but older, broken and bitter. I was getting dumber with each pass of the squeegee. I could see my life stretching out in one long endless pointless attempt to try and keep windows clean in the Oregon rain. In those old eyes of the reflection I saw how I'd go home in the evening worn out from work, wet, cold, and would lash out at Rae. She'd leave and I would come home to an empty apartment. My life would add up to nothing. Empty.

The rain was always going to win. The only way I could win this game is if I didn't play.

I looked over my shoulder and I'd like to say the clouds parted and the sun shone down on the answer. Not true. No angelic choir celebrated my escape from the squeegee. I looked over my shoulder and saw in the corner of the shopping center was the local Armed Forces Recruiter Station. All four branches had offices together.

I set my bucket down and walked across the parking lot. Riley saw where I was going and put my bucket in the truck. He then moved the truck to wait on me. I stood outside, almost in a trance, staring at the promotional posters in the window. I didn't want to be out at sea away from Rae for ten months out of the year so that ruled out the Navy. I wasn't crazy, or physically fit, enough to be a Marine. Truth was I was carrying around an extra fifty pounds. I put it off to being happy with Rae. The reality was I had let myself go and was horribly out of shape.

I didn't want to be in the Army because I felt like I had too much intelligence to be a grunt. My father retired from the Air Force, and I was familiar with the life, so it seemed like a natural fit. I didn't get the same sense of Destiny I had with the *band* but it felt like the right move.

The military is a fine thing for people, like me, without clear direction to what they wanted to do with their life. I knew that I wasn't happy, and I knew Rae deserved better than I was providing even if she'd never say as much to me. I wanted her to be proud of me. I wanted to feel proud of me again. I was a washed-up failure. A didn't quite make it almost rock star. Worse, I still didn't know what I wanted to do with my life. All I knew was my current choices brought me to the end of the road. It couldn't go on like it was. Radical change was necessary. What could be more radical than a wanna be rock star joining the military with all of its structure and discipline? Maybe Uncle Sam could help me find what I was missing.

The Air Force recruiter told me the Air Force wanted cops and mechanics and I was too fat anyway, so I needed to get out of his office. And don't think I was going to go somewhere else because he was the only Air Force recruiter in Lane County. Fuck you very much.

I turned around and went back out the door, past Riley's questioning look, and into my final option. The Army. The recruiters were having a naughty discussion about some celebrity in heels and a push up bra when I walked through the door.

"And every time she opened her mouth, I'd stick my dick in it!" The recruiter was saying. He turned around and saw me watching them. His face flushed red, and he apologized. I told him I heard nothing. The recruiters burst into testosterone fueled laughter and they asked what they could do for me.

I told them I was an older guy who was out of shape, but I was willing to work. "Ohhhhhhhh really?" The recruiter said to me with a gleam in his eye.

"We'll just see about that."

I began working out with the Army recruiters in the morning for their morning PT sessions and again with the guys in the delayed entry program in the afternoons. I ate grilled chicken salad for dinner. I ran everywhere I went. Four months down the road the guys in the recruiters' office were telling me I was now the standard by which they were going to judge potential recruits.

"I don't want you to die!" Rae said to me over a dinner of frozen chicken pasta with veggies and garlic sauce.

"Baby, I'm not going to die." I said, setting my fork down. "Too ugly."

"Bullshit. I like the muscles, but I need you. Don't you know that?"

Rae was not happy. She didn't want me to go to war. She liked the physical changes I was going through, but she was afraid she was going to lose me when I went into the military. I loved her. I told her I was doing this for her. Yes, I was doing it for me too, but I wanted her to be proud of me. The soldier was in vogue across the country with the exception of Eugene. Eugene is still the place where hippies came to die. There were way too many hippies here for the military to get much support. The entire town existed under a perpetual fog of patchouli and marijuana. Lots of hemp sandals in Eugene.

The people weren't openly hostile, but they would rather look at anything other than a soldier in uniform. Rae and I went Christmas shopping at the mall and a guy threw himself into a display to get out of my way. I was wearing an Army T-shirt. The people t treated soldiers like barely domesticated animals which at any moment might spring into a killing frenzy. They acted like the military was to be tolerated but never trusted. I wasn't even in the Army yet and I experienced this covert anti-military attitude every time I left our apartment. Rae was scared this hippy dippy silliness was going to be our life. No amount of convincing would change her mind.

My weight dropped from two hundred and forty pounds to two hundred even. I could ship to Basic Training at one hundred and ninety two pounds or less. The recruiting staff no longer had any doubts I was going to lose the eight pounds. They scheduled an ASVAB test for me so I could start thinking about what I wanted to do in the Army.

They scheduled an ASVAB test to measure my ability and future occupational success.

We were scheduled to test once we arrived at the recruiting depot in Portland. I followed the group into the building and down a long industrial hallway. We were taken into a classroom at the far end of the hall. We were told to take a seat but maintain a computer between each person. There were few enough of us, it wasn't difficult to maintain the spacing.

After receiving our instructions SSG Walker left the room and we were allowed to log onto the computer and begin our testing. The recruiters made such a big deal over it. I thought there was going to be advanced calculus or particle physics at least. A sample question showed a picture of a wrench. Beneath the picture was the question, "This is a picture of a ?" There were four choices: A)1863 B)Purple C)Wrench D)Cow says "MOO!"

After forty-five minutes I raised my hand to let the monitor know I was done. He asked me several times if I was sure. He asked if I wanted to go back over any sections. I told him I was fine, and he shook his head and collected the scratch paper I used for some basic fractions, not calculus, and escorted me out. The other guys taking the test were watching me out of the corner of their eyes, some openly staring, all of them with the same kind of disappointment the monitor had on his face. So many sad faces, I tried not to laugh.

I was told to wait in the lobby for SSG Walker to come get me. I waited. He came. He looked concerned I was finished so quickly. I told him it wasn't exactly a hard test, but he shook his head and mumbled, "Alright." Then he drove me over to the hotel and said I could order dinner or lunch, but only one meal, and I could watch television until the group got back.

I decided to save my meal for dinnertime so I wouldn't go to bed hungry. Being no stranger to waiting in hotels I stretched out on the bed and fell asleep. A few hours later the phone in the room rang. SSG Walker wanted to talk to me about my ASVAB score. He asked if I had a hard time with the test and to be honest with him. I told him it was simple. He asked if I was sure, and I got the feeling I was being baited. He said he was going to smoke the shit out of me, and I should meet him outside.

I went outside to meet him, and he was holding a copy of my score. Nearly perfect. Only one question missed. He said he was going to smoke me for both missing one question and getting a higher score than he did. Up to that point SSG Walker had been the recruiting station's record for the highest ASVAB. I qualified to pick any job in the military I wanted. Things were finally falling into place. Fuck being a cop or a mechanic.

SSG Walker told me he was going to go visit the Air Force recruiter and thank him for running me off. Then he was going to show him my test score and let him know how motivated I was, and the weight was almost gone. That was a conversation I wish I could be there for. The first time I ran with SSG Walker we did a mile, and I threw up four times. I hadn't been able to run more than a couple hundred feet at a time. Now I could do two miles in less than fifteen minutes.

After taking the ASVAB I went with the recruiter to discuss what actual job I was to do in the Army. My score was high enough I could pick any path I wanted but I had no idea what I wanted to do. The guy at the Military Entrance Processing Station or MEPS saw me coming a mile away. He said with my scores I should consider something in Military Intelligence. That sounded good and the first thing that caught my eye was a codebreaker job. That came with an eighteen thousand dollar signing bonus and a year in Monterey California at the Defense Departments Language School. With visions of Rae in her bikini enjoying the California sun I told the guy to sign me up.

Just one catch, he said, I had to take a test called the DLAB, the Defense Language Aptitude Battery. He scheduled a test for me and, as luck would have it I was able to go that day. The DLAB is a test to help determine how successful a person will be at learning a new language. The tricky part about the DLAB is it's a test in a fictional language made up specifically for that test. I had to test, read, and write, in a language never before used by humankind. I had never taken a more difficult test. I probably couldn't have told you my name afterwards. I needed a 95 out of 100 for the codebreaker job. I got a 91.

It wasn't good enough. A ninety fucking one wasn't good enough. Those four points were too many for me to get the job I wanted. Like everything else I could get within eyesight of the goal but couldn't quite finish. Denied, always denied. The guy told me not to worry, because if I wanted to be in Military Intelligence then what I should go for is Counterintelligence Special Agent. The Army had a shortage of Counterintelligence Agents.

I could be like James Bond. Of course, there was a five year commitment and there wasn't a signing bonus. And I wouldn't be going to California, I'd be doing my Advanced Individual Training, Army speak for job training, in Arizona. There would be lots of sand, but I'd find the surf lacking. The guy had me with the James Bond line and we both knew it. I signed the contract.

The ride back from the recruiting depot was a straight shot south on a rainy, foggy Interstate 5. The guys in the DEP program were discussing their scores; several of them were happy they finally scored high enough to be admitted. I sat in the back watching the evergreens hiding in the mist and didn't talk much. The guys figured I hadn't done well on the test and were giving me space. One of the guys told me it was alright because he had to take it three times before he scored high enough to get in. Silence was preferable to making these guys, good guys really, feel stupid. I let them believe I had completely bombed the test. SSG Walker didn't say anything to the contrary but every so often would make eye contact with me in the rear-view mirror and shake his head slightly. Snarky fucker.

I was happy I'd scored well even if I wasn't going to be a codebreaker, but Rae still wasn't convinced this was a good thing. She didn't want me to leave her alone while I went to basic. She didn't want me to go to war either. I didn't blame her. I would have rather spent my time with her, but I had to have some direction in my life. The military was going to provide us with a living while I figured out the next step. What could possibly go wrong there?

The night before I shipped out the recruiters drove us to Portland and put us in a hotel. Rae and I got a room and we stayed there instead of with the roommate SSG Walker had arranged for me. I wasn't going to be with a woman for at least ten weeks so I wanted to spend as much time with her as I could. If the rumors were true, I wouldn't even be able to get a hard on for most of the time. I wanted to take advantage of her sweet skin while I could.

In the morning a small group of five of us boarded the bus to the airport. I had my ticket in hand, but I drug things out as long as possible so I could have a few more minutes with Rae. I was already missing her and even though she was trying not to, she couldn't quit crying. At the last minute I got on the bus. I ached missing her. All I wanted to do was get back off the bus. I had signed papers and raised my hand to defend the Constitution from all enemies, foreign and domestic. Hey, my first contract! I was contractually obligated. Rae stood in front of the hotel crying and waving until I could no longer see her.

People talk about a moment when you get to Basic Training where you immediately regret the decision to come. Everyone has it to a greater or lesser degree. Even people who were excited to get away from their hometowns, in trouble with the law, needing direction or just wanting something different all experience this *Oh Shit!* moment. For me it wasn't when the plane landed, and we were herded onto a bus bound for Fort Leonard

Wood Missouri. It wasn't even when the bus stopped, and we were herded into the 43d AG Reception Battalion.

We were given a sandwich after filling out some paperwork and calling home to let them know we had arrived safely. Since it was around two in the morning, we marched to a large open bay filled with bunk beds and wall lockers. I was given a top bunk and stored my things in the wall locker with the number that matched my bunk. I lay on the bunk staring at a ceiling made of wire mesh. The lights were on and the sound of shouting and slamming lockers and people moving echoed throughout the cavernous space. Staring at that ceiling, the wire was brown and smooth, giving the mesh a slick almost wet look, is when I had my moment. I'd trapped myself in a cage. I was listening to the chaos with the light in my face, missing Rae, and I couldn't stop thinking, "What have I done?"

The thought echoed over and over, bringing no sleep or comfort. Over and over the thought echoed until screaming in my skull. I was going to be a rock star. What the hell was I doing here? I should be into the Cycle by now. I was in the Army. I wasn't going to be leaving the Army for at least five more years. What had I done?

That was the last night of basic I had time to think of anything. I was too tired afterward to do anything

other than sleep. The first week was all in processing
at the reception battalion. Loads of paperwork needed
to be completed. Further medical screenings as well as
inoculations had to be done. They stood us in a line facing
a gauntlet of army medical personnel, all holding needles.
We would take a step, get stabbed, and take another step
for another pair of stabbings until we had cleared the
gauntlet. Most soldiers had blood running freely down
their arms by the time they got to the last shot.

The last shot was special, and we got that one in the
ass. My butt cheek was sore for a week afterward, not
fun when you run everywhere every day. It was also my
suspicion this is where the chub killer was introduced into
our systems. Some thought it came from the eggs, or some
nefarious chemical in the drinks. I don't believe so. I think
one of those smiling medical personnel administered a
shot which killed any attempt of a hard on for the next six
weeks.

The chub had always been up before me. We were old
friends, lifelong companions, and had seen and done a lot
together. For most of my time in Missouri he wouldn't
look at me, only stared sadly at the floor, and occasionally
ran some water. It was terrifying. My first phone call to
Rae, I told her the army had broken my dick. She said
she hoped that wasn't true because my dick was the only

thing she liked about me. I missed her so much it became a physical ache in my chest. I imagined her scent, lilac and feminine. I missed the soft silk of her red hair and the flash of amusement in her green eyes like electric jade as we joked across a table. We had several conversations throughout my time at basic and she started every one with, "How's the chub?"

I was the first guy in my company to have the effects of the drug wear off. Standing in line for breakfast when he finally broke free from his chemical constraints. Everything in training is controlled. You don't do anything without someone telling you the way it was to be done. You're told how to move, how to speak, when to do anything, how to walk, how to run, you know nothing unless the Drill Sergeant teaches it to you. This includes standing in line. I didn't know how to stand in line until I was taught.

Nothing sexy about breakfast but we had to stand in line as close to the soldier in front of us as we could in a staggered formation. Meaning one soldier stood to the left and the soldier behind him stood to the right, packed in tight as we could get it. Nuts to butts.

There was a female soldier behind me who was subtly twisting back and forth at the waist. Subtle movements were necessary so as to not draw the ire of the ever watchful

Drill Sergeants. She was bored and was probably still trying to loosen up from the morning's PT session. But what I felt was her breasts dragging back and forth across my back. I've always been a chestnut and that's all it took. I had my first raging hard on. It had been seven weeks. I was so excited I wanted to run around the cafeteria and show people.

I wanted to scream at the top of my lungs, "*My dick works again!! Wooooo!!! Take cover Missouri!!*"

Back at the bay and first thing I told my bay mates was I'd gotten a hard on in the breakfast line. All the guys were cheering and slapping me on the back. Some of my bay mates ran up and down the hall spreading the good word. Hopefully that meant the chemical tyranny was coming to an end. For a solid week I had guys with hope shining in their eyes coming up to me every day asking if I had woken up with wood. It was a weird kind of celebrity.

"Yes, yes, my dick was in fact hard this morning. Yes, I can get hard. Thank you. Thank you very much. Tell your sister, I'll show her."

Then a guy in the next bay broke through and after that it happened with greater and greater frequency. When I was able to tell Rae that things were working again, I heard her whisper, "Oh thank God," but I don't think she meant for me to hear it. I laughed. She cried.

We took a basic PT test while in reception to prove we could handle basic. That test consisted of a timed two-mile run, at least ten push-ups and thirty sit ups. I had been working out with the recruiters for months while I dropped weight, so the initial PT test wasn't a problem.

I did my run in time to qualify for the first tier group. The names of the soldiers in this group were sent to the drill sergeants as the top athletic performers. These were the guys that the drill sergeants would look at most critically to begin with before backing off and concentrating on those soldiers who needed the most help. I was kind of relieved the scrutiny would be over quickly. I didn't want to stand out, but I didn't want to be at the back of the pack either. Comfortably anonymous in the middle was my goal.

At the end of the five-day work period Reception was over, I got my orders to transfer to my basic training battalion. My journey to become an adaptable physically capable soldier was set to begin. I had my paperwork done and I'd received my gear. I completed the medical screenings and passed the initial PT test. I had my smart book that I read while waiting to go. It was full of things

I would need to know to become a soldier. A surprising number of things are necessary to know in order to become a soldier. It's not all push-ups and shoot bad guys.

While I waited for my bus ride, they let us get comfortable. We watched military themed movies, like Black Hawk Down and Enemy at the Gates. We could work out in a gym if we had permission and an escort. Otherwise, there were always push-ups and sit ups which could be done by the bunk.

I made a couple of friends in reception only to find out they failed the push-ups portion of the initial PT test and were going to another battalion to strengthen them before basic. Or failing that, send them home. There was an entire battalion's worth of future soldiers headed where I was headed, and I didn't know any of them. Awesome.

We were all in uniform from our clothing and bags and boots to our bald heads, to the matching fear on our faces. Everyone looked the same. These guys were all younger than me, with different life experiences. The only thing we had in common, other than the army, was most of us came from poor families.

Maybe they were lost and looking for something like I was. Maybe they had families to support, and this was the only option. The factories all shut down and moved to other countries where the company could pay someone a fraction of what these American boys demanded. It could be some of them were in trouble with the law and their options were jail or military.

The doors of the bus shut, and the bus had just begun to move when two guys stood up. I heard the first of what would be many blasts of the Drill Sergeants. *"Get your face in those fucking bags! I don't want to see a single face looking at me! Get your face in the fucking bag now*!!"

I put my face in the bag I was holding on my lap because there wasn't room for it to fit by my feet. All of us had bags on our laps. All of us immediately buried our faces. This was the real deal. Nothing we'd heard prepared us for the ferocity these men and women were capable of. Two guys instantly cowed an entire bus load of recruits. And they'd done it in a matter of seconds.

When the bus got wherever it was, we were thrown unceremoniously off. *"Get the fuck off my bus! Run damn it! Don't be the last guy!"* No chance of that as I was seated near the front of the bus. I grabbed my gear and bolted. Outside there were more brown rounds directing traffic, screaming to get ourselves into a large warehouse. There were continued threats of don't be the last one, move it, sorry looking bunch of recruits, and other nastier obscenities. If you'd like to know what is really said and done, then please feel free to go talk with your local army recruiter and arrange a personal visit. All expenses paid, free meals, and plenty of exercise.

Once inside we lined up in formation and tasked with getting our bags in a perfectly straight line at our feet. We failed repeatedly. To correct our deficiency, we did a number of exercises to help increase our motivation. Push-ups and sit ups, flutter kicks, leg spreaders, more push-ups, and the military version of the jumping jack: the side straddle hop. I always called it a jumping jack, but the United States Army does not do jumping jacks. They do side straddle hops. Because fuck you.

Between each iteration of exercises, we got another opportunity to fix our bags. Our consistent failure to make a straight line required further rounds of exercises. This went on all afternoon. The Drill Sergeants cruised up and down the aisles, their brown round hats like the dorsal fins of colossal sharks waiting for some recruit to fuck up. When the recruit fucked up it was blood in the water. The Drill Sergeants would swarm the recruit screaming conflicting orders at him or her from all sides.

"Get down!"

"Stand up!"

"What the fuck are you waiting for? Get down!!"

"What the fuck are you doing?? Stand up!"

"Get down pri!"

"Stand the fuck up private!"

"What in the fuck are you waiting for? Move!"

I found a spot on the wall and stared at it and only it. I could still see those brown rounds cruising between the recruits, but I made no eye contact with anyone. I managed to avoid putting myself in the center of a swarm.

We were required to empty our canteens and hold the empty canteen over our heads. We held them up until everyone held them up. I held my canteen over my head for fifteen minutes until the last recruit had his in the air. My arm was shaking, and I was beginning to question my decision to drink as quickly as possible. A couple of brown rounds saw my shaking arm and began screaming, *"You gonna shake when an Iraqi sticks a rifle in your face?"*

There was no right answer, I kept my mouth shut and let the insult sting. Still there are nights when I wish I could see that Sergeant again and let him know I did not in fact shake. As the afternoon faded into evening we marched over to our respective companies. Our gear was checked, and our bunks and wall lockers were assigned. I was assigned to an eight-man bay that always seemed to smell like feet and ass no matter how much we bleached. When we were dismissed, I collapsed into bed too tired to think of anything, except Rae. I thought about Rae. Thus ended Day Zero, the real training began in the morning.

The days quickly fell into routine. We would get up in the morning earlier than I ever had in my life, dress and form up outside. We did morning PT be it calisthenics (side straddle hops) or a run and then march over to the dining facility for breakfast. That was my favorite meal of the day. Before every meal we stood outside the door, I'm still not sure why, until we got the go ahead to come in. Then we ran down the length of the building, turned around, ran back, and went inside. Stack up in line, nuts to butts, and wait to be served. We could get as much as we wanted but we had to eat everything we took. And there was a short time limit to eat.

I learned quickly to get a blueberry waffle or a box of cereal. I mixed blue and green Powerade and shoved it in my face as fast as humanly possible. Sometimes the Drill Sergeants cut our already short mealtime and if there was anything on the tray to throw away, woe to that Private. They were going to be smoked into oblivion.

I did my best to remain under the radar. I ate enough to keep body and soul together but little else. By the time I graduated from basic I had lost another thirty pounds. I was as fit as I'd ever been in my adult life. I could run all day long while carrying a hundred pounds on my back. I could throw a hundred- and eighty-pound man into the dirt hard enough to knock him unconscious. I was lean and mean.

Rae came to my graduation. When we were finally back at the hotel, she couldn't get over how skinny I was. She liked the muscle definition, but she wasn't used to me being so thin. OR so bald. We had to get haircuts the day before our families arrived and in basic there is only one type of haircut. Bald. There are men in the world that look good with a bald head. I am not one of them. I have a big head and combined with the horrible glasses I had to wear I looked like a child molester. Or a serial killer. Rae had taken my prescription and mailed me a decent set of glasses but for basic I had to wear the BCG's.

BCG stood for birth control glasses. Glasses so ugly they were guaranteed to keep you from getting laid. They didn't work on me, but Rae loved me, and we pretended the glasses didn't exist after she got a good laugh.

After breakfast we marched back to the barracks for a quick change of clothes and a shower if you could get one in time. Few could. I didn't even try. Form back up and march off to whatever the day's training was. Sometimes it was outside, sometimes it was the classroom. Classroom training was the worst because it was so easy to fall asleep.

Fall asleep and you and the guys next to you will spend the remaining training time holding a folding metal chair over your head.

Lunch might be an MRE in the field or if you were close to the dining facility you might get a hot meal. People have said that the Meals Ready to Eat are tasty and they enjoyed them. Those people are liars. There is nothing good about an MRE. Like most things in the military, it's best to suffer through as quickly as you can and pretend it wasn't as bad as it probably was. I also learned any meal, any hot meal, served in the Army can be eaten as a sandwich thus expediting the time it takes to eat.

Fried chicken? Fried chicken sandwich. Spaghetti and salad? Spaghetti and salad sandwich. You'd be pressed to name a food that a soldier hasn't eaten as a sandwich. It was fast and convenient and the sooner you were done eating the less likely you were to draw the ire of the NCO.

After lunch training resumed and there was usually more PT. Dinner might be another MRE, or the rest of the MRE you had from lunch, or you might be lucky enough to eat a hot meal. We didn't get many hot meals but the ones I got I was grateful for and I snarked them down like I was trying to set a speed eating record. Eat it now, taste it later.

There might be training at night, or you might get to go to bed. The Drill Sergeants told us we'd be thinking we'd never get to sleep with the sound of the floor buffer going but when we graduated, we'd think we'd never get to sleep without the whine of the buffer's motor.

This was completely true. The sound of a floor buffer still makes me sleepy. If you were a fireguard, part of the overnight detail was to buff the floors and clean the bathrooms. Each shift was an hour long, so you had to move fast. We kept the bathrooms always sparkling and the floors maintained a high gloss shine. The Drill Sergeants even remarked on how well we kept up the bathrooms and the floors and they almost never gave out a compliment. Usually, the best you could hope for was, "You didn't fuck up too bad Pri."

And then we'd do some push-ups.

The weeks worked themselves by. Routine set in like it tends to do. Monday through Saturday meant training and cleaning. Sunday meant whatever church you went to you could attend and then clean upon returning. My weekly entertainment was picking a different church service to go to. My favorite had to be the Wiccan service.

I signed up for several Wiccan services because I would go with a group into a park and nap under a tree. It was fantastic, God bless Wiccans.

Weeks eight through ten we got occasional phone privileges and I always called Rae. The first time I spoke to her after letting her know I'd arrived safely, she cried. She tried not to. She told me she missed me. She said she hated me. She called me a fucker for pranking her where she couldn't prank me back.

As we were packing to go to the hotel the night before I shipped out, Rae was in the bathroom crying. She didn't want me to know. I snuck into our bedroom and got all of her underwear except what she'd packed in the overnight bag and took them to the kitchen. I wet them down in the sink and stuck the wet ball into the freezer. She spent most of the day looking for her underwear. Rae told me she was going to the freezer to get some ice cream and meditate on what I might have done with her panties. She said she opened the freezer and there was a giant frozen ball of her underwear. She laughed and cried and laughed some more. Then she cried, watched Willow on DVD, and put the ice cream back beside the silken lacy ball.

I missed her badly. Knowing the time was close when I could hold her again made the still moments away from her that much worse. The Army did a good job working us until we were exhausted and couldn't do much more than drop into bed in the evening. Most guys I knew didn't even write letters home; they were just too tired. I identified.

I couldn't stay the night with her after graduation, but I was allowed to be with her until ten o clock in the evening. We made an immediate break for the car and headed to the hotel. She ordered pizza to have something to eat later. Lying in bed, smelling the wonderful scent of her hair, she told me she was pregnant. I was going to be a father. We lay in bed, and I laughed and she cried. We held each other. Then we ate cold pizza. She told me she hated me. I told her I loved her enough for both of us. Everything I did now was for her. To care for her. I wanted to provide and protect her. All I wanted was to be worthy of her love. I wasn't.

I wouldn't be able to marry her until I had progressed in my training. After leaving Missouri, I headed to Arizona where I would spend at least six months learning how to be a spy.

Seeing Rae was like coming back to life. Everything came back into focus, and I remembered what I was doing and why. Walking into the hotel with her was also nice because the room had taken on a slight combination of hotel cleanliness and her perfume. Being somewhere that didn't smell like feet and ass was heavenly. I knew I had made the right decision for us even if we both hated the time apart.

Now I was going to have a child and because of the military that child would have health care and dental care. Doctors' visits, glasses, colds, shots, broken bones, bug bites, and prescription medication would be covered for the baby. I had to marry Rae, but I planned to anyway, so she would be covered. I wasn't going to be a rich rock star, so I had to start thinking about how I was going to take care of my budding family.

Rae dropped me off at the barracks fifteen minutes early. In the Army, if you're early you're on time and if you're on time you're late. You better not be late. I regretfully parted from her but told her I'd see her in Arizona. I had my pay going into her bank account so she had access to my money. I had no expenses, and my military pay was more than sufficient to handle whatever bills she had.

The Army paid a basic allowance for housing based on the area I had enlisted from. For me that area was one of the most expensive in the country so the BAH was high.

I went upstairs where several of my new comrades had come back from their day of leave. Most of them were staying in Missouri but there were a few of us scheduled to go other places. The Drill Sergeants had given me my orders which included a plane ticket to Arizona. I packed all my things and in the morning all I needed to do was get dressed and get on the bus to the airport. Basic Training was over, but it still had one more gift to give.

Halfway through training the first case of conjunctivitis had broken loose. Pink eye. It happened every cycle. There were too many dirty bodies doing not enough cleaning. A breakout happened every time. I spent most of whatever free time I had bleaching down walls, door knobs, and any other surfaces I thought might carry pink eye. I didn't want it and I managed to avoid it the entire time I was at Basic. Until the morning I was scheduled to leave, I woke up with one eye gummed completely shut. Fuck.

In this age of terrorism there are few things that can move you quickly through airport security. One thing is to be traveling in your freshly pressed Army Class A uniform. Another thing is a nasty blatant case of highly contagious pink eye. If you're fortunate enough to have both get ready to rocket through security. Nobody will touch you, your luggage, or your plane ticket.

A TSA agent pulled the group of us out of the line to get us on to our various connections. He was going to inspect our duffel bags. He came to mine first and I told him after he finished touching my things he should go and directly wash his hands. I pointed to my eye and told him that it was highly contagious, and it itched like all hell. He snatched his hands away from my bag like he'd touched something hot. He told me to go ahead and close it up and have a nice flight. It would have been funny if it weren't for the thick goopy boogers that kept sliding over my left eye. Rae never got it so I can't help but think it was a parting gift from Basic Training.

The lady taking the tickets received the same speech from me and refused to touch my ticket. She told me what to tear off and drop in the slot and what to keep. I couldn't blame the lady for wanting to move me through fast as possible. This shit was nasty. I couldn't wait to get rid of it.

Traditionally new arrivals at AIT got smoked by whatever Drill Sergeant happened to be on duty. The Drill Sergeant, a surprisingly cute blonde, stopped me before inspecting my duffel and asked if I had pink eye. I told her I woke up with it that morning in Missouri. She demanded I go to sick call in the morning, gave me a slip and told me the procedure, and tasked me with getting rid of it. She said she would not have disease in her barracks.

When I got back from the doctor that morning I had my room assignment. I took my stuff to my new room and met my roommate. He looked at me and asked if I had pink eye. It's awful and having dealt with it for a solid twenty-four hours I understood his fear. The doctor had given me drops to clear the infection and I was to report back when I'd taken them all so he could give me a clean bill of health. Two days into the medication I was better. My roommate became convinced he was getting it. I was past the contagious part, so I told him he was probably fine. He wasn't convinced. He walked to the mirror over our little sink and began to soap up his hands with Dial anti-bacterial soap. He then proceeded to scrub what he thought was the infected eyeball with his soapy hand.

His eye jiggled as he scrubbed. He rinsed, got fresh soap on his hands and scrubbed the other one. My butt squinched up. I couldn't stand looking but couldn't look away. The guy was hardcore. It was amazing and horrifying at the same time. We became instant friends. Ryan was his name, and he was a tall blue eyed blonde from Georgia. Those eyes were currently blood shot, red, and swollen from the Dial treatment but his smile was open and full of Southern boy charm. I never met anyone else who scrubbed their eyeballs on the suspicion they might have an infection.

He never got pink eye.

Training in Arizona was conducted at a much slower pace than training at Basic. I wasn't allowed to do PT for the first three weeks after arrival because I needed to acclimate to the higher elevation. Mornings were beautiful and I fell in love with the desert all over again. I loved morning PT even if I didn't like to exercise. Watching the sun rise was a treat. It would light up the pinks and reds in the stone of distant buttes making them appear to be on fire. The sweet smell of the desert's night blooming flowers is still with me. Even with the heat I completely understood how people could come to love a place so deceptively barren. Being under the thumb of the Army wasn't enough to dampen my growing affection for the Arizona desert.

A month after arrival the Drill Sergeants didn't require us to be counted outside our rooms at night. They let us sign out of the barracks for the weekend. They didn't care what we did after five pm. I was unused to freedom. It felt strange, like a trap, I always waited for an NCO to pop out of nowhere and scream at me. Still, it was nice being treated like an adult again. There were places we weren't allowed to go as military personnel and there were things we weren't allowed to have on base, like a car, but other than a few tolerable restrictions we were allowed to do whatever we wished.

Rae came down from Eugene for more weekends than she didn't. I guess she liked having at least limited access to me. I know I liked having more access to her. I got permission and we got married. Nothing fancy, that wasn't us. We went to the Justice of the Peace and got it taken care of. We bought two rings from a pawn shop in Sierra Vista. Hers had a small diamond, mine was a plain white gold.

When I graduated spy school she was showing. She told me the dogs were missing me, Boston condescended to share the bed with her, but she thought my German Shepard liked her better. They shared countless quarts of vanilla ice cream. IF that dog was going to sell me out for anything, it would be for vanilla ice cream. He had a problem.

After graduating from the Army's spy school, we received orders to our new duty stations. We were given our orders while in formation and then dismissed so we could trade if we so chose. Some people were going to Germany, or New York state, or staying there in Arizona. I was headed back to the Pacific Northwest. My duty station was Fort Lewis, Washington, just outside of Seattle.

Rae was thrilled because she had wanted to stay on the west coast. I did too but I had been hoping for Hawaii. That still counts as west coast, right? My roommate was going to Georgia which probably meant he was getting fast tracked to the desert. We were given two weeks of leave after training to rest, relax, and move to our new duty stations.

Breaking the lease at our old apartment was not a big deal with orders from the military. I had other places to be. The military sent a truck and packed up our stuff for the short trip north on Interstate 5 to Seattle. Getting the two of us and the dogs into base housing was much easier than I thought it was going to be. During my welcome to Fort Lewis briefing, I was told that married couples might wait upwards of six months to a year in order to get into base housing. I told Housing I was in a hotel off base and we were running out of money. If we didn't get some help, we were going to be homeless. We were moved into base housing within a week on the condition that we be willing to relocate.

No problem. We moved into a section of older housing scheduled to be demolished within a two-year time period. They actually got to us less than a week later and we were moved, again, to a house in North Fort Lewis normally reserved for senior enlisted and officers. American Lake was directly across the street. My neighbors were both senior NCO's that liked me probably because I had such a good-looking wife who liked to lie out in her bikini. Bikini's make a lot of friends. Her pregnant belly made her even more beautiful.

My unit was deployed when I arrived. I was part of the rear detachment. The acting first sergeant signed me up for the dodgeball team before he met me. The first game was my first night at the unit. I reported for dodgeball duty and Rae got a good laugh at how serious the Army took its gaming. Everything was hyper competitive and always taken to the next level. When we walked into the gym, we saw teams running basketball style pass drills. Passing drills. For dodgeball. We got blown out in the third round by one of those drill running teams. Maybe we should have run some as well.

I found out there was a Counterintelligence Agent of at least Specialist rank needed for immediate deployment to Iraq the next day. I wasn't of high enough rank, nor were any of the CI people that were in the rear detachment. At the end of the week, I was promoted to Specialist along with four other CI people newly arrived at the unit.

The following week was a bad one for the Counterintelligence Agents as they were struck down with a rash of injuries and ailments. There were back problems and knee issues. One guy had problems deploying because he was on blood thinners. Another had dental issues which made him unsuitable for deployment. Out of all the newly arrived personnel there was only one Counterintelligence Agent of sufficient rank who managed to survive the plague of injuries. I'd never use the word malingering. Only one soldier emerged unscathed from under the black cloud of bad teeth, bad backs and bursitis filled knees. Me.

Monday, two weeks after my epic dodgeball adventure, I began the process of preparing for deployment. Mostly what this meant was tons of paperwork following another delightful gauntlet of shots reminiscent of Basic Training. Except this time the medical personnel were much more personable and were willing to tell me exactly what it was I was being shot full of. From Anthrax to tetanus, I was fully immunized and ready for my third world adventure. My paperwork was in order. Rae had settled into our new lakeside house.

She and I both knew with me joining an Army at war there was a better than average chance I would someday go to a war zone. But like with Queen Hill Penitentiary there is a difference between knowing something on an intellectual level and staring down the slobbering maw. Most nights we made love and tried not to talk about it or if we did, we tried to make light of it. I told her how she wouldn't even want me back because I was going to fuck up the routine vibe she would set up. We took long walks around American Lake holding hands and dog leashes. We loved hard.

I also knew I wasn't going to be there for the birth of my first child. That one hurt. That one hurt a lot. She knew it too and knowing her family wasn't going to come to the birth or support her in any way made things much more difficult for her. My family thought of love as cool indifference with the occasional guilt trip thrown in for flavor. Her family was mean. Like alcohol-abusive-afterschool-special-flowers-in-the–attic-kind of mean. If she trusted you enough to tell you about her family, you wouldn't believe it. Her family locked her out of the house barefoot for hours in the winter for putting her feet on the couch. She had scars where she had been chased and burned with a cigarette lighter. That scar was a perfect circle inside a perfect oval. You could even see the tiny inner circle the gas came out of. Someone, she never told me who, held a lighter alight for a good long time before jamming it into the flesh on the back of her neck.

I wouldn't want any of those bastards around my kid anyway.

The unit was supposedly going to help her. The only problem was being new to the unit, no one in command knew us. How were they going to take care of someone who only existed on paper? We hadn't been there long enough to make any friends. I knew my neighbors liked her in the way older men like all sexy younger women but that didn't exactly leave me with warm fuzzies.

Bottom line there really wasn't anything I could do except leave her. I was contractually obligated to obey. Go where the Army told me to go. I wasn't the only soldier in history to leave a pregnant young wife behind. The guys in the rear detachment who met Rae liked to make jokes about how they were going to take good care of her. Maybe they were trying to be funny and set my mind at ease, but it didn't help. What I wanted to do was go AWOL until my baby was born. But going to military prison wasn't going to help her keep a roof over her head and losing all the medical benefits was something I wasn't willing to do. I did what I was told to do.

What the fuck, run amok, the only option was to get on the fucking plane.

Our last night together before deployment, we didn't sleep at all. I made love to my wife and then I held her close until the sun came up. We didn't talk. I could sleep on the plane. I had my bags packed by the door waiting for me to pick them up on the way out. Rae would drive me to the unit, the unit would drive me to the airfield, once at the airfield I would be flown to Hawaii, then to Kuwait City. From Kuwait City I'd catch a ride to Baghdad.

I was wrong about sleeping on the plane. Even though I wanted to, the altitude made my ears ache and no matter how fiercely I chewed my Cinnaburst gum I couldn't find any relief for it. The flight took longer than any human being should reasonably expect to spend in a pressurized aluminum tube. The seats were made of rough red cargo net. It was cold the entire time. I should have enjoyed the cold because the Middle East is a couple of blocks down the street from hell. Stepping off the plane in Kuwait City was an experience unlike anything I'd ever known. The heat was so intense I wondered if the plane caught fire. Then there was the smell. Nothing in the world can compare to the smell of a third world country. Interwoven with the stench of unwashed humanity was the subtle bouquet of rotting sun blasted garbage mixed with open sewer.

My sense of smell died right there on the sunbaked tarmac.

Even before I hit the hanger sweat popped out on my back and ran down the crack of my ass. I was herded toward a large hangar with the group of soldiers I'd arrived with. Once there we were given bottles of water and told to hydrate. When the bottles were all empty, we were given another bottle and told to hydrate more. Mine must not have been the only sweaty butt crack. The hangar was a kind of permanent/impermanent in processing station.

There was activity everywhere. Soldiers were directed in every direction. Trucks of all sizes moved in all directions on the tarmac. Helicopters were landing or taking off, throwing dust everywhere. It was the organized chaos of the military.

I waited in line, because the Army taught me to hurry up and wait, after hydrating some more with a group of soldiers who were all as bored and tired as I was. While we waited for our individual orders to be inspected and sent on our individual ways, I noticed a private playing with a M203 grenade launcher. He was showing another soldier how to load and unload the weapon. There wasn't much to it, open the tube, load the tube, close the tube, and pull the trigger.

Not exactly open-heart surgery.

I wondered how many times he'd taken the ASVAB. I had hitched a ride with a Striker brigade because my unit was already here. Now the issue for me was how to get where they were. Hopefully the guy looking at orders would be able to direct me to where I was supposed to be. The line was moving in the syrupy slow way only government lines can. I kept watching the private with the grenade launcher because he kept loading live grenades into the weapon. It was making me a little nervous and as I looked around, I noticed there were several other soldiers within the hangar watching him as well. They weren't even pretending to be doing something else. The private was so engrossed in his weapon he hadn't noticed the crowd staring at him.

Then it happened. I knew it was going to happen. Everyone knew it was going to happen. It was like a signal went out to every soldier in the area there was a nearby idiot that was about to engage in close quarters idiocy. The private was slamming the tube closed with a round chambered and he pulled the trigger.

There was a hollow POONK as the round fired off. The grenade bounced off an iron ceiling support and then ricocheted off the concrete floor. As it pinged off the walls, the soldiers ducked and ran. Soldiers by the doors cut out to put distance between them and the inevitable boom. Soldiers packed in too close yelled warnings if the grenade bounced their way. The round ended up hitting the floor and spinning out the rest of its momentum like a top without detonating.

I was with a group who weren't close to one of the large open hangar doors. We found ourselves beside a smaller entrance for personnel which became immediately impassable with a crush of panicked bodies. There were two windows on either side of the door. A soldier threw his duffel bag through and then followed it. I followed his example and bailed out the other window as the grenade spun on the concrete. Any second I knew it'd explode. I had time to wonder if there'd be enough of me to ship home.

The UXO, unexploded ordinance, guys needed to be called to deal with the grenade. They took about four hours to show and scoop the grenade into what looked like a metal trash can via a small remote-controlled vehicle. The grenade didn't have time to arm before losing momentum. We were lucky. Had the round detonated it would have killed everyone within five meters and everyone up to one hundred and thirty meters would have had an extremely sucky day. It was a miracle nobody got hurt either by explosion or by a high explosive round traveling at two hundred and sixty-nine meters per second.

This little escapade also caused the complete stoppage of in processing. We had to wait for UXO and then we had to wait for the lines to reform and for everyone to generally get their shit together. What should have been a two-hour exercise in boredom turned into an eight hour exercise in boredom with fifteen seconds of abject terror thrown in for spice. Most of my time in the war was not unlike the first time taking the stage at a biker bar.

A senior NCO wanted to know who broke the windows. Having learned my lesson about the dangers of volunteering I kept my mouth shut and shuffled on by. The private who caused the whole ordeal was still doing pushups when I left. He's probably still there, pushing. Another soldier took his weapon.

There was little else of note after getting myself checked in. Word had been sent forward Military Intelligence personnel would be passing through. Being MI offered a certain mystique we often took advantage of. No one but us really understood what exactly it was we did. I didn't quite understand having just landed but it was something I was quick to pick up on.

After getting settled in I discovered another perk of being MI. We had the greatest collection of tech nerds. That meant we had access to phones and computers which could be used to communicate back home. Most soldiers had long queues they waited in to call home. Phone cards were required and there were never enough to go around. Plus, those phones were notorious for shitty connections. Calls frequently disconnected and soldiers had a hard time hearing their loved ones.

I talked to Rae in one form or another almost every day.

Time passed like it does, slowly. I was having an uncanny amount of success as a Counterintelligence Agent. My sources were consistently accurate, and I was catching bomb makers at the rate of nearly one a week. Nobody else could boast about such numbers. The unit hadn't been anywhere near as productive before my arrival. I was good at catching bad guys. Who knew?

I found out I was going to leave my comfy little network of golden sources, most of which I recruited, to a new batch of CI. I was attached to a Special Forces unit that had need of MI personnel, specifically Counterintelligence. I took pride in my body, and in my job, and in myself. I felt like what I did mattered.

Once again, I was shuffled off to another unit, this one in country. I was still technically part of the 201st MI Brigade but was on loan to SF. Don't get confused here, I'm not Special Forces and make no claims to be so. Those guys are cut from a completely different cloth entirely. I have way too much fuck it in my veins for SF. Those guys don't know how to quit.

Whenever they weren't on an actual mission they were training for a mission. When they weren't training for a mission they were thinking about missions. When I wasn't on mission I thought about Rae, food, video games, my dogs, Rae, more food, and then probably Rae. The Army handed a dilatant to people that were all business all the time. I was good at my job, but I was also good at fucking off. A successful Agent should be fun.

I went with the door kickers to interrogate the people they cuffed up and dumped on the street. They could kick doors, cuff people, and dump them on the street much faster than I could figure out who was an actual bad guy, who had intel, who liked to waste time, and who had nothing to do with anything. There was no possible way I could sift through all the folks as fast as they sat them down.

When the word came down that we were to go door kicking I would groan. When SF were close by, I had no worries. Being surrounded by the toughest men on the planet tends to lend a certain sense of security. If anything went wrong, I had no doubt they would handle it in a swift proficient military fashion. The trouble came when they pulled away and started down the street, around the corner kicking doors leaving me alone with other CI weenees armed only with clip boards. In a hostile country in hostile neighborhoods where people hated the American invaders we were alone with pissed off people in cuffs. More pissed off people were spectating and the guys that were pissing people off were a block and a half away. None of the MI personnel were as fast, as strong, or as fearless as the elite soldiers we were attached to.

On rare occasions SF didn't get the cuffs on quite as tight as they should have. I'm not going to say one of those guys might have been a little sloppy in his duties, maybe moving a bit too fast, but maybe, just maybe, someone was moving a bit too fast. The guy waited until I was right in front of him to spring up, free of the plastic cuffs, pull a knife from his boot and scream something about a salad bar.

One CI agent grabbed the arm with the knife, and I tackled Salad Bar in the knees. The three of us fell to the ground. I held onto the guy's legs and prayed the other Agent could keep control of the knife. The third CI Agent stood by watching the melee like it was a scheduled brawl on World Wrestling Entertainment. He was also the only one armed out of our little trio and he seemed to have completely forgotten he was wearing a sidearm.

"*Shoot him!*" Knife Arm screamed.

"*For fucks sake shoot this motherfucker!*" I still had his legs wrapped up spreading my own to keep him from rolling over. He was bucking and wriggling like electricity coursed through him. I gripped onto his legs like my life depended on it all the time thinking any minute the knife was going to get free and I'd feel eight inches of cold blade sinking into my back.

"*Shoot!*" I screamed.

"*Fucking shoot!*"

CI number three kept staring vacantly. His mouth was slightly open, and his breathing quickened. Is he getting some kind of sexual thrill, a good bone on, I wondered while being thrashed on the concrete. Knife Arm was holding his own. I hadn't felt the bite of the blade yet. I couldn't look up and see what was happening because I was struggling to keep the guy immobile. Salad Bar was thin, but he was strong, legs like banded steel, and he was panicked. The seconds were crawling by. Finally number three snapped out of whatever fog he'd been in.

He unsnapped the safety strap and pulled the weapon. He pressed it into Salad Bars temple. Salad Bar stopped struggling immediately. He let go of the knife and lay there calmly like he hadn't just been trying to kill us. He completely relaxed and I rolled him over and put the cuffs back on him. Tight.

Back at the camp I screamed at the SF commander his men almost got us killed. We were left alone without support in a hostile zone, and someone got sloppy. They weren't supposed to be able to get out of the cuffs but *surprise!* Not only had he got out, but he was armed, and it had taken all three of us to subdue him. The commander wasn't impressed. I told him we weren't all Special Forces trained.

He agreed.

It was like arguing with a wall. Outside the commander's tent were three of the door kickers who had been on our door kicking safari. They were laughing and joking about how the MI weenees had finally seen some action. All three were excellent soldiers but they were completely useless human beings. Most of the time I avoided them preferring the company of other MI personnel or I would mind my own business and think about Rae.

They continued harassing the three of us over the next few weeks. One went so far as to shoot me in the back with a Taser while I was leaving my tent. If you've never been hit with a Taser allow me to describe the process. Two metal needles with fishhook like barbs are fired at a high rate of speed into the target's flesh. The needles are connected to wires that conduct electricity at extremely high voltage, although low wattage, throughout a target's body interrupting the nervous systems normal electrical activity. Muscle control is all but impossible to maintain. It burns. It hurts. And it still feels like you're being shocked even after the current ceases.

I began to think of them as Larry, Moron, and Curly. The Three Special Forces Stooges. They brayed like donkeys when I hit the sand. I couldn't even put my hands down to catch myself. I flopped like a fish. A rock opened a gash by my eye that would later scar. I was completely unaware of what happened until they pulled the barbs and yanked me back to my feet. Totally blindsided. This shit had to stop.

Being CI I was taught the value of rapport; I'd been sizing up and ducking trouble for years. I knew within the dynamic of the Stooges; Moron was the boss. If I took him down the others would be reluctant to mess with us in the future. Plus, after the Taser, I had to get him. Some things you can't let slide.

Iraq is full of spiders, rodents, snakes, scorpions, and all manner of creepy crawlers. There is the Camel Spider, the granddaddy of military myth, which always reminded me of the face huggers from Alien. The Sand Mantis, predator of the dunes, shared its domain with Oriental Hornets and Black Desert Ants that came in all kinds of colors besides black. Those ants also carried a painful bite. The sands hid Desert Hairy Scorpions, the much feared but rarely seen Death Stalker scorpion, and the more common Fat Tail. There were Sand Spiders in abundance along with bottom feeding Mole Crickets. Fog Drinking Beetles and Jewel Beetles could be seen skittering around at night.

I would, however, need the aid of my creepy crawly friends to set the stooges straight.

Counterintelligence work gave me the opportunity to meet all kinds of people. The children of Iraq were a particular kind of amazing because if you managed to befriend one then you could count on their ability to find things a foreigner couldn't. I paid an eight-year-old friend two dollars to find me some jelly and a bottle of alcohol. I thought he might have trouble with the booze because Iraq is a dry country. He came back in twenty minutes with a case of Smuckers Strawberry and a bottle of Captain Morgan Spiced Rum. I couldn't even get Smuckers at what passed for the PX, never mind the rum. Who knew where he got it? It was best not to ask.

I paid him three more American dollars. He was thrilled. He wanted to know if I wanted sexy woman pictures. I thanked him and told him no; the jelly would be enough but if I needed anything else I'd look for him first. He ran off smiling and waving his five dollars. Cute kid, I thought, I hope he bought something fun with his five dollars. More likely, he probably gave the money to his father for food or some other necessity. A little bit of American money could go a long way. Hopefully that five dollars helped things be a little less hard for him.

I made a show around Moron of finding and "confiscating" the rum. I told a story about a source trying to bribe me with alcohol so I wouldn't take a weapon stash from him. Plausible enough as there were open weapon caches all over the country. We often paid a bounty on weapons and explosives. Some people supported their families by selling weapons a little at a time from bunkers they'd discovered. It wasn't unusual for a man bearing an armload of rifles to show up at the gate in the morning only to show up again and again, day after day, until he emptied the cache.

I acted like I'd followed the man to the cache and then taken the weapons along with the rum. It was the kind of dick move I knew Moron would appreciate. I told him I didn't drink rum so I was going to turn it in for disposal. He didn't like that at all. He asked who else knew about it. I told him nobody. He asked if he could have it or if I'd be willing to sell it to him. I pretended I was debating with myself, that I didn't want to get in trouble. If he got caught with it, I didn't want things to come back on me. He sensed I was close to giving in and pressed.

"No, no, it won't come back on you. I'll share it with Hickey (Larry) and Cox (Curly) so we won't get drunk. If we get in trouble, it won't come back on you."

He then upped his offer from fifty dollars for the bottle to a hundred. I acted a little unsure but like I really wanted the money. Truthfully, I could give a fuck about the money. I didn't really buy anything there. Everything was provided. What I wanted was for him to believe the money mattered. He pushed the cash into my hand and took the bottle. I held on for another second then relented. I let go of the bottle and moved on to stage two.

A few hours later they were all three dead drunk, passed out in their tent. Exactly how I needed them. Somebody would have woken up and pounded my face into oblivion. The rum insured I would be able to do what I needed to do without the risk of my face becoming modern art. Creeping into the tent I saw the empty bottle hanging loosely from Moron's hand. The three collapsed on their cots and hadn't even bothered to pull their bug netting. They also hadn't bothered getting in their sleeping bags. I found Moron's boots at the foot of the bunk.

I took them both and filled them with Smucker's Strawberry Jelly all the way to the top. I put the boots back at the foot of his bunk and propped the tent open with two now empty jars. Now the plan truly began to take effect.

My attack was two pronged. The first being the obvious hassle of having to clean jelly out of his boots, har har, the other would start as soon as the insects caught the scent of the sugar.

The screaming began around five am. Slightly earlier than I expected. This was worth getting up for. I made my way down the row of tents. The screaming was mixed with rough male laughter. A small crowd formed in front of the stooges' tent, and I had to force my way to the front. All around were soldiers laughing so hard they couldn't stand.

Looking into the stooges' tent I saw the plan worked better than I hoped. Insects everywhere. Crawling on the bunks and on the walls. Bugs covered the windows. On both sides of the mosquito netting. The jelly called to the bugs that ate sugar and then the bugs that ate those bugs showed up to feed. The rum had kept the stooges asleep while an armada moved into their tent.

There were bugs in their clothes, crawling on them, and in their hair. No matter how tough a guy you think you are I guarantee you will be completely unnerved by all those legs crawling on you. They had unmanned all three completely. Moron was thrashing around in the middle of the tent trying to wipe off every area of his body at the same time and not accomplishing much. He was bouncing from foot to foot and screaming.

He had a high-pitched squeal like a girl and along with the dance he was doing in the middle of the tent soldiers were falling over in hysterics. He had forced his feet into the boots and jelly ran down the sides. With each hop, jelly was flung on the walls and pooled on the ground.

Larry and Curly had enough presence of mind to get out of the swarm but stripped completely naked in the sand outside. There were catcalls almost constantly and their butt cheeks were red from a near continual string of ass slaps.

I had no idea how they were going to get the bugs out of their tent, but it wasn't my problem. I waved at Moron and asked him if he needed some deet.

"You! You did this!"

"Why Sergeant, I have no idea what you're talking about." I opened my eyes wide, the picture of innocence.

He screamed and slapped at a mantis that crawled up onto his cheek, *"Ahhhh Ahhlll These fucking bugs! Fucking everywhere*!!"

"You might want to consider closing your tent flaps at night. You might get a bug problem."

"You!! I'm going to kill you! Fucking bugs!!"

"Sergeant, do you really want to escalate things? Maybe you should leave MI alone from now on. I don't know, just a thought."

I've never been a nice guy.

I walked away laughing and listening to the squeals and catcalls from some of Americas finest fighting men. I made quite a profit, and those three idiots learned messing with MI was more trouble than it was worth. We wouldn't have to deal with their bullying, or anyone else's, for the duration.

A few weeks after the insect invasion saw the SF guys on their best behavior. We conducted our business kicking doors and arresting bad guys in peace. Other than the usual dose of mind-bending terror waiting for the bombs or snipers there wasn't much out of the normal routine. I got the word from the commander of the SF unit I was to be returned to my unit. I wondered if insectageddon had anything to do with that decision. He didn't mention it and I thought it prudent not to ask. Better to let it die.

I thought about Rae as I climbed into the truck. Not that this was in any way unusual, I thought about Rae all the time. I thought about our child who had come into the world three weeks ago. We had a little girl and named her Elora. She was beautiful like her mother, thankfully, and Rae told me she had my green eyes. It was hard to tell from the pictures I had. She had fat apple cheeks and her mother's happy disposition and thick red hair, for a baby.

I couldn't wait to meet her.

All my gear was loaded into the back of the truck. I wouldn't be back here hopefully ever. I positioned the rear-view mirror and warmed up the glow plugs. I put my belt on and checked to make sure my gunner was set, and the rest of my crew was ready to roll. Headed back with me were the two other CI Agents I was working with when Salad Bar tried to stab us. I put the private with the sidearm in the backseat and had Private Knife Arm on the gun. If anything should happen, I wanted someone on the weapon capable of thinking and acting fast. Private Sidearm wasn't quite there yet.

We had been operating in Western Iraq and now faced a long dangerous drive back east. Part of that drive would take us through the Sunni Triangle. Road tripping through some of the most dangerous ground on earth. Flat, brown, dusty, and uninspiring, the bleak landscape always left me with a sense of foreboding. It always felt like something awful was on the verge of happening. Or something awful had just happened. Five minutes early or five minutes late could make the difference between life and death, and you never knew which.

I hated this place. What was I doing here? All I ever wanted to do was get high, play music, and get paid. Maybe throw in the occasional naked romp and I'm good. I had no business in a foreign land. I didn't like sending people to jail, or worse. I wanted to be home, my home, with my lady and my baby girl. Not that I could do anything about it now. I was here. I was obligated. I wasn't going anywhere.

I was keeping my fellow soldiers safe from bad people who liked to make things explode. I couldn't get behind the mission, but it felt good keeping my battle buddies from being harmed. I didn't care about politics. I thought we really didn't have any business I could see. Problems Iraqi people had should be solved by Iraqi people. I didn't enjoy being a member of the world police force.

Grim thoughts. Unpatriotic. But you feel how you feel and there isn't much you can do to stop it. I drove along, mile after dusty mile, looking at nothing and brooding. I tried to think of Rae but missing her only made my mood blacker.

We had been sent here by men who used war as a means to an end. Men who either didn't care or didn't understand boots on the ground meant actual lives on the ground. War was a buzz word with no real meaning behind it for them, the way prison used to be for me. I was fucking around in the desert while my baby girl grew up not knowing her daddy. I knew it was a bit melodramatic, but I had a daughter out there in the world I hadn't met and a wife who needed her husband. I missed Rae. All I wanted was her. And my little family. What could I do? I'd signed up, sworn the oath, and taken the money. I was stuck until my contract was up. I rode and thought about red hair and sweet smiles.

The HMMWV or Humvee is the military's all-purpose truck. Fifteen feet long with a wheelbase of ten feet ten inches weighing in at a mere seven hundred pounds, the Humvee is as fine and faithful a truck as you could want.

A powerful 6.5-liter V-8 which can haul a payload of 5100 pounds never failed to growl into life for me. There is no end in configuring the truck. You can swap out armor, doors, weapons, and whatever else you might need or want in a few minutes. The convoy moved east through the Sunni Triangle without incident and was within a stone's throw of Baghdad when the bomb detonated. I loved that truck and was completely heartbroken when the back end blew into the air with a roar of fire and twisted metal.

The nose of the truck ground into the pavement, sparks spitting as momentum carried us forward. The hood, never designed to take the weight of the vehicle, bent up breaking the windshield. My seatbelt bit painfully into my shoulder and my helmet kept me from busting my forehead into the steering wheel. The rear end dropped back to the ground and the vehicle was still.

I sat in my seat, numb, my hearing gone from the massive explosion, trying to figure out what happened. My brain wasn't processing. A massive BOOM caused the world to go crazy for a moment. I looked to my right to make sure my fellow soldiers were alive. Sidearm stared at me like I had something to do with what just happened, like it was my fault. Blood leaked from his nose and ears, but he didn't seem otherwise harmed. Knife Arm was gone. I could only assume he had been thrown clear when the bomb threw us into the air.

I tried to open the door. I had to move. It was jammed tight; the frame must have bent. I wished we'd had the resources to up armor this truck. There was supposed to be armor on the way but so far, we hadn't had any. It didn't make sense to send soldiers into battle without armor but that is the government at work. I used my knife to cut an x through cloth, plastic, and vinyl. It wasn't hard. Shrapnel had shredded both doors on the driver's side and the roof.

I fell onto the road. My legs weren't working. I looked down and saw blood, my blood, pooling on the asphalt below me. There was a series of metal shards sticking out of my leg and lower back. Spines on a porcupine. How did I not notice that? It didn't hurt. Nothing hurt. I couldn't hear. From my prone position I could see Knife Arm off the side of the road, his legs sticking up out of the ditch. He wasn't moving.

The rest of the convoy stopped. Soldiers were running back to collect us and burn what remained of our Humvee. Looking at it, I thought it was well fucked without the burning. The front end looked like it had been kicked by a petulant giant. The rear end of the truck, gone. The rear wheels weren't there, and neither was the back end. Some roaring beasts had risen from the dunes and bit the back end of our truck off. The trailer disappeared in a literal flash.

My head rolled back to the soldiers who were trying to carry me out of the danger zone. Another group surrounded Knife Arm. I couldn't tell if he was alive. Sidearm had been helped from the wreckage. Soldiers guided him over to another vehicle. He looked confused, like he wasn't quite sure where he was. As they helped me into the bed of yet another truck, I saw a soldier drop an incendiary grenade into the driver's seat.

"Aww now don't do that," I said, reaching out a hand. The world went dark.

I ride waves of sound.

I feel the music all around me. Sweet, sad, urgent, undeniable the music washes over me in wave after wave like lying on the exact point where the ocean meets the land. Here there is nothing but music. Time and stars and life burn dark, the music carries on. I'm part of an endless song sighing, talking, laughing, and screaming. One wave carries me soft and sweet, Rae waking me in the night to hold her. Another wave crashes down lonely and full of regret for a soul I helped bring into the world. Someone I will never know. I love you, Rae. I love you Elora and I'm sorry, I'm so sorry.

I'm pulled in all directions and none by endless song. I see Gideon's living room. There is a single plate, a single fork, and a single knife in the middle of the room. A lamp without a shade rest in the corner. Otherwise, the house is empty. I know these are the only things Ashley left him.

Vito stands on a dirt pile with a shovel in his hand. He wipes the sweat from his forehead and looks East thinking about things that almost were. Chadwick has a heart attack at work sitting at his desk. An accidental flash showed him the new girl doesn't wear panties. It's the last thing he sees. Raven paints houses and believes there will be another chance. He might even be right. Dexter retreats to his farmhouse until the battle stress claims him. Virginia summer heat liquifies his body. His soul finally finds its peace.

I ride the waves of sound.

Gideon sits alone in a small apartment at a card table that doubles as his dining room. He's holding his guitar listening for the song. The music has closed the door to him. He no longer feels the endless waves I now ride. The music left him, denied him, and I leave him waiting at his table.

I'm a young man sneaking out my window to run the night with the neighbor's daughter. Our song is vibrant and mysterious and filled with the infinite possibility of youth. I swing my long hair as the crowd sways with me. The lights dance in time with the melodies flowing through me. I'm an old man sitting on the porch watching the sunset, Rae beside me, a cup of coffee warming arthritic hands. My life is behind me. My songs are slow and comforting. I'm a soldier fighting up Victory Tower for the first time. My song pounds triumphantly. I am all these songs and yet I am none of them.

I feel the pain at the loss of my first love as a child. The unfathomable depth of passion which can only be reached in one who hasn't lived or loved for long. The deep crushing regrets of one who has. I feel all the joy, all the loss, and all that ever was or ever will be. I am a part of it and it is a part of me. This music. My song. I ride the waves.

I hope. I love. And I want. I still want.

About the Author

Jeremy Eads was first published at six years old.

Since then he's gone on to be a traveling musician, soldier, spy, and software engineer.

You can find him on Facebook at OldSchoolScary or lurking over at Wicked House Publishing or Unveiling Nightmares.

When not writing, Jeremy is promoting novels, missing his kids, working on stories, more marketing, or writing.

He lives in southwest Virginia.

THE LODGE

A demon runs a bed and breakfast in southwest Virginia where sin never needs a reservation.

A guilt-ridden retiree, two little boys, and a pair of meth-making cousins will challenge America's most wanted black widow, a haunted southern town, and the Devil himself.

The quest for salvation will lead to the darkest parts of themselves as well as the beating black heart of Summit Valley, Virginia.

The Maple Lodge, a B&B where the turndown service is to die for.

Reptile

There's a creature prowling Summit Valley thirsty for blood, and it has already claimed multiple victims. Night after night, the body count rises with no clues to the predator or the reason for the attacks.

Newly blessed or possibly cursed with strange powers he doesn't yet understand, Mark Branton fears he might be responsible.
Mark's grasp on his sanity is slipping.

Is he a savage murderer with no recollection or are darker powers at work that he may not be able to stop, regardless of his powers.
Reptile, it's time to hunt.